CONFESSIONS
OF THE SULLIVAN SISTERS

CONFESSIONS

OF THE

SULLIVAN

SISTERS

NATALIE STANDIFORD

SCHOLASTIC PRESS ■ *NEW YORK*

Copyright © 2010 by Natalie Standiford ▪ All rights reserved. Published by Scholastic Press, an imprint of Scholastic Inc., *Publishers since 1920*. SCHOLASTIC, SCHOLASTIC PRESS, and associated logos are trademarks and/or registered trademarks of Scholastic Inc. No part of this publication may be reproduced, stored in a retrieval system, or transmitted in any form or by any means, electronic, mechanical, photocopying, recording, or otherwise, without written permission of the publisher. For information regarding permission, write to Scholastic Inc., Attention: Permissions Department, 557 Broadway, New York, NY 10012. Library of Congress Cataloging-in-Publication Data Available ISBN 978-0-545-10710-5 ▪ 10 9 8 7 6 5 4 3 2 1 10 11 12 13 14 ▪ Printed in the U.S.A. 23 ▪ First edition, September 2010 ▪ The text was set in Cochin with Neutra Text. Book design by Kristina Iulo

FOR

MY FAMILY:

MOM, DAD, KAKIE,

JOHN, JIM, AND

GREG

THE SULLIVAN FAMILY'S CHRISTMAS BEGAN IN THE traditional way that year. All six children gathered at the top of the stairs in order, from youngest to oldest, and waited for the signal from Daddy-o that it was safe to come downstairs and inspect the work of Santa. Never mind that the oldest Sullivan child, St. John, was twenty-one. The youngest, Takey, was only six, and Daddy-o insisted on keeping up the annual rituals so Takey wouldn't feel as if he'd missed everything.

The signal — "Joy to the World" sung by Nat King Cole — burst through the stereo speakers, and the six children — Takey, Sassy, Jane, Norrie, Sully, and St. John — trooped downstairs to the family room and rummaged under the tall Christmas tree for presents. Afterward they waded through the sea of discarded wrapping paper to the kitchen for a pancake breakfast cooked by Daddy-o. (Miss Maura had the day off, though she always stopped by with her husband, Dennis — known to the Sullivan children as Mr. Maura — to say hello and drop off presents around noon.) Ginger contributed her signature dish, sliced grapefruit halves sprinkled with Splenda. Slicing the grapefruit was the most work she did in the kitchen all year, unless you counted transferring caviar from the tin to the silver serving dish on New Year's Eve.

After breakfast, everyone retreated to their bedrooms to try on their new Christmas clothes and get ready for the big family dinner at Almighty's. The Sullivans lived in a very big house, but Almighty — their grandmother Arden Louisa Norris Sullivan Weems Maguire Hightower Beckendorf, known to everyone in Baltimore as "Almighty Lou" — had a house that was a bona fide mansion, with a fancy name to match: Gilded Elms.

Christmas Eve at Gilded Elms was a party for family and friends. But Christmas Day dinner was a quieter occasion, usually just for Almighty and the Sullivans. That year, an unexpected guest joined the family at Almighty's Christmas table: her lawyer, Mr. Calvin Murdoch. Mr. Murdoch had the silent, nodding, overly polite demeanor of an undertaker. Each of the Sullivans wondered what he was doing there while they quietly chewed on their turkey breast and passed around the homemade raisin bread.

In time, they got their answer.

After dinner, Almighty gathered her nearest and dearest in the library for a special announcement. She wore a simple black dress, which set off the bold white stripe in her iron-gray hair.

"I have recently learned that I may not have long to live," she declared to gasps of surprise. "There is a tumor in my brain. If it doesn't grow, I might live out my natural life as I was intended to, active and sentient. If, however, it grows — and the doctors say it has a distinct possibility of doing so — then I will quickly decline. Therefore, I have revisited the affairs of my estate, financial and otherwise. In other words, I have changed my will."

The family members gathered around her sat perfectly still, with a studied lack of emotion. No one wanted to appear upset at the possibility of a change in Almighty's will. Such a change, however, would affect the fate of everyone in the room to a great degree. Almighty was very rich, and her son, his wife, and all of their children were completely dependent on the money she controlled.

"Alphonse," Almighty continued, looking to Daddy-o, who'd been named after his late father, "I fear your entire family has been cut out of the will."

The Sullivans gasped in horror. They couldn't help themselves. This was just too awful.

"Now now, there is no need for alarm," Almighty said, even if no other reaction seemed sensible.

"Mother, why?" Daddy-o asked.

"One of you has offended me deeply," Almighty explained. "I'm not going to name names. But unless that person comes forward with a confession of his or her crime, submitted in writing to me by New Year's Day, I will donate your share of my fortune to my favorite charity upon my death."

"Which charity is that?" Ginger asked.

"Puppy Ponchos," Almighty replied.

The Sullivans collectively restrained themselves from groaning. Puppy Ponchos provided rain ponchos for the dogs of people too poor to buy dog raincoats for themselves. In a city full of needy people and animals, it was the most useless charity imaginable. No one in the Sullivan family understood why Puppy Ponchos was more deserving of Almighty's money than they were. After all, hadn't they put up with her for all these years? Didn't that count for something?

"If the offending party submits the proper confession in time," Almighty continued, "I will reinstate the family in my will. Or at least consider it."

Almighty had spoken. And if Almighty wanted a confession, a confession she would get.

When the torturous dinner was finally over and the Sullivans had returned to their house, they gathered in the kitchen for a family meeting.

"Who could have offended Almighty so much?" St. John asked. "Which one of us could it be?"

"One of the girls," Sully said.

"One of the girls," Daddy-o repeated.

"Definitely one of the girls," Ginger concurred.

Almighty had always been tough on the girls. And each of them had recently done something to upset their grandmother, no question about that.

And so it was agreed that the three girls — Norrie, Jane, and Sassy — would spend their Christmas break writing out a full confession of their crimes, to be handed to Almighty by midnight on New Year's Eve.

After that, they would have to hope for the best.

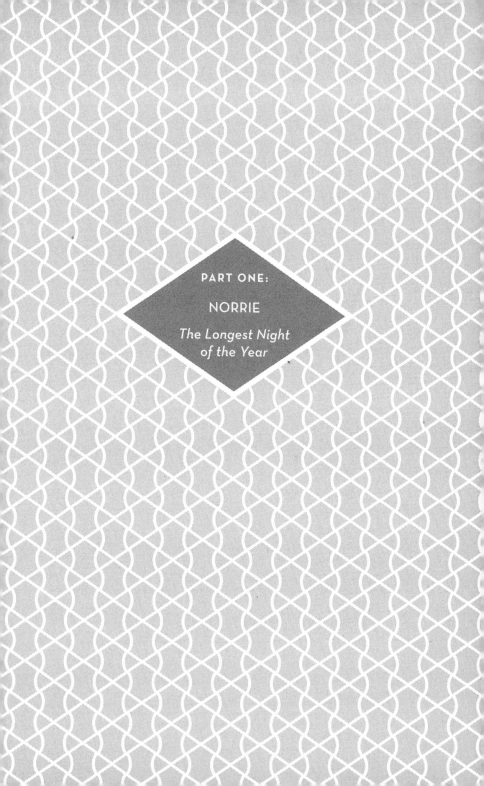

PART ONE:

NORRIE

*The Longest Night
of the Year*

Dear Almighty,

I confess.

You know what I did, and you know why—I did it for true love. Have you ever been in love, Almighty? You've been married five times—but have you been in love? You can't resist it. You're in its power. Helpless.

I tried to be good and dutiful and do what the family needed me to do. But I fell in love. Being in love made me crazy. That's all I can say in my defense. I will tell you the whole story, from the beginning, and hope that will help you to understand, and to forgive me. (I hope I remember to take out all the curses. I'm trying to train myself not to curse anymore. But some people, like Sully and Jane, just don't sound like themselves if they're not cursing. So a few might have slipped in. If so, I'm sorry.)

I will return to my old dutiful self if it will save my family from poverty. I can do it. Dear Almighty, if you lift this curse from our heads I promise to be good for the rest of my life.

ONE

✆ ✆ ✆

TO YOU, HE MUST HAVE SEEMED TO COME FROM NOWHERE.
But everybody comes from somewhere. And it's not always
Baltimore.

We met in September in a night class at Hopkins: Speed
Reading. I wanted to learn how to read faster. That night I sat in
the second-to-last row. I still had on my uniform from school — the
navy blue cotton jumper with SMPS stitched over the breast in
white thread.

I did my calculus homework while I waited for the class to
start. The room filled up and the teacher came in and started
talking about speed reading, but I wasn't finished with my calculus homework, so I kept doing it while she talked. Not much of
what she said was getting through to me — I'd been having concentration problems lately; that was partly why I wanted to learn
how to speed read. But that wasn't the only reason I was distracted. I also felt this heat coming from behind me, as if someone
were watching me. I half turned to the left and saw an old man
with a mustache, who wasn't paying any attention to me at all. I
half turned to the right and saw a tuft of frizzy black hair. That

was all I could see without turning all the way around, which seemed rude.

Through the whole class, the heat distracted me. Finally the teacher told us to take a ten-minute break. I stood up and turned around casually, very cool. This guy was sitting there, the guy with the frizzy black halo of hair, and he beamed up at me in such a warm way that it was no wonder I felt heat. He had a pale brown, creamy-skinned face with alert brown eyes and a short, wide nose that for some reason reminded me of a frog. A very cute little frog, topped with that hair.

"Hi," he said. "I noticed you're doing calculus homework."

"Yes," I said. "I guess I shouldn't do that if I want to learn to speed read."

"I think it's really cute," he said. "That you're doing calculus homework."

"It isn't cute at all," I told him. "There's nothing cute about calculus."

I wondered how old he was, then I wondered briefly if he realized I was still in high school. I say briefly because it only took me a second to realize that, duh, I was still wearing my uniform. Also, the homework was a dead giveaway. Sometimes I'm such an idiot.

"I think I'll get some water," I said. I wandered out into the hall and found a water fountain. I stared at it for a few seconds, as if I couldn't remember how a water fountain worked. Something was fogging up my brain circuits. I was really beginning to worry about myself.

I finally remembered how to use the fountain and drank some water. Then I went back into the classroom and sat down. The guy in the seat behind mine nodded at me. I really liked his hair. It looked like what licorice cotton candy would look like, if they made licorice cotton candy.

The teacher started talking again, passing out an article for us to test our current reading speeds. My current speed turned out to be a hundred and fifty words a minute, which is pretty slow for a supposedly smart person.

I felt a tap on my shoulder. "What score did you get?" the cute guy behind me whispered.

I didn't want to tell him, because my score was so low I was afraid he'd think I was mentally challenged. But I told him anyway. My first instinct is usually to be honest, which is a terrible weakness if you think about it.

"What's your score?" I asked him.

"Four hundred words a minute," he said.

I cursed — to myself — because Licorice Halo's score was so much higher than mine, plus he had to be older, at least in college, and I hated to start out at a disadvantage that way.

And then I realized what I was thinking, and wondered, *Start out what?* Why did I care what this total stranger thought of my intelligence?

But I did, and that's when I knew I was doomed.

When class was over, he looked at me as if he wanted to say something but was thinking the better of it, so instead of saying something, he just nodded and left. I figured it was the uniform that turned him off. Some people find Catholic school uniforms scary. I cursed myself again for being too lazy to change before class — an adult night school class, what was I thinking? — and vowed to wear civvies the next week. I also vowed to find out his name so I wouldn't have to think of him only in terms of his hair.

When I got home that night, Jane was in my room, smoking out the window. That drives me crazy. Next year when I go away to college it'll be her turn to have the Tower Room and she can smoke her lungs out if she wants. But no matter how many times I yell at her she won't stop, so I've kind of given up.

A police helicopter was circling the neighborhood, and Jane was watching its searchlight. "Can you see anything?" I asked. Sometimes, when the police copters come, you can catch sight of someone running down the street in the glare of the searchlight. But it's hard to see much from up in the Tower Room in summer, when the leaves are so full it feels like a tree house. In winter, when the trees are bare, you can see the neighbors' houses and the lights downtown.

Jane turned away from the window and blew a stream of smoke at me. "You look different."

"Different how?" I asked.

She shrugged and took another puff. "I don't know. Just different."

"I am different," I said. "I don't think I'll ever be the old Norrie again."

She didn't react much to that, since we Sullivans are all very dramatic, as you well know, Almighty. You're the Drama Queen.

It's hard to top the striptease Jane did in the middle of the school musical last year, or that time St. John announced that he was leaving for Paris in the morning to live there forever. Did you know about that? Daddy-o was afraid to tell you his twelve-year-old son had run off to Paris alone, because you're always criticizing him for being too lax with us. It all blew over in a week. A friend of Daddy-o's met St. John at the airport, and after a week of cafés and museums he flew home and declared that Paris was lovely but overrated.

So my announcement that I suddenly felt "different" didn't have much impact. Jane said, "I didn't know speed reading could change a person so much. And so speedily! Will the new Norrie trade rooms with me so I can smoke whenever I want?"

"No," I said. "There will never be an incarnation of Norrie who will give up the Tower Room before she leaves for college. And you shouldn't smoke anyway."

"I know I shouldn't." She blew a stream of smoke out the window.

I didn't tell Jane anything about the guy I'd met in Speed Reading class that night, because it was too early. I wanted to give the thing, whatever it turned out to be, a chance to happen first. Besides, if I told anyone, that would make it real, and I wasn't ready for it to be real yet. I knew that *real* meant trouble.

TWO

⊠   ⊠   ⊠

THIS WAS BACK AT THE BEGINNING OF THE SCHOOL YEAR, WHEN I still thought I had a crush on Brooks, and the fall stretched out before me like a short, smooth road to the Cotillon. Robbie was just a gritty piece of sand that had slipped under my shell. An irritant.

There was a party that Saturday, the last summer party of the year, at Matt Bowie's farm in Stevenson. Matt Bowie has all the big parties: pool parties with kegs and jam bands in the fields behind his grandmother's house in summer; apple-picking parties in the fields in fall; ice-skating parties on the pond, with bonfires and spiked hot chocolate in winter; and Hunt Cup picnics in spring, where we sit on the hill and watch the horses run the steeplechase across his family's fields. You probably sat on that very same hill once, Almighty, watching the riders with Matt Bowie's grandmother. Or maybe you went to one of their annual Christmas parties, in the big house with the cage elevator and a wreath on every door.

Sassy, Jane, and I wore bathing suits under our shorts, threw towels over our shoulders, and hopped into St. John's old baby blue Mercedes sedan, which he left in the garage when he moved to New York. He inherited it when Daddy-o upgraded to the new cream-colored Mercedes, but I guess it's mine now.

The day was warm and hazy with pollen. I rolled down the windows and drove barefoot, heading due north straight up Charles Street. We stopped in Homeland to pick up Claire, who sat in the front seat next to me, propping her feet on the dashboard. Jane insisted we stop in Ruxton to get her annoying friend Bridget, so we did that too. Before long we were in horse country, the rolling hills a fading green.

Cars already lined the road when we pulled up to the reservoir and parked beside the cemetery where all those Bowies are buried, way back to the 1600s. Kids were splashing in the water and lying on the grass in the sun. Matt swayed over the reservoir on a rope swing and yodeled as he hung suspended in the air, then dropped into the water. We draped our towels over the sun-warmed headstones and stripped off our shorts.

"I'm going in," Sassy said. She ran straight toward the water, yelled "Geronimo!" and jumped in.

"She's always hot," Jane said. "I need to warm up first."

Jane, Bridget, Claire, and I walked over to a sunny spot beyond the trees and set up our towels. At the end of the row of sunbathers lay Bibi D'Alessandro and some other girls from Jane's class. Bibi had snagged the prime spot, Eliza Bowie's tombstone. When the sun hits it just right it's like lying on a warm stone table. Bibi used to be Jane's best friend but they had some kind of feud, I forget about what. I'm sure it was all Jane's fault.

A few Radnor girls were splayed out at my feet, with Lily Hargrove at the center. I'm not friends with Lily, but everybody knows who she is. She's effortlessly skinny with long, glossy chestnut hair and mysterious almond eyes, but mostly she has that *thing* — I can't say exactly what it is but it's like *knowing* you're hot makes you even hotter.

I do not have that thing. I have a feeling there's something old-fashioned about my looks, not in a good way. There are boys who think I'm cute, but old ladies *flip* over me. Not you, but every other old lady in the universe. They're always coming up to me to say how beautiful I am. It's my skin; they love my pale, rosy skin. Boys don't notice skin. I've never heard a boy say, "Hey, check that girl's foxy skin." There's a girl at our pool named Kelsey Mathers who practically has acne but all the boys drool over her anyway. Once, I pointed out Kelsey's pimples to Sully and he said he didn't know what I was talking about. "Acne? Check out her ass!" (I was going to write "bottom" instead of "ass" in deference to your delicate sensibilities, but then it wouldn't sound like Sully talking, would it?) I guess a good ass blinds boys to other deficits.

Sorry if you think this is vulgar, Almighty, but I decided if I'm going to confess to you I'm going to be completely honest and tell everything, even things you might not like to hear about.

I said hi to the Radnor girls. They squinted up at me, shading their eyes from the sun.

"Oh, hi," said Phoebe Fernandez-Ruiz. She tugged her red scarf out of her hair. Lily Hargrove turned her face toward the swimmers in the water.

Brooks and his friend Davis Smith climbed out of the reservoir and walked over to us, dripping. I felt Claire tense up beside me. I have a feeling she likes Brooks. Lots of girls like Brooks. I had a huge secret crush on him myself. At least I thought I did. I used to like playing with him when we were little, at family picnics or Easter egg hunts, until we were about ten and he didn't want to play with girls anymore. That's when I started missing him a little bit, and thinking about him. It didn't help that you and Ginger always talked about him as if he and I were going to get married someday.

He's not that cute if you really look at him, you know, but nobody really looks at him. I mean, maybe if you showed a picture of him to a girl who never met him, she might shrug and say, "Yeah, so?" But anybody who's met him knows. I can already kind of see where his bald spot is going to be in twenty years, maybe ten. I can picture him as an old man: He'll be charming and everyone's favorite uncle or dad, the kind of guy who still wears his tweed suit from college and sails and writes poetry for special occasions, like the rehearsal dinner for his daughter's wedding or the baptism of his first grandchild. I don't know why that is so appealing, but it is. You can look at Brooks Overbeck and see the future, and that future is bright and comfortable, full of parties and travel and glittery Ivy League people. A lot like your life, and my parents' life, and his parents' life. I guess that's why so many girls like him. Who wouldn't want that?

Davis kissed Lily and she said, "Ew, Dave, you're getting me all wet." Brooks shook his hair like a Labrador and spattered us with water. We all screamed happily except for Jane, who put on her sunglasses and rolled over onto her stomach with an exasperated sigh.

"What d'ya know, girls?" Brooks said. "Nice to see the Sullivan clan out and about."

Brooks's father always says "What d'ya know?" and now Brooks always says "What d'ya know?" (Doesn't that ever get on your nerves?)

"Spare me," Jane muttered.

"You didn't have to come," I said to her.

"I wanted to go for a swim."

"So go for a swim."

"I will. Come on, Bridget." She stood up, gave Bridget a little kick, and walked petulantly toward the water, where Sassy and some other kids were splashing and having chicken fights.

"Oh no," Lily said. "Here comes that St. Haggie's slut."

I bristled, since the Radnor girls are always calling us sluts just because we're Catholic school girls and the boys think that's sexy for some reason and it makes the Radnor girls jealous. I looked back to see which "slut" was coming toward us.

Shea Donovan. Who actually *is* kind of a slut.

Shea stumbled toward us through the graveyard wearing flip-flops, very short cutoffs, and a T-shirt sawed off at the rib cage over a pink bikini top. Her dark blond hair hung in her face and her eyes were covered by aviator sunglasses. As usual, she was slouching slightly, with this way of ducking her head, ready to flinch, like a dog who's used to being hit.

"I heard she's going out with some guy who's, like, thirty," Phoebe said.

"Is that true?" Lily asked me.

As if I'd know. "Maybe. I don't know her very well."

"She's hooked up with every boy on T&A's lacrosse team," Phoebe said.

Shea had arrived, so the gossip stopped. She glanced around in search of a friendly face.

Sassy ran out of the water then and grabbed her towel. "The water feels great! Hi, Shea. Sit in the sun with us."

"Okay." Shea spread her towel near Sassy's.

Shea's kind of pretty in an off-kilter way, her nose and mouth not quite centered on her face. But the girls at school don't consider her pretty. Her only friend is this other slutty girl, Caitlin, who wears a lot of eyeliner. There's something about them. . . . They seem contagious, as if you could catch misery from being around them. I don't know why I get that feeling. They might not be unhappy at all.

After a short swim, Jane came back to her towel, Bridget nipping at her heels. "It's frickin' cold," Jane grumbled. She sat her cold wet butt on my stomach.

"Ow. Get off me." I pushed her over. Since I was now wet, I figured I might as well swim. "Want to go in?" I asked Claire.

"Yeah."

We got up and dove into the water. The cold snapped me awake. I swam a few hundred feet out to the wooden float anchored offshore, letting the sun sink into my bones. Across the water I heard laughter and squealing. It didn't sound like anything unusual. It crossed my mind that maybe somebody had done something mean to Shea.

By the time Claire and I crawled back onto the shore, it was clear we'd missed something. I glanced at Shea, but she was hovering on the sidelines, watching. Bibi was the focus of attention. She stalked toward the road, blood dripping from her nose. Brooks, of all people, was trailing after her. Brooks's friends and the Radnor girls were laughing, and Jane and Bridget huddled on their towels, snickering. I zeroed in on Jane. She's always my prime suspect.

"What was that all about?"

"Just Bibi being Bibi," Jane said. "You know how she is."

"Not really," I said. "She's your friend."

"She *was* my friend," Jane corrected.

Brooks came back from the road, frowning, Bibi having left in disgrace. He opened up a cooler and hefted out a huge watermelon. "Who wants some? Last melon of the season." He dropped it on the ground and it broke into pieces. Davis reached for one and bit into it. Brooks passed chunks of watermelon around, and soon everyone was drooling pink juice and spitting seeds. Just like that. Whatever had happened, he was over it. That's part of his charm.

But was that enough for me?

Well, that was the question, wasn't it?

THREE

✉   ✉   ✉

THE NEXT WEEK, I WORE JEANS TO SPEED READING, TRYING TO look more like a college student even though I'd already blown my cover. When I got to class the licorice-haired guy wasn't there yet so I sat in the same seat. He came in just before the class started and sat behind me again. I could feel the heat. My cheeks and my nose got very hot, and I knew they were probably red. I hate when that happens.

The teacher tested our reading speeds again — it turned out she planned to do that every week — and this time my score was much less embarrassing. I turned around to wave it victoriously in my tormentor's face.

"Good job," he said. He flashed his score at me, which was even higher than the week before, still way higher than mine. But this time he'd written his name on his paper. Robinson Pepper. Had he done that on purpose so I'd see it? I scribbled my name on *my* paper and showed it to him.

"Hello, Norris," he said.

"Hello, Robinson," I said. "Everyone calls me Norrie."

"Everyone calls me Robbie."

I sighed happily. I was so glad to have an official name to call him. Now things could get started for real. Fate could begin to take its course.

I just want to clarify here that I didn't *consciously* think "Fate can begin to take its course." I wasn't planning a coup or anything. But looking back, I can see that was the moment when my life changed direction. I would also like to add that I'm talking about FATE here, not choice. Not free will. It was out of my hands. I'm not saying I didn't choose to do what I finally did — I'm only saying that I wasn't steering myself that way on purpose.

After class that night, Robinson Pepper asked me if I wanted to go get some coffee. Speed Reading was on Tuesday nights and I had homework to do, but what the hell. Heck.

We walked to a café on campus that was busy with Hopkins students taking study breaks. What follows is a re-creation of our conversation from my memory and from what I wrote in my diary later that night.

"So what does SMPS stand for?" Robbie asked me.

"Huh?" Oh right, the monogram on my uniform. It took me a second to figure out what he was asking. "Guess."

"Snooty Mean People Society?"

"Close. St. Margaret's Preparatory School."

"Oh. Is that a good school?"

"If you're Catholic. You must not be from around here."

"Because if I were, I'd know all the schools?"

"Obviously."

"No, I'm from New York. I'm down here for grad school."

"My brother lives in New York."

"I must surely know him then. What's his name?"

"Sinjin. St. John."

"Hmm. Is he a saint?"

"No. My father named him after the college he went to. St. John's in Annapolis?"

"That's that strange college where they make everybody study mathematics and classical Greek, right?"

"Yeah."

"So what does St. John do in New York?"

"He's a philosopher poet."

"Ah. A dying breed. We used to have a lot of those up there."

"I know it sounds ridiculous."

"No it doesn't."

"What are you studying in grad school?"

"Your turn to guess."

I sized him up. The hair was not conservative, so nothing business-y, lawyerly, or medical seemed likely. The oxford shirt and jeans were faintly preppy, which said to me *not Art.* "English?"

"Film theory. Basically the same thing."

"Why are you taking Speed Reading?"

"Because I have a lot of reading to do. You?"

"Same reason. What other reason is there?"

"You're so right."

There was an awkward pause while we sipped our hot coffees. I didn't usually drink coffee at night back then so I wondered what kind of effect it would have on me. (Five hours later as I lay wide awake staring at the ceiling, I got my answer.)

I tried not to stare at Robbie too much but I found him really fun to look at. He has very twinkly eyes — they're merry, like Santa Claus's — and his mouth is always moving, so the expression on his face changes every few seconds. They're nearly always pleasant expressions, in an astonishingly wide variety. I never knew one face could have so many different happy looks. His coloring is very harmonious — mostly variations of charcoal, brown, and tan, with his lips providing a nice slash of red for contrast. He kept looking at my face too, and I could only think that he liked it because of all the happy expressions flashing by on his. We were signaling back and forth to each other silently. This has never happened to me with another person, let alone a guy, before.

I could have sat there like that all night, not saying a word, but Robbie finally broke the silence. "I go to the movies a lot because, you know, that's what I'm studying."

"Makes sense," I said.

"I bring this up because I was wondering if you would like to go to a movie with me someday. Would you be allowed to? Or would you get into trouble? I don't want to get you into trouble."

"What movie?" I asked.

"Um, let's see. . . . What about *Vertigo*? There's a Hitchcock series at the Charles this month."

I said okay. I'd never seen *Vertigo* before but St. John used to have a poster of it in his room. Sully replaced it with a Yeah Yeah Yeahs poster when he moved in.

"Are you sure it's okay?" Robbie said.

"Why wouldn't it be?" I asked.

Now he wouldn't look at me. He fingered his napkin uncomfortably. "Well, isn't St. Margaret's Preparatory School a, you know, a high school?"

"Yes."

"The Johns Hopkins University Film Studies Program is a graduate school," he said.

"So?" I said. "What are you, bragging?"

"No, but I'd conclude from the fact that you're in high school and I'm in grad school that there may be a significant age difference between us."

"How old are you?" I asked.

"Twenty-five. How old are you?"

Twenty-five! Eep. *Should I lie?* I wondered.

"Seventeen." I couldn't lie to him.

He frowned. "I was hoping you were at least eighteen. I was under the impression that lots of high school girls are even nineteen these days."

"Sorry to disappoint you. But I'll be eighteen in November."

"Maybe we shouldn't go to the movies."

"Why not? Is there some law against twenty-five-year-olds going to the movies with seventeen-year-olds?"

"Not exactly. But won't your parents mind?"

"I don't know. They're hard to predict." I wasn't sure what Ginger and Daddy-o would think of Robbie. They live on their own planet. The age difference might bother them, but then again they might not even notice it. Daddy-o mostly objects to people he feels aren't interesting enough. He likes "aristocrats of the mind." Ginger's more of a local snob — the people she likes best are those she's known since birth. Robbie seemed a likely candidate for aristocrat of the mind, but since he wasn't from Baltimore, Ginger probably wasn't best friends with his mother in kindergarten. The best I could hope for was that they'd been sorority sisters in college. "I say we try it and find out what they think later."

His face flashed through five different happy expressions. "You're an adventurous girl. I knew it the minute I saw you."

I had never thought of myself as the least bit adventurous before. I was the dull goody-goody who never got into trouble and always got straight A's. The bossy, responsible big sister. But as soon as Robbie said that, I realized I *am* adventurous — like you, Almighty. It's just taken time for everyone to get used to thinking of me that way.

FOUR

⊠   ⊠   ⊠

JANE AND SASSY WERE WAITING FOR ME IN MY ROOM AS USUAL
when I got home that night.

"It's freezing in here," I said. Jane had the window open for
smoking, of course. I snatched her clove cigarette from her hand,
tossed it outside and shut the window.

"Hey, I was smoking that," Jane complained.

"You could set the whole house on fire," Sassy added.

"There's no respect for privacy in this family," I said. "Every
time I walk into my room, it's full of people."

"We're not people," Sassy said. "We're us."

"The Tower Room has always been the official clubhouse,"
Jane said. "It has been since St. John."

"Things change," I said. "The new rule is you have to ask permission before you can burst in here and fill the place with clove
smoke."

"Speed Reading really is messing with your head, Norrie,"
Jane said.

"Remember that rope ladder St. John had so his friends could
climb up for late-night parties?" Sassy said. She's often a few
steps behind in conversation. "Whatever happened to that?"

"He took it to college," I said. "Maybe Sully has it." It occurred to me that the ladder could come in handy again. If I — or somebody else — I wasn't thinking of anyone in particular — should ever need to sneak in and out of my room, for example. I reopened the casement window and stared into the darkness, four stories down to the ground. It's amazing none of St. John's drunken friends ever fell and broke their necks.

"Look at her, Sass," Jane said, nodding at me. "Don't you think she looks different lately?"

I turned my face toward Sassy so she could study me carefully.

"Yes," Sassy said. "Norrie, you've got cheekbones."

I went to the mirror. Sassy was right. Where only last summer — the last time I'd really checked — I'd still had puffy baby-face cheeks, now I suddenly had sharp angles in my face. I was beginning to look a bit like Ginger. I still have mixed feelings about that.

"I must have lost weight." I ran my hand over my face.

"It's the Speed Reading class," Jane said. "Something happened in that class that changed you forever, and now it's showing up in your face."

"What happened in Speed Reading?" Sassy asked.

"She won't tell us," Jane said.

"Yes I will," I said. "Just not yet."

"What?" Sassy jumped up and down on the bed. "You have to tell us! Now!"

"No."

"Let me guess," Sassy said. "You met a boy!"

"No I didn't," I said. "How did you know?"

"Lucky guess," Sassy said. "Throughout history, big changes always start with a girl meeting a boy."

"No they don't," Jane said. "They start with somebody being assassinated."

"But that starts with boy-meets-girl," Sassy said.

"No, it's not love that starts trouble. It's greed," Jane countered.

"Shut up, you two," I said.

"Norrie!" Sassy looked shocked. You know Ginger — she has seizures if anyone says "shut up," "heinie," "wiener," or "booger" in her presence. She'd rather we talked like sailors than like ill-bred suburban first graders. We've been trained to find those words shocking.

"I'm sorry," I said. "I just got tired of hearing you two talk about me as if I were about to start World War Three. Sassy is right. I met a boy."

"I knew it," Sassy said.

"Ho-fucking-hum," Jane said.

But Sassy was excited. "In Speed Reading? Who is he?"

"His name is Robinson Pepper," I told them. "Isn't that the loveliest name you ever heard?"

"Robinson Pepper?" Jane said.

"It's spicy!" Sassy said. "Where does he go to school? T&A?"

Did you call St. Thomas Aquinas "T&A" in your day, Almighty? Did you call the boys who go there "T&A-holes?"

I didn't think so.

"No, thank God," I said. "He goes to Hopkins."

"A college boy?"

"Not exactly," I said.

The buzzer buzzed. Ginger has a button right next to her bed that rings a buzzer in the Tower Room, left over from the olden days when a maid slept here. I don't know how often she buzzed St. John and Sully but she loves to annoy me with it.

"Ginge must have heard us knocking around up here," Jane said. "Better go see what she wants."

I wearily pushed myself off the bed. Ginger almost never wants anything interesting or important. It's usually something like "Have you seen my Chinese silk robe?" or "Be a love and scratch my back," or "Darling, do I smell smoke?"

"I know what she wants," Sassy said. "Brooks called tonight."

"Uh-oh," Jane said. "Bachelor Number One."

In all the years we've known each other (our entire lives), Brooks never called me at home — until that night. He texted me and e-mailed me and maybe called my cell to tell me about a party. So I pretty much knew this had something to do with the Bachelors Cotillon. It was only September but I figured he was laying the groundwork like a good escort should. Your friend Mamie raised him well.

"You could do worse," Sassy said.

"Hardly," Jane sniffed. "Brooks Overbeck is a raging bore."

"I think he's nice," Sassy said.

"Exactly," Jane said.

The bell buzzed again. "Better go see what she wants before she comes up here," Jane said, stubbing out her second cigarette.

I went downstairs to Ginger and Daddy-o's room. Ginger sat in bed propped against about a hundred pillows, bracelets dangling, reading *Vanity Fair*. Daddy-o was downstairs in his study, writing a monograph on images of virginity in late medieval painting.

"You rang?" I said to Ginger.

"Yes, love, I didn't know if you were home yet. I wanted to tell you that Brooks Overbeck called for you tonight."

"You could have left a note on the kitchen table," I said.

"I know, darling, but I wanted to make absolutely sure you got the message." She glanced at the clock on her bedside table. "It's too late to call him now, but you might want to ring him tomorrow after school. Don't call him from school on your cell; that's rude."

"How is it rude?" I asked. Ginger has made up her own etiquette to cover new technology like texting and e-mails. She has all these rules but she's the only person who follows them, or even knows about them. "Wouldn't it be even more rude to make him wait all day until I call him back?"

"Now that you put it that way, definitely don't call from your cell," Ginger said. "You don't want to seem overeager."

"Don't worry, I'm not." The words just popped out. They even surprised me. Just a few weeks earlier I would have been excited to get a call from Brooks.

"You're not? But darling, you need an escort to the Cotillon, and I can't think of a better one than Brooks. Aren't you thrilled?"

"I'm not sure I want to go to the Cotillon," I told Ginger.

She dropped her magazine in horror. "Not go? Darling, you have to! You're the first girl in the family. We haven't had a deb yet, and already you want to drop out?"

"I just don't see the point of it."

"There is a point, a big point," Ginger said. Then she paused.

"Well?" I said. "What is it?"

"Tradition. Generations. All that. What were all those dancing lessons at Miss Claremont's for? If you don't come out, Almighty will be very disappointed. And no one wants Almighty to be disappointed."

I sighed. I don't know if you realize it, but you are often used as a threat in our house.

"I don't want to disappoint anyone," I said. "But I'm not excited about going."

"Not excited? Cue the violins." She resisted pantomiming a violinist, and for that I was grateful. "Poor Norrie. You'll be the girl of the season — especially if your escort is Brooks. I hope you'll call him tomorrow, lovey dove."

It's just a party, I told myself. *It's just a party.*

I didn't always feel this way about the debutante thing, I swear. When I was younger I looked forward to dancing waltzes and fox-trots with handsome boys in white tie and tails, and practicing my curtsy in my white gown and gloves. But somewhere along the line the Cotillon lost its romance for me. I know everyone — the boys, the other girls, the "bachelors," and the older socialites — too well. Maybe that's the trouble.

I wanted to be more enthusiastic; I really did. It worried me that I wasn't. I worried about Brooks too. I liked him. I still like him. But whenever I'm with him I feel detached, like I'm watching myself be with him instead of just being with him.

"Call him tomorrow," Ginger repeated, gazing at the glossy pages of her magazine in a lustful trance.

I left her room and went back upstairs, where my two side-kicks were waiting for me.

"Was it about Brooks?" Jane said.

"Yes," I replied. "I'm supposed to call him." I fell onto my bed, knocking my head against Sassy's foot.

"But what about Robinson Pepper?" Sassy asked.

"What about him, indeed," I said.

I didn't know then what would happen, Almighty. And I wasn't planning anything yet. But I do admit I had a feeling the road to the Bachelors Cotillon was not going to run as smoothly as I'd once thought.

FIVE

✉   ✉   ✉

I DISOBEYED GINGER AND CALLED BROOKS FROM SCHOOL THE next afternoon. Claire wanted to coach me.

"Keep your options open, that's all I'm saying," Claire said. "I'd kill to get a phone call from Brooks Overbeck. The only reason you're resisting him is because your mother likes him."

"Don't you think that's a red flag?" I said. "What kind of boy does a mother like? Never an exciting boy or an interesting boy. Always a *nice* boy. Nice to the parents — which can be the fakest kind of creep there is."

"Look, just call him and see what he wants," Claire said. "Whatever it is, you don't have to say yes."

I got out my cell and called Brooks. He didn't pick up. He was probably in class. I left a message: "Hi, Brooks, this is Norrie. My mother said you called last night so I'm, um, just calling you back. Okay, bye."

"Dork," Claire said.

"What?"

"You just are."

We went to the library to read magazines. I was in the middle of an article about how to survive an alien invasion — not that I was worried, but I like to be prepared for anything — when I felt my phone vibrate.

"It's him," I told Claire.

"Take it," she ordered.

I took the phone outside the library. "Hello?"

"Hey, Norrie, what d'ya know?"

"Brooks?" Who else?

"Yeah."

"What's up?"

"How's it going?"

"Good. How are you?"

"Good."

"So, you called me last night?"

Claire materialized by my side to eavesdrop and nudge me with her elbow.

"Right," he said. "My school's having a thing this weekend, like a dance thing. Want to go with me?"

"Um—" A dance at Holman? Would that be fun or hellish? "Which night?" I had promised to see *Vertigo* with Robbie on Saturday night.

Claire double-poked me with her bony elbow. Ow.

"Friday night. We don't have to stay if it sucks. Ryan Gornick's having an afterparty."

"Friday night?"

Claire nodded vigorously to indicate that I should say yes.

"Okay, sure," I said.

"Awesome. I'll pick you up at eight. It's not formal or anything."

"All right," I said. "See you then."

"*Ciao.*"

Ciao? I clicked off.

"What did he say?" Claire asked.

"He said '*ciao*,'" I told Claire. "When did he start saying '*ciao*'?"

"I don't know. He must be going through a phase. So?"

"He said '*ciao.*' Instead of 'hi,' he says 'What d'ya know?' and instead of 'bye,' he says '*ciao.*'"

Claire frowned impatiently. "Did he ask you out?"

"He asked me to the Holman dance Friday night."

"The Lily Hargrove mob. That will be fun."

"Are you being sarcastic or serious?"

"I'm not sure. What's wrong? You don't seem excited about your date."

"I feel like he's asking me out for the wrong reason," I said.

"He likes you. What other reason could there be?"

"His parents could be making him ask me," I said. "Just like my parents are making me say yes."

Which they were, because of you, Almighty. Because Brooks's grandmother is your best friend, and because you've been planning this since I was born.

SIX

⊠　　⊠　　⊠

AT EIGHT, BROOKS DROVE UP IN HIS BMW. HE CAME INSIDE TO
say "What d'ya know?" to my parents, who were on their way
out to dinner. Daddy-o shook his hand warmly and Ginger kissed
him on both cheeks. Sassy and Jane hovered in the foyer,
watching.

"Ready to go?" Brooks asked. I had to admit he looked nice.
He has very regular features and straight teeth. I'd just read that
even, regular features are universally recognized as beautiful. So
no matter what I think of Brooks as a person, I'm genetically
programmed to find him attractive. I resent that.

"Bye, you guys," Sassy said, her voice dripping with
insinuation.

"Have fu-u-un," Jane said, even more suggestively.

"*Ciao*, girls," Brooks said.

"Bye," I said to my sisters. "Have a good time stuck in the
house watching TV and texting your friends."

"Oh, we will," Jane said.

We went outside and got into the car. It was a pretty night, and
warm. Brooks had the sunroof open. I was wearing a dress —
not a fancy one, since the dance wasn't formal — and a beaded

cardigan. Brooks wore jeans, a button-down shirt, and a blue blazer, no tie. It felt strange sitting next to Brooks alone in a car. I didn't know what to say to him. I glanced at his hand on the gearshift and fixated on the wiry golden hairs on his fingers. When did Brooks get so hairy?

"So, I guess you've been taking Italian lessons, huh?" I finally said.

He grinned. "Why do you say that?"

"Well, I noticed you've been saying 'ciao' all over the place. I don't remember you doing that before."

"It's just a little thing I picked up somewhere."

"Cute," I said.

We pulled into the Holman School lot and parked among all the other shiny cars. There was no band, just some guy with a playlist programmed on his laptop, which was plugged into big speakers. The auditorium had been halfheartedly decorated with red streamers and a sign that said HOLMAN HARVEST PARTY. A few boys stood behind a long table, ready to serve soft drinks and pizza. The utter lameness was no surprise. Boys' schools give terrible dances. St. T&A's are the worst. But I'd never been to a Holman dance before and I'd thought it might be a little cooler since Holman is the fanciest boys' school.

Brooks shook his head in disgust. "We're not long for this dump."

I nodded noncommittally, but I was relieved. The dance looked like the outer waiting room of hell.

Brooks led me to a back corner, where his friends and their

dates had exiled themselves. Brooks's best friend, Davis Smith, was with Lily Hargrove.

"Gornick already left to pick up the kegs for the party," Davis said. "We're so out of here."

Lily sighed and propped her long body against the windowsill. "I don't know why you guys even bother pretending to have dances."

"Yeah, sorry we don't have Chanel gift bags and take-home flower arrangements like you get at Radnor," Davis said.

"At least our auditorium doesn't feel like a hospital cafeteria," Lily said.

"Oooh, now you've really cut me to the bone," Davis said.

"You should hold your dances off campus, like at the Peabody Library or someplace," Lily said, ignoring her date's sarcastic tone.

"Are we leaving or what?" said a pouty girl I didn't know.

"What do you think, Norrie?" Brooks asked.

"Well, do you want to stay?" I didn't, but I didn't want to drag him away from his own school dance if he wanted to stay longer than five minutes.

"Do you?" he asked.

Lily rolled her eyes. "We're leaving."

"That's fine with me," I told Brooks.

"It's just that, you know, I asked you to a dance, and we haven't even danced one dance."

"It's okay," I said. "I don't mind." I really didn't.

"I'd stay for a while if you wanted to."

"I know."

We all went outside to the parking lot and got back into our cars. I touched the hood of Brooks's BMW. The engine hadn't even had time to cool yet.

"Sorry about that," Brooks said. "I should have known it would be a waste of time."

We drove out to Ruxton. Ryan Gornick's house looks like a fancy farmhouse, with a small pond out back and even a windmill. People were already swarming around a keg on the back patio, kids who didn't go to Holman or just hadn't bothered with the dance.

Ryan's father — I guessed he was Ryan's father; he was the only person there over forty, including his wife — stood by the patio door greeting the kids as they came out through the kitchen. He wore jeans, sneakers, and a T-shirt that said THUG LIFE. He nodded his head to the hip-hop music playing not too loudly through the outdoor speakers. His wife, Ilsa — Ryan's stepmother — brought him a bottle of German beer. She's in her thirties, tall and leggy and vaguely Scandinavian-looking.

"What d'ya know, Dr. Gornick?"

"Brooks, dude, good to see you." Dr. Gornick patted Brooks on the back and shook his hand. "You playing soccer this year? We need you, man. Who's this lovely young thing with you?" He grinned at me, his white teeth glowing in the twilight.

"This is Norrie Sullivan," Brooks said. "Norrie, this is Ryan's dad, Dr. Gornick, and Ilsa."

"Hi, Norrie." Ilsa smiled warmly at me.

"Brooks, please, call me Joe," Dr. Gornick said. "Grab a seat, relax, have a beer." He waved us toward the patio, where a cool breeze blew the tiki torches.

Dr. Gornick is notorious for hanging around at Ryan's parties. Ilsa is a psychologist and likes to talk to the girls about their self-esteem and their feelings.

I sat on the cool stone wall, and Brooks brought me a plastic cup of beer. Lily and Davis and some other kids stood nearby, warming themselves by the fire in the outdoor stove.

The patio was slowly filling up with people. A tall, brawny boy I didn't know walked in with his arms around two girls from my school: Shea Donovan and Caitlin Evers. The boy looked around the yard as if he expected recognition, as if he wanted to crow, "Hey, everybody, I'm here! And I brought two hos with me." Shea was wearing a blouse unbuttoned low enough to see her electric-blue lace bra, and Caitlin seemed to have had eyeliner tattooed to her face.

"Oh God," Lily said. "It's Tim Drucker. And look who he dragged in."

Phoebe Fernandez-Ruiz made a face. "Why are Catholic school girls so slutty?" Then she looked at me as if she just remembered I was there. "Whoops. Sorry. I don't mean you, of course, Nora."

"It's Norrie," Brooks said, playfully tossing his empty beer cup at her to show he didn't take her infraction too seriously.

She smiled and stood up. "I'll get you a refill. Nora?"

"No, thanks."

People got drunker as the night wore on, especially Dr. Gornick. He and Brooks, Davis, and Tim Drucker were reliving every shot of the previous year's championship lacrosse game. Dr. Gornick was everybody's buddy. When a song he knew came on, he sang along at the top of his lungs. Whenever a girl walked by he would stare at her ass. Ilsa didn't seem to notice. She sat in the kitchen having heart-to-hearts with whichever girls she could corral as they passed her on the way to the bathroom. "Brownie?" she'd say, holding out a plate of them. "I just took them out of the oven."

Lily and Phoebe got friendlier too. "You live in that big house with the tower, right?" Lily said. "My older sister said she went to a secret party there once in the Tower Room. St. John lowered a rope ladder and everybody had to climb up four stories in the middle of the night."

"I was there," I said. "I was twelve, but I heard the noise and sneaked in and St. John let me stay."

"Didn't your parents hear it?" Phoebe asked.

"Guess not," I said. "My mother sleeps with a mask and earplugs, and my dad snores. They can be pretty out of it sometimes."

"They must be," Lily said. "I wish my parents were like that. They watch us like prison guards."

"Bull —" Phoebe said. "They give you grief, but you and your sisters do what you want in the end."

" 'Cause we're not afraid of them anymore," Lily said. "What can they really do to us?"

"That's true," Phoebe said. "It's not like getting a time-out is a big threat."

Near the keg, Dr. Gornick put his arm around Shea's shoulders. "You're the sexiest girl out of this whole bunch, you know that?" he said. Shea swayed slightly.

"Shea Donovan is wasted," Phoebe said.

"I'm so shocked," Lily said.

Ilsa came out from the kitchen with her plate of brownies, looking for victims. She crossed the patio to her husband and offered everyone treats. Then she put her arm around Shea's waist. Dr. Gornick let her go, and Ilsa led Shea to a picnic bench.

"Looks like Shea's in for one of Ilsa's pep talks," Phoebe said.

"Oh God, poor girl," Lily said. "'Where do you see yourself in ten years? You don't want to be dependent on a man.'"

"She should talk," Phoebe said. "If she married that creepy Dr. Gornick for any reason other than money, she's crazier than I thought."

"*Joe*," Lily corrected. "Call him Joe."

We all laughed. But then Ilsa waved us over.

"Jesus. What does she want?" Phoebe said.

"Girls! I need your help for a minute. I've got brownies. . . ."

"Enough with the brownies," Lily said. But we all got to our feet and joined Ilsa and Shea at the picnic table.

"I'm trying to explain to Shea that she doesn't have to behave in this self-defeating way," Ilsa said. I half expected Shea to burst into a rage and yell at Ilsa for humiliating her in front of everybody, but Shea just sat and swayed. She looked more than drunk, like maybe she'd taken some pills or something.

"These girls get plenty of attention from boys — right, girls?" Ilsa waved a hand toward me and Lily and Phoebe. "But they don't have to resort to wearing their blouses unbuttoned or doing whatever boys want."

Shea gaped at us under her blond eyebrows as if she was trying to figure out who we were.

"Ilsa, I don't think she's getting it," Phoebe said.

"Maybe this isn't the best time for a lecture," I said.

"Lecture? I'm not lecturing her. This is girl talk. Right? A heart-to-heart."

Shea started crying. She just sat there with tears running down her face, her nose dripping, quietly sobbing. She kept her hands at her side, not bothering to wipe away the mess on her face.

"Oh my God." Lily turned away.

Ilsa put her arm around Shea. "That's right. Let it all out."

"Let go of her," I said. "You're embarrassing her. I'll take her inside." ·

The party had stopped dead. Everybody was staring at Shea. Brooks ran over. "What's wrong?"

"Shea's upset," I said.

"Shea, do you need a ride home?" Brooks said. "Because Norrie and I are leaving, and we can drop you off if you want."

Shea moved her head, but I couldn't tell if she was shaking it or nodding.

"Where's Caitlin?" I asked.

No one seemed to know. Tim Drucker made a rude gesture and pointed toward one of the upstairs windows.

"Forget it," Brooks said. "Caitlin will find a way home. Let's get Shea out of here."

"There's no need for that," Ilsa said. "I've got this under control, kids."

Brooks helped Shea, still crying, to her feet. "I really think she should go home."

Ilsa rose and towered over us. "Young man, we're the adults here, and this is our house. I'm a professional. I can handle this."

"I'm a dude man!" Dr. Gornick, oblivious, was howling the lyrics to a song.

Brooks and I helped Shea to his car. I gave her a Kleenex and she finally wiped her wet face.

"Thanks, you guys," she said. "For a few minutes there I felt like I couldn't talk. Like I had a gym sock on my tongue."

"Are you okay?" Brooks asked.

"I think so. I think Tim slipped something in my beer."

"That jerk," I said, only I used a stronger word than "jerk." We eased her into the backseat of the BMW. "Do you want some water or something? Are you sure you're all right?"

Shea shook her head. "I'm okay. I dumped the beer when I noticed it tasted funny."

"We'll drive you home," Brooks said. "Where do you live?"

"In Lutherville," Shea said.

Lutherville was not on our way home, but Brooks didn't seem to mind. I didn't mind either. I like driving down the dark, winding roads out in the country at night. There's something romantic about it — even with a drunk girl passed out and snoring in the backseat. Maybe especially then.

"It was nice of you to come to Shea's rescue," I said to Brooks.

"Ilsa's always doing that, trying to psychoanalyze girls in the middle of a party." He didn't look at me, just kept his eyes on the road. "It's not right."

"They're both jerks," I said. "Ilsa and Dr. Gornick."

"I used to wish my parents were cool like Dr. Gornick," Brooks said. "But now I'm glad they just stay on their side of the fence. Who wants your dad singing classic rock at your parties? I don't care if he does supply half your friends with Valium."

"Dr. Gornick gives kids Valium?"

"That's what Tim Drucker says."

We drove in silence for a few miles while the dark wooded road morphed into a commercial strip. "Do you have any idea where we're going?" I asked.

"No. Better wake up Shea and ask her."

I shook Shea gently. "Hey, Shea, how do we get to your house?"

She groaned and opened her eyes and dragged herself up to a sitting position. She stared out the window as if she didn't recognize this landscape at all. But she did.

"Turn left on York Road," she said. "Then left on Othoridge."

She slumped back down on the seat. When we stopped in front of her house she tumbled out the door, muttering, "Thanks, guys," and stumbled toward the ranch house. We lost her for a minute on the lawn, but then she reappeared in the pool of light on the porch. The door opened and she vanished into the world beyond it.

We headed back to the city, a good twenty-minute drive. I didn't know what to say to Brooks so I turned up the radio.

When we got to my house he kissed me on the cheek. He didn't try anything else, and I didn't expect him to. He is a well-known gentleman, and I must admit, Almighty, he deserves his good reputation. I sometimes suspect that he's extra-careful around me, though, since anything that happens between us is sure to get back to you and Mamie.

"Thank you for coming to the lamest dance ever with me," he said.

"I forgot all about the dance," I said. "Seems like months ago."

"We only stayed for five minutes. I think we set a record."

"Well. Thanks for a nice evening."

"Let's do it again sometime, Norrie. Soon."

"Okay."

He got out of the car and went around to open the door for me. Then he walked me up the concrete path to our front door. He kissed me on the cheek again.

"Well, *ciao*," he said.

"*Ciao*," I said. I don't know how to say anything else in Italian except *abbondanza*! And that didn't seem appropriate.

SEVEN

⊠   ⊠   ⊠

THE NEXT NIGHT WAS MY FIRST DATE WITH ROBBIE. THAT WAS A busy weekend.

I met Robbie at the Charles Theater at seven. He didn't need to buy tickets because he works there as a projectionist and curates the Vintage Film Series.

I noticed on the poster that the Hitchcock movie we were about to see was part of the Vintage Film Series. "So it was your idea to show *Vertigo* tonight?" I said.

"Uh-huh. We're doing twelve straight weeks of Hitchcock."

We went inside to buy popcorn. The girl behind the counter cooed, "Hi, Robbie," and gave us the popcorn and Cokes for free.

"Hi, Aileen," Robbie said. "This is Norrie."

"Hi, Norrie." Aileen smiled at me but underneath her smile I saw suspicion or jealousy or annoyance — it was hard to tell exactly what.

I liked the movie; it was kind of scary and sexy. Afterward, we stood awkwardly outside the theater while the crowds poured onto the sidewalk around us. I waited to see what would happen next.

"Well," he said, "I guess you need to get home now?"

"Not really." ·

"You don't?"

"No. It's cool." Ginger and Daddy-o were out, so I wasn't worried.

"Oh. Okay. Want to get something to eat?"

"Yes!" I wished I hadn't said that so enthusiastically, but I couldn't help it.

"Do you like bouillabaisse?"

"Mais oui!"

"Then follow me." We walked, down Charles to Mulberry and headed west.

"Where are we going?" I asked.

"Maurice's. Have you ever been there?"

"No, but I've always wanted to go." St. John goes there sometimes. "Is it true their specialty is ostrich?"

"Mwah!" Robbie kissed his fingertips. "It's ostri-licious. Will you try it?"

"Maybe," I said, adding, *"Abbondanza!"* and throwing my arm in the air for no good reason.

Robbie laughed. "You sure have lots of lust for life."

"I'm not usually so energetic and happy, I swear. I mean, I'm a happy person generally, I'm not depressed or anything, but I try to keep things under control —"

"That's okay, Norrie. I like it. Don't you get sick of everybody acting cool all the time?"

"Yes, I do. I never thought it before, but you're right. It's tiresome."

"Totally tiresome."

"If we become friends, I promise not to act cool," I said. "If I like something, I'll gush about it without holding back my enthusiasm. If I hate something, same thing."

"*If* we become friends?"

"Okay, *when* we become friends. Now. We're friends now. I like you! Okay? I like you and I'm not pretending I don't in order to look cool."

He didn't laugh. I really thought he was going to laugh.

"Thank you," he said. "I appreciate that. I like you too."

"That wasn't very gushy," I complained.

"*You* promised not to act cool. I didn't."

"No fair, Robinson Pepper!"

"When I'm in a gushy mood, I'll gush. I promise. Right now, I'm hungry."

"Mmm. Me too."

The neighborhood started getting sketchy. We turned down a dark alley and stopped in front of a small brick house with a pink door and bright blue shutters on the windows. The main window was obscured by stained glass. There was no sign over the restaurant. There *was* a sign over the burned-out storefront across the street, which said: CHOP CHOP KARATE SHOP.

Robbie rang the doorbell. A man's eye appeared in a peephole. "Who is it?"

"Robbie Pepper. Two for dinner?"

The door opened. A bald, skinny, old man in an apron appraised us, then let us in. "Right this way, sir."

The restaurant was dark, lit only by candles. I touched the

patterned wallpaper. It was snakeskin. Tom Waits played quietly through the speakers.

"Your waitress will be right with you." The old man disappeared into the kitchen.

"That's Maurice," Robbie said. "This place has been in his family since the 1920s. It used to be a speakeasy."

I looked around. There was a collection of odd figurines on a shelf in one corner, and bronze sculptures mounted here and there on the walls.

A pretty waitress gave us menus. "Hi, Robbie," she said.

"Hi, Marissa," Robbie said. "This is Norrie."

Marissa and I said hi to each other. I thought I saw that same look in her eye that I'd seen in Aileen's. Competitive.

"Let's get a pitcher of sangria," Robbie said.

Marissa said, "Sorry, Robbie, but does Norrie have ID?"

He turned to me and blinked as if he didn't understand the question. I shook my head.

"Oh. Right. Sorry. Norrie, what would you like to drink? That's nonalcoholic, I mean."

"Coke, I guess." I felt like an infant. Marissa's smug smile didn't help. "No, ginger ale."

"Two ginger ales," Robbie said.

"Are you sure you don't want a glass of wine?" Marissa asked Robbie. "We've got a nice Sangiovese tonight."

"No, thanks," Robbie said. "Ginger ale's good."

Marissa shrugged, like *Whatever you say, cradle robber,* and left us to our menus. My happy, gushy mood faded away. I suddenly felt self-conscious and uncomfortable.

The doorbell rang and this time Marissa answered it. A large group trooped into the restaurant and started for a table in the corner. As they passed by, a rangy guy with long hair and glasses looked at us. "Robbie!"

"Hi, Robbie," one of the girls in the group said.

Robbie introduced me to them while Marissa impatiently tapped a pile of menus against one hand, waiting to seat them. "This is Doyle, Katya, Josh, Bennett, and Anjali."

"You guys should come sit with us," Doyle said.

Robbie glanced at me. "Is that okay?"

"Sure." I was curious about his friends and hoped they'd save us from awkwardness.

Under Marissa's withering gaze we moved over to the corner and squeezed into a round booth. Doyle — the guy with the glasses — immediately ordered two bottles of wine. Marissa made a point of swooping my wineglass out from under my nose.

"Larissa Dalsheimer is up for the Sondheim Prize," Katya said. "Can you believe that? She paints pornographic scenes on children's blocks. Could she be more obvious?"

"Her stuff is crap," Doyle said. "But she'll win, you watch."

"Erotic stuff always wins prizes," Anjali said. "It's supposed to be so *subversive*."

"Larissa gave me one of those blocks," Josh said. "I like it." That made sense to me, since Josh, with his shaggy blond hair and ironic hipster mustache, looked like a porn star. An ironic porn star. Or at least how I imagine an ironic porn star to look, since I've never seen a porno movie. (Honest, Almighty. I swear!)

"You probably modeled for it," Doyle said.

Josh sat back and grinned. "I'm not saying one way or the other."

"Don't press him, Doyle," Bennett said. "You'll just encourage him."

Katya is an artist and the others are grad students like Robbie. They wear their piercings and tattoos and the unnatural colors in their hair in the blasé way of people who run together in the same tribe.

"So, Norrie, are you in school too?" Katya asked.

"Oh yeah," I said, hoping to leave it at that. Unfortunately, the look on her face told me her curiosity didn't end there, so I added, "Robbie and I met in a class at Hopkins."

"Really?" Anjali said. "You look kind of young to be out of college already."

"Uh, yeah, I know," I said. "Everybody says that."

Robbie laughed. "She's not out of college. She's still in high school."

"What?" Bennett burst out laughing.

"Robbie!" Anjali gasped.

My face burned with embarrassment. Jane calls it "Instant Sunburn," when I blush so fiercely my whole head turns red.

"We just went to a movie together," Robbie said. "What's the big deal?"

"No big deal," Doyle said. I had a feeling they were thinking it was rude to talk about this in front of me. And I guess it kind of was. So they stopped. But I knew they'd all be talking about it later. To defuse the situation, I said, "It's not like we're dating or anything."

Robbie looked kind of sheepish at that, but didn't contradict me. What I'd said was true — the literal truth, if not the spirit of the truth. Meeting Robbie had given me cheekbones, and that had to mean something. But nothing concrete.

Josh poured a glass of wine and reached across Anjali to set it in front of me. "*Josh* . . ." Anjali muttered.

"What?" Josh flashed me an innocent smile. Everything about him seemed designed to make him look harmless, from his boyish curly hair and slight yoga body to his T-shirt with a pink flower on it. All sweetness and light he was, as Miss Maura would say. But was he? "I'm just trying to make her feel welcome."

Marissa stopped at our table. "You guys ready to order?" She looked at me first. I'd barely glanced at the menu, but it didn't matter. I knew what I wanted.

"I'll have the ostrich."

I did it just to show I wasn't a little picky-eater kid. I really wanted spaghetti, but that's what a kid would order. Besides, I was curious to see how ostrich tasted. I was adventurous now.

"She's a brave little toaster," Josh said.

"Josh, why do you have to be such a prick?" Anjali said.

"What'd I say now? Is this about some feminist thing? I'm more feminist than you'll ever be, Anjali."

Anjali rolled her eyes.

"Norrie doesn't mind, right, Norrie?" Josh said. "She doesn't want us to treat her differently just because she's a little younger."

Robbie looked me in the eye to gauge how I was taking Josh's teasing. "It's okay," I said. "I've got two older brothers."

"Told you she was tough," Josh said.

A new song played softly through the speakers, an accordion and a man's low French voice. "Ooh! Charles Trenet!" Bennett cooed, neatly changing the subject.

"He's no Aznavour," I said.

Robbie looked at me in surprise. Everyone did.

"My brother St. John and Daddy-o and I had a Battle of the Charleses, Trenet versus Aznavour. We played all their records, one after another, and voted. Aznavour won."

They all gaped at me.

"You can close your mouths now," I said.

"What kind of high school kid knows Charles Aznavour?" Bennett said.

"You have a brother named St. John?" Doyle said.

"Who's Daddy-o?" Katya asked.

"He's my . . . father." I never realized how weird it sounded until then.

"Norrie's full of surprises," Robbie said.

I guess I was just as exotic to them as they were to me.

"My grandmother likes those old French music hall singers," I explained. I'm happy to give you credit for everything, Almighty. "Sometimes she plays her Aznavour records when we go over for —" I was going to say "tea," but decided not to. Between high school, Daddy-o, St. John, and my familiarity with French pop songs, I'd been exotic enough for one night. "— To visit."

"Now that we've got that straight . . ." Doyle said.

"You really think Aznavour's better?" Bennett asked me. "Did you know Trenet said, 'I make songs like an apple tree make apples. They come from inside me'? How can you not love that?"

The conversation resumed, and now I had a place at the table. I still felt self-conscious, but it was so much fun to listen to them talk that I didn't mind. They came from other places, and their world was the *whole* world, not just a few miles of North Baltimore filled with private schools and dilapidated mansions. The whole, wide world. I forgot all about Brooks. It was like our date had never happened, like he didn't exist. Nothing existed outside of that secret restaurant. I had stumbled into a new world and left the old one behind.

EIGHT

⊠　　⊠　　⊠

JANE AND SASSY AND GINGER AND I WENT TO YOUR HOUSE FOR tea after school that Tuesday. I usually like tea at your house, but that was the beginning of The Tension.

It was a nice October afternoon, the air just starting to crisp up. The grass in Sherwood Gardens was turning brown, and the trees that lined your long drive were shedding their leaves. Bernice was putting watercress sandwiches on the silver tea tray when we walked in.

"Hi there, girls," Bernice said. "Mrs. Beckendorf is waiting in the library. Better scoot on in there because you're late and she's in one of her moods."

"Oh, *lovely.*" Ginger snatched a sandwich off the tray and popped it into her mouth. You're hard on Ginger, but admit it, Almighty: It can't be easy having you for a mother-in-law.

I love your library. Week after week I walk in and am amazed all over again. All those thousands of books, two stories high, and the sunlight pouring in through the tall windows, making the air sparkle with dust motes. Through the French doors, I saw Wallace pottering around outside on the terrace, moving plants from one place to another and watching Raul blow fallen leaves into a pile. Every once in a while, Wallace glanced in and gave us that quick two-fingered salute, like "Wallace Beckendorf reporting for duty."

You were sitting at the head of the tea table as always, with Buffalo Bill on your lap and a Schubert string quartet on the sound system. No zesty French pop songs that day.

We kissed you hello and sat down. You glared at us for a few tense moments, grimly stroking Buffalo Bill's stiff Schnauzer fur. At last you said, "Good afternoon, girls. Norris. Jane. *Sa∂*kia." You always pronounce Sassy's name in that peculiarly emphatic way, as if it tastes funny in your mouth. Don't you like it? Once, I heard you sniff that Saskia sounded like the name of a European actress. Ginger agreed. The difference is that Ginger thinks that's a good thing.

"And Virginia. Who is no longer a girl and should begin behaving as if she is aware that middle age has arrived and she is not a dewy-eyed debutante. Yes, it happens even to her."

Ginger went pale but I doubt she was surprised.

"I'm speaking of that abominable dress you're wearing," you said. "Don't you think a woman of your age should cover her knees?"

Maybe Ginger's dress was a bit on the short side, but come on, she has good legs. She plucked her napkin off the table and placed it over her knees.

Bernice brought in the tea tray and you poured out steaming cups of Earl Grey for all of us. Sassy reached for a sandwich. In spite of the fact that you hate her name, Sassy is the only one of us who never seems intimidated by you. Not counting the boys, of course.

"Virginia, how is my dear Alphonse?"

"He's very well," Ginger said. "Skipping through life as usual."

"Glad to hear it. And, girls, how are you doing in school this year? Saskia?"

"Pretty well, Almighty." I happened to know this wasn't true — Sassy was practically flunking math — but I wasn't about to mention it and spoil your wonderful mood.

"Jane?"

"Just peachy."

"I hear that note of sarcasm in your voice, young lady. Don't think I don't. Your report card will come out soon enough and then we'll see how peachy everything is. Norris, how are you faring in your last year at old St. Maggie's?"

"Fine so far, Almighty," I replied.

"Good. Now. I have issues to discuss with all four of you, Saskia first. What's this I hear about you being immortal?"

Sassy blinked. "Where did you hear that?"

"From your baby brother, Theodore — once I stopped him from torturing poor Bill here. Out with it."

"I'm not immortal, Almighty. I mean, probably not. It's just that I've had a lot of accidents lately and I never seem to get hurt."

By then I knew that Sassy had been hit by a car, but she'd made it sound like nothing, just a tap. And anyway she seemed fine. I didn't realize she felt this made her immortal.

"Count yourself lucky, child. My advice to you is to be more careful and you won't have so many accidents. You are not immortal except in the sense that our souls will ascend to heaven when we die, thanks to the sacrifice of our dear Lord. If we're lucky. And girls who go around committing blasphemy are not good candidates for heaven."

"No, ma'am."

Jane spread jam on a piece of toast. Your face clouded over.

"Jane, if you don't learn to hold your knife properly, no man will ever want to marry you."

Jane wanted to wave that knife in your face like a switch-blade — I know she did — but only set it on her plate and defiantly chomped on her toast in the most unladylike way she could. You suppressed your annoyance admirably.

"Now, Jane. Father Burgess tells me that you've been giving Sister Mary Joseph a terrible time in Religion class. I don't need to ask if this is true; I can see by the wicked, gleeful look in your eye that the situation is even worse than I thought. If you're not careful, Jane, you'll be expelled from St. Maggie's. How would you like that?"

"I'd love it!" Jane cried. "I want to go to public school."

You laughed. "You'd last about a minute with those hoodlums."

"Ha. You don't know Jane," Ginger drawled.

"I don't want to hear any more bad reports about you this year, Jane."

Jane glared at you, and you glared back. Two powerful wills facing off. After an endless moment, Jane looked away. You won that round. But I'd never count Jane out.

"Now, on to Norris."

Ulp.

"Your debut. Have you chosen your escorts for the Cotillon yet?"

"Well, there's Daddy-o and St. John," I said. "You've already arranged that, I think."

"Yes, and your third escort will be Brooks Overbeck. What I'm asking, Norris, is if you have sent him an invitation yet. Time is a-wasting."

"Not yet, Almighty."

"Well, what are you waiting for? You're not thinking of asking another young man, are you?"

Your beady blue eyes bore into me. You were onto me, and you wanted to make sure that I knew that you knew.

A lot goes on under the surface at these teas, doesn't it?

"I believe Brooks has already made some kind of overture to you, to let you know he'll gladly accept your invitation. Correct?"

"Well, he asked me to a dance —"

"Sounds like an overture to me. Get that invitation in the mail."

I couldn't speak. I was angry and afraid. I thought, *Who does she think she is, telling me what to do with my life this way?* It was just a stupid date to a stupid dance. I had nothing against Brooks Overbeck, but I didn't like being ordered to go out with him. Next, I thought, you'd tell me we were getting married in June.

"We've been to Downs and ordered the invitations," Ginger said, trying to stave off a fight.

"Mamie Overbeck has already told everyone that Brooks is escorting Norris to the Cotillon," you said firmly. "I believe she's even told the society reporter at the *Baltimore Sun*. That means it will happen. If it doesn't happen, Mamie will be annoyed, and I'll be annoyed. Brooks will be hurt, and your debut to society will be ruined, forever besmirched by your selfishness or laziness or whatever it is that is keeping you from doing your duty to this family, Louisa Norris Sullivan."

I'd sat through your lectures and orders before, Almighty, and I'd left your teas in tears. But never like this. Maybe it's because I was older now, or maybe it had something to do with the change that happened in Speed Reading class, but this time you went too far.

I knew that anything I said would steel your resolve and make you more stubborn, which would only make things worse for me.

"Do you hear me, Norris?"

"I hear you," I croaked.

"Good." You smiled, but you weren't happy. "Now that most of our business is over, let's enjoy some of these lovely cakes Bernice made for us. More tea, Virginia?"

The Schubert CD ended. "Norris, we need some more music," you ordered. "Put on *La Sonnambula*."

I found the CD — Maria Callas singing *La Sonnambula* — and put it on. Opera music blasted into the huge old library. I turned it down.

I choked down a cucumber sandwich and swallowed my tea while I stared at that giant portrait of you as a young girl that hangs high on the library wall. You posed in your riding outfit with your beloved horse, King, two spaniels at your feet. You were maybe sixteen when that portrait was painted; younger than I am. I wondered: Did people call you Almighty Lou yet, at that age? Or were you still just Louisa?

After tea we went outside to say hello to Wallace. He wore a sun hat that day, even though it was October, to protect the pink and white skin on his head.

"Hello, girls! Have a nice tea with your grandma?" he asked.

Sassy gave Wallace a hug. We all liked him. He didn't seem to have any idea he was married to a saber-toothed tiger, and that was what was endearing about him.

■   ■   ■

That night as I lay in bed in my Tower Room, I thought about the Cotillon. I pictured myself in a white dress like a bride, dancing with Daddy-o, then with St. John, and then with Brooks. But every time Brooks spun me around he turned into Robbie.

You sat in a place of honor at the head table, scowling at the dance floor and telling Robbie the infiltrator to get out of Brooks Overbeck's way. The music changed from a waltz to the melancholy aria from *La Sonnambula* as the room grew bigger and bigger and spun around me until I fell asleep.

NINE

⊠ ⊠ ⊠

BY THE END OF OCTOBER I ASSUMED THAT ROBBIE WOULD SIT next to me in Speed Reading class. My reading speeds were inching up but not as much as they should have been. I kept getting distracted by the words. I'd see one I liked and would stop to admire it. Robbie was the star of the class. He had the highest numbers every week.

"Why are you even bothering with this stupid class?" I asked him. "You're already a speed reader."

"I wasn't before I started," he said. "And besides, I like my classmates."

After class he told me that Katya was in a group show at the Cader Gallery and he was going to the opening party Friday night. "Want to come?"

"Yes," I said, and then I started thinking about what I'd said yes to and added, "Wait — I take it back." Katya had been nice to me that night at Maurice's, but a lot of Robbie's other friends were bound to be there too. Including maybe snide Marissa, creepy Josh, and the jealous Charles Theater girl. What if I felt weird there?

"Too late," Robbie said. "You said yes. You can't take it back." Then he looked at me more carefully. "Why do you want to take it back?"

"I'm afraid your friends will be mean to me in such a subtle and sophisticated way I'll barely know they're doing it," I confessed.

"I'll protect you," he said.

"Then I'll go."

■ ■ ■

Jane wanted the Mercedes that night so she dropped me off downtown, and I met Robbie just outside the gallery. It was packed. People spilled out onto the street, laughing and smoking cigarettes. The first person Robbie saw when we walked in was Doyle.

"Hey — we're all going over to Carmen's for dinner after this," Doyle said. "You guys in?"

Robbie glanced at me. "Sure," I said. "Dinner is good."

We wandered around looking at the art. Katya's piece was a video monitor mounted inside an elaborately painted gold frame. The video showed a girl dressed up like the *Mona Lisa*, sitting still as if posing for a painter.

"Do you like it?" Robbie asked me.

"Yes, I do."

"It's so late eighties," Doyle whispered to us. "But I won't tell Katya that."

We found Katya in the middle of a crowd of her friends and congratulated her. I felt shy. Waiters passed around bottles of beer and plastic cups of wine. The room got hot and crowded and stuffy. Robbie said something to me but I couldn't hear him over the noise, so he shouted whatever it was and I still couldn't hear him.

"LET'S STEP OUTSIDE FOR SOME AIR," he yelled.

I nodded and we threaded our way through the people. Just as we got to the door, who should come in but Ginger and Daddy-o. They looked out of place yet somehow perfect, Daddy-o in a bow tie and one of his old tweed suits, and Ginger draped in mink and crimson lipstick. It hadn't occurred to me that they'd be at Katya's opening, but it should have. Sometimes I forget that the medieval artifacts Daddy-o works with and pieces like Katya's video are part of the same world.

"Well, well, look who's here!" Daddy-o said in his jovial way. "I didn't know you ran with the art crowd, sweet pea."

"Who are you here with?" Ginger asked. "Claire?"

They smiled reflexively at the sight of me, their delightful daughter, but looked a bit baffled as they took in the young man standing beside me and realized he wasn't Claire in any way, shape, or form.

"Darling, who's your friend?" Ginger purred.

I summoned my manners. "Ginger, Daddy-o: This is Robbie. Robbie, these are my" — gulp — "parents."

Robbie shook Daddy-o's hand. "It's very nice to meet you."

"Robbie *who*, darling?" Ginger asked.

"Pepper," Robbie said. "Robinson Pepper."

Ginger accepted his offered hand at last. "Charming to meet you."

"What do you think of the show?" Daddy-o asked. "Should we bother braving this mob or simply turn around and head for dinner?"

"It's good," I said.

"Definitely worth a look," Robbie said. I was proud to see that he didn't seem rattled by suddenly meeting my parents. He held his own with them, cool for cool.

"Would you two like to join us for dinner after we have a look round?" Daddy-o asked. "We're only going down to the Prime Rib, but I still say they have the best steaks anywhere."

Oh no. God no.

"We can't," I blurted.

"We're invited to a friend's for dinner," Robbie said.

Ginger raised one of her overplucked brows. "Oh? A friend? And I don't suppose *that* would be a Miss Claire Mothersbaugh, would it?"

"Who?" Robbie said.

"No, Ginger, it's a friend of Robbie's. Don't worry, I won't be home late."

"Who's worried?" Daddy-o said. "You can't stay out late in this town no matter how hard you try. Nothing stays open past two!" He pressed Ginger forward, into the crowded gallery. "We'll see you in a few minutes."

Oh no they wouldn't. I waved them off and we stepped outside into the chilly night air, pungent with cigarette smoke and car exhaust.

"Well, that's that," I said. "We can't stay. We have to get out of here."

"But Carmen's dinner doesn't start for another hour."

"We can kill some time, get a coffee or something."

"Was it that bad? What did you tell them you were doing tonight?"

"They didn't ask. I guess Ginger just assumed I was doing something with my friend Claire. Or maybe one of my sisters told her that, to cover for me."

"Are you going to get in trouble now?"

"I don't know," I said. "They could bombard me with annoying questions. Or they might never mention this night again. It could go either way."

"I thought they were nice," Robbie said.

"They know how to talk to people," I said. "They're always 'nice.'"

Robbie scuffed the sole of his shoe on the dirty sidewalk. "Well, let's walk down to Carmen's. By the time we get there we'll only be a little bit early."

We walked downtown. Robbie took my hand. I was nervous about what Ginger and Daddy-o would say when I got home, but I tried to push that out of my mind because I was also nervous about my ability to make it through a whole evening with Robbie's friends without looking like an idiot.

"What are your parents like?" I asked. "I bet they don't go around calling everybody 'darling.'"

"That's for sure," Robbie said. "My mother's a psychiatrist. She's half Jamaican and half Jewish — she calls herself a Double J — and she's very cutting and blunt. She wants everyone to be honest and face the truth all the time. It's brutal. I really appreciate people like your parents, who take the trouble to pre-tend to be nice, even if they don't mean it. You have no idea what a wonderful thing that is, Norrie. It's so civilized."

I'd never thought of it that way. I always wished Ginger and Daddy-o would stop talking around things and just say what they're really thinking. But you never have trouble speaking your mind, and I don't always like that either. No offense. So maybe Robbie had a point.

"What about your dad?" I asked.

"He's as bad as my mother. Maybe worse. He's a market-research consultant. He studies people's facial expressions to see how they feel about commercials and products. He used to be a psychologist but he makes more money helping big corporations dupe the public. The worst part is he can look at your face and say, 'Your upper lip just twitched! Anger! You're angry. Don't try to hide it from me, young man. Why does it make you so angry when I say those pants make you look like a girl? Do you have some-thing against girls? Perhaps some unresolved Oedipal feelings?'"

"Ouch."

"Maybe denial is the reason your parents are still together," Robbie said. "Mine split up when I was ten. Two aggressive people can't live in the same house for long, analyzing every word and facial twitch. They tear each other apart."

We strolled through Mount Vernon Place. People poured out of the Peabody Library, having just seen a concert. A group of music students sat on the edge of a fountain, their instrument cases propped up in front of them, passing around a bottle in a paper bag.

"I really like Baltimore," Robbie said. "It's so chill."

I pointed to the Walters Art Museum. "Daddy-o works there."

"I love that you call your father Daddy-o. It makes him sound so fun and not scary."

"He is fun and not scary. He likes to have a good time. Your dad sounds scary, I have to say."

"I make him sound worse than he is. If you met him you'd like him, I think, because he's smart and you like smart people. He'd like you. He can read faces, and you have one of the great ones."

We stopped at a second fountain — the one with the Sea Urchin statue. The rushing water chilled the air. Robbie looked down at me. I could read his face very easily. Maybe he'd learned to telegraph his feelings clearly, having been raised by crazed psychologists. He wanted to know if I'd mind if he kissed me.

"No," I said. "I wouldn't mind."

He leaned down and kissed me quickly and lightly on the lips. "That's enough for now," he said. Then we continued on our way downtown.

■ ■ ■

Carmen lived in a loft near Fells Point. It turned out we weren't early after all. People were already drinking wine in the kitchen and helping Carmen make salad. Carmen wiped her wet hands on her canvas apron. She kissed Robbie and pinched his cheek, murmuring "Robbila, Robbila," like a Jewish grandmother, then shook my hand. She's small and wiry as a dancer, with long black hair and rich dark skin and full red lips. She's sexy, and I felt jealous of her immediately. It turns out I had good reason to, but I didn't know that yet.

Robbie introduced me to everyone. There were too many names to remember, but they all seemed to remember mine.

"Wait . . . Sullivan?" a shaved-headed girl said. "You're not from that evil family, are you?"

"Yes I am," I said, thinking she was making some kind of odd joke. "We're all evil. How did you know?"

She wasn't joking. "From that blog, you know? Myevilfamily .com? This girl named Jane Sullivan tells all about her rich family who lives up in Guilford somewhere —"

Jane. I should have known this would have something to do with her. Should I admit that she was my sister, or pretend to be from a completely different Sullivan family? It's a common name, after all. I could've gotten away with it.

"I'll show you." The girl went to a Mac on Carmen's desk and typed in www.myevilfamily.com. There at the top of the page was a drawing of our house. In a side column, under "About Me," was a caricature of Jane, probably drawn by her friend Bridget.

"That's my sister," I blurted.

"Really?" the bald girl said. "That's hilarious. Listen to this" — she started reading out loud from one of Jane's entries — "'Almighty was born with lots of money. I've already told you some of the evil ways her ancestors earned it. But she has even more money now. How did she get it? By marrying people.' She calls her grandmother 'Almighty.' Is that not a riot?"

"Do you really call her 'Almighty'?" a guy asked me.

"Everybody calls her that." I never gave it much thought until that night.

"You have to read the whole thing," the bald girl said. In my mind her name had become "Shavey." "It's the context. You know, this poor little rich girl bitching about her terrible family —" She paused. She must have remembered that the poor little rich girl's sister was standing right next to her. "Sorry. I mean, you think it's funny, don't you?"

"I haven't read it yet," I admitted. "But when I do, I'm sure I'll be in stitches."

Katya and the rest of the gallery contingent arrived, and the loft began to fill up with people. Robbie knew most of them. I was enjoying my uncomfortable anonymity when it was shattered by the entrance of Shea Donovan. Even worse, she walked in on the arm of Josh. He wore yoga pants and a T-shirt that said BE PRESENT. She wore jeans and a sweater. She didn't look all that slutty, really. Not that night anyway.

"God save us, Josh is here," Anjali muttered to Robbie. "With that little kid." I tried to take it as a compliment that she'd already forgotten to think of me as a little kid too.

"I know that girl," I told Robbie. "She goes to my school."

"She has crap taste in men," Robbie said. "Josh is a skeeve."

"Yeah," I said. "She likes skeeves."

"Dinner's ready," Carmen announced. The long table was spread with tall candelabras and all kinds of delicious food, from curried chicken to vegetable samosas to salmon teriyaki and pork dumplings. Some people settled at the long table to eat, and some filled their plates and made satellite groups on the couches and cushions scattered through the living room.

I sat next to Robbie at the long table and we passed the dishes around. Music was playing and the room was buzzing with talk and laughter. Robbie grinned at me and I felt warm and happy all of a sudden. I pressed my hand on the top of his head. It was an irresistible urge. His curly black hair flattened under my hand. I laughed.

"Why are you doing that?" he asked.

"I don't know. I can't help it." I lifted my hand and his hair sprang back into its usual fan shape. "Does it bother you?"

"Not when you do it."

Then we laughed the strangest laugh, like we were co-conspirators. I've had that feeling with my sisters before, but never with a boy or even Claire.

Carmen sat down next to me. "Hey, you two. So. Norrie. You're Robbie's new girlfriend?"

She was staring at me intensely. I got the feeling her interest in this question was not casual.

"We just met a few weeks ago," Robbie said.

"That doesn't answer my question," Carmen said. "Which was directed at Norrie, not you, Robbie. Don't do that thing."

"What thing?" Robbie asked.

"That thing where you think you know everything and you answer questions for everyone, even those that weren't directed at you," Carmen said. "Norrie's old enough to speak for herself — aren't you, Norrie?"

She was smiling, but her incisors suddenly made me think of a wolf's teeth.

"Of course I am," I said. I had to stop playing the shy little girl or people like Carmen would eat me alive. "Robbie and I are friends."

"How did you meet?" Carmen asked.

"In a class at Hopkins," I said.

"Oh? Do you go to Hopkins?"

"No."

"Then what were you doing there?"

"What is this, an interrogation?" Robbie asked.

"I'm just curious about your new friend, Robbie," Carmen said.

Robbie scowled. An electric current ran between them — some history I didn't know about. I'd been hoping to pass as a Hopkins undergrad, but I got the feeling Carmen already knew my true story. She just wanted to hear it from me. So I'd know she knew, and Robbie would know she knew.

"It's a night class." I hesitated to add the humiliation — not even a night class in, say, Existential Philosophy or Particle Physics but, "Speed Reading."

"Speed Reading! You must both be whizzes at it by now. As I remember, Robbie already reads pretty quickly."

"I wanted to go even faster," Robbie explained.

"I'm sure you did," Carmen said. "More wine?" She topped off our glasses. "Robbie, what's the name of that girl Josh is with, do you remember? Shawn, or Sinead, or something?"

Robbie gave me away. "Norrie knows her. What's her name?"

"Shea."

Carmen's wolf grin was wide and triumphant. "You sure get around for someone I've never met before. Did you meet Shea in Speed Reading too?"

"We go to school together," I said. "We're not friends or anything. I hardly know her."

"Isn't that interesting. Don't be a snob, Norrie. You have more in common with Shea than you do with anyone else in this room." She rose quickly with the bottle of wine and offered to refill someone else's glass.

"Sorry about Carmen," Robbie said. "She can be kind of a bitch."

I got up to go to the bathroom. Shea and Josh came out of the bathroom together, rubbing their noses. At the sight of me Shea brightened and got friendly.

"Norrie! What are you doing here?"

"Hi, Shea. Same thing as you, I guess."

"Your boyfriend is cute! Josh says he's supposed to be very smart."

"He's not my boyfriend, exactly —"

"What do you mean? I saw him sitting with his arm around you. What are you doing here with him if he's not —" A memory flickered across her face. "Wait — Brooks. You were at Gornick's party with Brooks, and now you're here with this guy. . . ."

For as long as I've known her — and I've known her since seventh grade — I'd never seen Shea so talkative. At school she's always chewing gum and hiding behind her hair and slouching around as if she doesn't want anyone to see her. At parties, with boys, she's all body language. But here, suddenly, in this exotic world of grown-up people who intimidated me, she was chirpy and cute. *No wonder she likes being with older guys,* I thought, *if she feels more animated around them.*

"I'm just hanging out with Robbie," I said.

"You know what? I really want some wine," Shea said. She tottered off to the kitchen counter where the wine was. Josh followed in her wake.

■　■　■

By the time Carmen's homemade spice cookies were served, the music was louder, the windows were open, and people were dancing lazily in one corner of the room. Shea and Josh were planted at one end of the long orange couch, making out as if they'd forgotten they were in a room full of people. The next time I glanced in their direction, they were gone. I thought they'd left, but about half an hour later I saw Josh back on the couch, talking to Katya.

"I'm working on keeping my mind here and now, and not letting it drift, you know?" Josh said. Katya nodded absently, her eyes wandering around the room. "I'm in a constant struggle with my ego. I'm always trying to tamp it down but it pops back up by itself."

"Maybe that's just human nature," Katya said.

"Josh is lying to Katya," Robbie whispered to me. "See how he's smiling with his mouth but not with his eyes?"

"Yeah . . . ," I said. Robbie was right — Josh's smile looked stiff. "So you mean he's not in a constant struggle with his ego?"

"I think he let his ego win a long time ago," Robbie said. We snickered.

"Human nature is no excuse." Josh stretched, then rested his hands on the waist of his pants.

"Look!" Robbie whispered. "He just made two classic flirting signals!"

"But she doesn't like him," I said.

"How do you know?"

"I don't know," I said. "I'm just getting a vibe."

"Her legs are pointed away from him," Robbie whispered. "That's a signal she doesn't like him. You picked up on it unconsciously."

"I keep reminding myself in meditation: Other people don't matter," Josh said. "My consciousness is the universe."

"That's how you tamp down your ego?" Katya said.

Carmen ran out of her bedroom screaming in disgust. "Josh! Where's Josh?" She zeroed in on him. "Josh! That little lush you brought over puked in my bed! Right on my pillow!"

"Shit," Josh muttered as Carmen dragged him back into her bedroom to show him the damage.

A few minutes later Josh pulled a stumbling Shea toward the door. Her eyes were heavy-lidded. She burped. "I've got to take her home. Sorry, Carmen."

"What? You're not going to clean up after her?"

"What do you want me to do? She's in bad shape. I'll make it up to you. Send me the laundry bill or whatever."

"She's never coming here again, do you hear me?" Carmen pushed them out the door. "That's what you get for fooling around with little baby sluts." *Slam!* She whacked the door shut.

A few people glanced in my direction.

Carmen turned her fury on me. "Maybe you should go too, Robbie, before something else happens. I don't want to be responsible for corrupting a minor. You want to be a glorified babysitter, that's your business."

"Norrie's fine, Carmen," Robbie protested. "I—"

"Don't worry, Robbie, I get it," Carmen said. "I was too much for you, and since you can't handle a real woman, you go for a high school girl. Nice and dumb and easy to scam. Right, Robbie?"

My face was flaming hot. I wanted to defend myself, but what could I say? Besides, it was obvious now that the electricity I'd noticed between Robbie and Carmen was an ex-girlfriend vibe.

"Norrie isn't like Shea," Robbie said. "Just because they're the same age—"

"— and go to the same school —" Carmen said.

"— doesn't mean they're the same kind of person," Robbie finished. "Norrie is not dumb and nobody's scamming anybody. You want to see a real scam artist, look in the mirror."

"I'm so grateful we broke up!" Carmen said. "It was the best thing that ever happened to me."

Robbie grabbed my hand and we flew out of there. She slammed the door behind us too. "How dare she talk to you that way?" he said. "Or to me? Or to anybody?" He kicked open the door to the stairwell and raced down a few feet ahead of me. When we got outside in the cold night air he said, "I didn't mean for things to turn out that way."

"Why didn't you tell me about her before?" I asked.

"We broke up months ago. Maybe she isn't as over it as I thought."

It was after midnight. The city was quieting down. A gang of boys watched us from across the street.

"Now what?" Robbie said. "We walked all the way down here. I left my car up near the gallery. How am I going to get you home?" He had figured on one of his friends driving us back to the car, but he hadn't counted on making such a speedy and humiliating exit.

"Maybe we can catch a taxi," I said. We weren't far from the Ritz, and I knew we could probably find one there if we didn't hail one on the street.

As it turned out, a cab drove by as we headed for the hotel. We flagged him down and he drove us up Charles Street to Robbie's car. We were quiet as we drove north through the city. The glasphalt sparkled like a street of stars. When he pulled up in front of the house, he laughed and said, "Look at this place! So you really *are* part of that evil family on the website."

The light was on in the Tower. "That's us all right — the evil family."

I waited for him to kiss me good night, but he hesitated. Maybe Carmen's words were echoing in his head, especially "babysitter." They were definitely banging around in *my* head.

"There's a big difference between you and Shea, you know," he said. "I mean, people don't respect Shea. She's always wasted and she doesn't know what she's doing half the time. She just lets things happen to her."

"People don't respect me either," I said. "At least, your friends don't."

"They don't know you." He leaned toward me and brushed my cheek with his lips. "I'm just trying to say don't worry about what my jealous ex-girlfriend thinks. She's only trying to make me mad. Okay?"

I wasn't convinced, but I said, "Okay."

I opened the car door. Robbie didn't get out to open it for me the way Brooks would have. But I didn't mind. I was perfectly capable of opening it myself.

"I'll wait till you get inside," he said. "See you in class on Tuesday."

"See you in class."

I ran inside the house and waved from the front door. He waved back and drove away.

Upstairs in my room, Jane and Sassy waited.

TEN

✉   ✉   ✉

"JANE, WHAT THE F — ?" I THREW MY BAG ON THE DRESSER, pulled my sweater over my head, and cursed her out. I was warm from climbing the stairs and being kissed and feeling annoyed. "My Evil Family? Dot com?"

Jane grinned. "How did you find out? Is it famous yet?"

"In a way," I said. "One of Robbie's friends showed it to me. She recognized my last name and asked me if I was one of *those* Sullivans. I wish I wasn't."

"It's just a little thing I started," Jane said. "Bridget has one too. Hers is called bridget2nowhere.com."

"Very clever," I snapped. "But why?"

"Because everybody looks up to us," Jane said. "And we're shrouded in mystery and mythology. Almighty spreads these stories about our ancestors and how great they were. I thought people should know the truth. Anyway, I haven't written anything about you . . . yet."

"You better not."

"How was the opening?" Sassy asked.

"Crowded," I said. "And guess who was there? Ginger and Daddy-o."

Sassy gasped and Jane laughed. "You're kidding! Did they meet Robbie?"

"Yes. They were very polite."

"What did Robbie think of them?" Jane asked.

"He thought they were charming."

"Everybody always says that," Sassy said.

"Yeah, if they only knew the truth," Jane said. "That's exactly why I'm writing this blog —"

"Please," I said. "Like you know the truth about anything."

Sassy tried to keep the peace. "Where'd you go after the opening?"

"To a party at this girl Carmen's house — and she turned out to be Robbie's ex-girlfriend."

"Holy crap."

"Yeah. Shea Donovan was there too. It was one of those nights when you can't go anywhere without running into somebody."

"You mean, like, every night?" Jane said.

"Shea got wasted and threw up in Carmen's bed."

Jane cracked up. "Poor Shea," Sassy said.

I put on my nightgown and nudged Jane over to make room for me on the bed. Sassy picked up a hunk of my hair, twirled it around in her hand, and let it drop. She likes to play with my hair.

"The thing is," I said, "I keep thinking about Shea, and me, and what it means that we're, I don't know, in the same world. If we're both dating these older guys, does that make me ... like her?"

Sassy twirled my hair some more. Jane thought this over.

"You mean, are you a slut like Shea? The answer is definitely yes."

I bumped her with my hip so hard she almost fell off the bed. "Really. I can see what people think of Shea. The girls at the party were putting her down. But what do they say about me? And how does Robbie think about me? Do you think he sees me as a malleable little high school girl he can use and then dump? Like I'm too young to know what he's up to? I mean, why is he with me? Why really?"

I didn't really expect them to have any answers. I wish I had an older sister.

"You have two choices," Jane said. "You can play it safe, break up with him right now, and you won't get fooled and you won't get hurt. Or you can keep seeing him and find out what happens. It might be good, it might be bad."

"What do you think I should do, Sass?"

She stopped playing with my hair and stretched her legs out from under her nightgown. "I think you should give him a chance. Keep your eyes open. If you chicken out, won't you always wonder what would have happened?"

I noticed a brown spot on Sassy thigh, about the size of a quarter. "Where'd you get this bruise?" I touched it lightly.

She flinched but said, "It doesn't hurt."

"How'd you get it?"

"I got hit by a car," she said.

"Again?" I said.

"Sassy, what's wrong with you?" Jane said. "Don't you ever watch where you're going?"

"I do," she said, looking sheepish. "They just come out of nowhere. It's like I have a magnet inside me that attracts cars."

"Did you hit your head? Are you hurt anywhere else?" I asked.

"No. Don't worry, I'm fine."

I looked at Jane, who shook her head.

"Really, I'm fine," Sassy said. "Cars can't hurt me."

"Sassy, no."

"Not that immortality stuff again."

"How else do you explain it?" she said. "I fell through a hole in the space-time continuum, and in this parallel universe I can't be hurt. I'm unkillable."

"You're un-sane," Jane said.

"Sassy, please don't think you can just walk in front of moving cars and be okay," I pleaded. "You're just as killable as the rest of us."

"Okay," she said. But I could tell she wasn't convinced.

■　■　■

"Who's the boy, Norrie?" Ginger asked.

I went downstairs at 10:30 the next morning. Takey had finished his cereal hours earlier and was already out with Miss Maura at a soccer game. Sassy, Ginger, and Daddy-o were quietly eating eggs and bacon. Jane followed me downstairs a few minutes later.

"What boy?" I said like an idiot.

Ginger sighed dramatically and rattled the charm bracelet on her freckled arm. "The boy you were with at the gallery. He was terribly good-looking. Though I'd like him better with a haircut."

"Oh, him? That was Robbie."

"I remember his name, darling. That's not what I'm asking."

"I thought he seemed like a very nice young man," Daddy-o said. "Refined."

"You could tell that just by looking at him?" Jane asked.

"Of course, lovey. How else?"

"What is it with boys and crazy hair these days?" Ginger shuddered.

"I'd think you'd like that crazy long hair," Daddy-o said. "Reminds you of your own youthful adventures."

Ginger and Daddy-o can easily lose the thread of a conversation and go off on some tangent like "Hair Styles of 1977." But not this time.

"It reminds me of my youth a little too much," Ginger said. "So—? What school does he go to?"

"School?" I said.

"Yes, Pie. You know, that place where you go to learn nine months a year?"

I had a feeling that Ginger and Daddy-o would like Robbie just fine, as long as they didn't find out too much about him.

"Well . . . he goes to Hopkins."

"College boy, eh?" Daddy-o said. "What's he studying?"

"Film," I said.

"Film?" Ginger said. "That sounds like a perfect waste of time. But wasting time is what college is for, I suppose."

As long as they accepted the information they had so far and probed no further, I might be all right. Leave it to Sassy to spill the dirt.

"I want to meet him," Sassy said. "I can't imagine going out with a boy who's older than St. John."

Daddy-o slapped the newspaper on his plate, and Ginger let her bracelet clank on the table. "Older than St. John? What are you talking about?"

"Ha-ha," Jane gloated. "There are no secrets in this family — anymore."

I glared at Sassy, but immediately felt guilty about it, because I knew she felt sorry and didn't mean to be such a blabbermouth. Jane, on the other hand, was going to get it.

"I thought you said he was a college boy," Daddy-o said.

"He must be pretty stupid if he's older than St. John and hasn't finished his degree yet," Ginger sniffed. "Is it a learning disability or does he take a lot of drugs?"

"He's in graduate school," I explained.

"Exactly how old is this gentleman?" Daddy-o asked.

"Twenty-five."

Daddy-o frowned, pondering this. "That's quite a bit older than you, Norrie."

"Where did he go to high school?" Ginger asked.

"I don't know," I said. "He's from New York."

"New York!" Ginger got up and threw herself onto the chaise longue. You know the green one by the breakfast nook? We keep it there in case she's seized with an urge to lie down. "A twenty-five-year-old film student from New York . . . with a learning disability . . . who takes drugs. Oh, darling, how awful. What kind of future could he possibly have?" The age difference in and of itself didn't bother her. It was the slackerish nature of his chosen profession. And maybe the drugs, which were a figment of her imagination but now would be stuck in her mind forever.

"What about St. John?" I said. "Who's hiring philosopher poets?"

"St. John comes from money," Ginger said. "There's always a future in money. Does this Robinson Pepper have money?"

"I don't know," I said. I doubted it, and I didn't care.

"At least he lives the life of the mind," Daddy-o said. "That's something." But I could tell by the way he picked at a nonexistent crumb on his chin that he felt uncomfortable with the situation.

"What if you end up marrying him?" Ginger said, off on her own tangent. "You don't want your last name to be 'Pepper' . . . Norris Pepper . . . It's too . . . *redolent.*"

"I could keep my own name."

"It's annoying when women do that," Daddy-o said. "It makes everything so complicated."

I slurped my cooling coffee. "We're not getting married. I just met him a few weeks ago."

"You hardly know him," Daddy-o said.

"He's already having a bad influence on you," Ginger said. "Since *when* do you slurp your coffee that way?"

Jane burst out laughing and slurped hers too.

"My slurping my coffee has nothing to do with him." I slurped again. "Anyway, you have nothing to worry about because I'm not going to marry anyone."

"Me neither," Jane said.

"Nonsense, darling, you'll marry someone lovely and suitable," Ginger said. "You too, Jane. Sassy, thank you for not making such a ridiculous declaration in the first place."

"I didn't have time to," Sassy said. "I might not get married, who knows? And what's suitable?"

"Suitable is like Brooks Overbeck," Jane said, clearly trying to cause mischief.

"Exactly," Ginger said. "Norrie, this Pepper person isn't a boy, he's a grown man. He'll either toy with you and toss you aside—"

"Oh, he had better not do that," Daddy-o said, his jowls shaking.

"— or he'll want to get serious with you. You don't want to get all wrapped up with someone like this now, Norrie. You'll miss out on all the marvelous boys your own age, like Brooks. You'll have plenty of time in your twenties to date aimless losers who think they're creative and can't make a living. And besides, who are you going to take to all the debutante parties this year? Not some crazy-haired grad student from out of town. He doesn't even own a proper seersucker suit, does he? I'm assuming he doesn't."

Jane smirked, triumphant because this conversation fed so beautifully into her theory that our family is evil.

"I have no idea what kind of clothes he's got hanging in his closet," I said. "For all I know he's got a Starfleet captain's uniform hidden in there. If he wants to wear it to a debutante party, that's up to him."

Ginger was really pissing me off. Daddy-o less so, because I could tell he was seriously thinking this over, until his brain got tired and he wished it away. But Ginger was putting all kinds of obstacles in my path, silly obstacles that were all about her and what she wanted.

"End it now, darling. That's my advice. This little adventure of yours isn't going to go anywhere."

"I agree," Daddy-o said. "This situation makes me very uncomfortable. I don't like thinking of you with a man who's older than my oldest son." He picked up his newspaper and gazed into its depths, ready to wash his hands of this whole affair and go back to his absentminded preoccupations. "I don't want to forbid you to see him, Norrie — one can't legislate one's heart's desires, after all — but I certainly wish you'd stop so our lives can go on again as usual. Thank you, dear."

Ginger studied me for a long time. At last she said, "Norrie is just trying to get some attention, that's all. To worry us and rebel a little. Aren't you, darling? You haven't been a bit rebellious until now, and everyone's entitled at your age."

She turned her face away and closed her eyes. "And, girls — this goes for all three of you, and you too, Al — I hope this won't get back to Almighty. She doesn't need to hear the sordid details of your love life, Norrie. It would only upset her, and no one wants that."

"Certainly not. No one wants that," Daddy-o chimed in.

See how we keep things from you, Almighty? But now I'm telling you everything. I'm not leaving anything out.

Conversation over. Daddy-o was buried in his newspaper, and Ginger covered her eyes with her forearm as if she had a terrible headache. Sassy shrugged and looked sheepish. Jane grinned mischievously. I pointed at the ceiling — universal code for "My room, now" — and the three of us went upstairs for a Tower Meeting.

"This isn't over, is it?" Sassy said on the stairs.

"No, it isn't," I said. "And, Jane, this had better not end up on that stupid blog of yours."

"Freedom of speech. You can't tell me what I can and can't write about, Mussolini."

I pressed her against the wall and said in my most threatening voice, "I'm your sister. If you care about my happiness and well-being, you will not write about my private problems in your blog."

"Understood," Jane said. "Unless it becomes a public matter. Then it's out of my hands."

"Make sure it doesn't become a public matter," I said between clenched teeth.

"Will do, Mildew."

"Think of it this way, Jane," Sassy said. "If you spill Norrie's secrets, she won't confide in you anymore. How would you like that?"

She tried to hide it, but I saw a flash of horror cross Jane's face. She hates to be left out. I gave Sassy a grateful smile. Sometimes she knows exactly the right thing to say.

ELEVEN

⊠　　⊠　　⊠

I FELT THE DIFFERENCE AS SOON AS I WALKED INTO SCHOOL
on Monday morning. Girls said hello to me as always, but there
was a tentativeness to their greeting, as if they were keeping
their distance. They looked at me with curiosity or scorn, when
no one had ever been curious or scornful toward me before. What
was there to be curious about? I was just another girl like
them, even less interesting than they were since I never got into
trouble and always seemed to be on the right track: the boring
track.

But word of Carmen's party must have gotten out, because
everybody knew about it. I could feel it. I had become a different
person in their eyes. I had become a pariah. I had become Shea.

Claire met me at my locker and confirmed my suspicions.

"Norrie — really? You were at a party with Shea and two guys
in their twenties? How did this happen?"

"How does everybody know?"

"Caitlin must have blabbed. I think she's jealous of Shea."

I didn't see how anyone could be jealous of Shea.

"Why didn't you tell me about it?" Claire asked.

I didn't need to tell Claire about it, because I had Jane and Sassy. And then there was Brooks . . . Claire wouldn't understand. Also, I feared the Caitlin effect: that Claire would blab and everybody would get the wrong idea.

"I don't know," I said. "It was weird. The girl who had the party turned out to be Robbie's ex, and I think she still likes him or is mad at him or something. Then Shea threw up in her bed and that didn't help at all —"

"Are you, like, friends with Shea now?" Claire asked. "Because that's what everyone's saying. That you and Shea are going to parties downtown together and picking up older guys."

"*That's* what everyone thinks?" I was shocked. How could my own classmates change their image of me so suddenly? "That's crazy. I went to a party and Shea just happened to show up. Doesn't that happen to you all the time?" This city is a big spiderweb that catches you no matter where you go. That's how it seems to me, anyway.

"I've got to meet this Robbie guy," Claire said. "I don't see how you can like anybody else when you could have Brooks. But that's just me." I knew that's what she'd say. She's on your side, Almighty.

How could I explain it to her? I liked Brooks, but I had the feeling he was just being polite when he paid attention to me, that he was just playing his role, doing his family duty and making his grandmother happy by playing prince to my princess.

Robbie changed everything. Even if I wanted to, I couldn't squeeze myself back into the old snow globe everybody wanted to keep me in. The glass was already broken.

TWELVE

⊠　　⊠　　⊠

AND NOW, ALMIGHTY, I'M GOING TO WRITE A PART OF THE story I never planned to tell you. I feel very uncomfortable about it. Not embarrassed, just uncomfortable. But I promised myself I'd tell you everything, and this part is important.

Maybe if you could forget that I'm your granddaughter and try to think of me as a person you don't know, or a character in a book . . . it might help you get through this without having a heart attack.

One November night after Speed Reading class, Robbie asked me out again. Just the two of us. And to make sure we wouldn't be disturbed by ex-girlfriends or wastoids I go to school with, he offered to cook dinner for me at his place. He lives in a studio apartment in an old building in Charles Village that's filled with other grad students. He wrote down the address for me. Friday night.

I told Miss Maura and Ginger that I was spending the night at Claire's house. I didn't tell anyone else what I was doing — not even Claire. I had a feeling something big would happen that night, and I didn't want any interference.

Robbie lives in a run-down brick building, twelve squat stories dotted with windows. The lobby has a dingy, chipped mosaic floor that was probably pretty once, a long time ago. The elevator is slow and creaky. I rode it up to the seventh floor and rang Robbie's buzzer. He opened the door wearing a plaid apron, his hair standing straight up from the steam in the kitchen.

His iPod was playing some old-fashioned music: a baby-voiced woman singing playfully about peeling a grape. I gave him some flowers I'd brought and he kissed me on the cheek.

The apartment is tiny, with a loft bed wedged in one corner, a desk underneath it, and a little kitchen with a window that looks into a courtyard filled with dozens of other windows, lit and unlit, a fascinating hive of students buzzing in their tiny cells.

I sat at the kitchen table, which was set with an open bottle of red wine, a bottle of sparkling mineral water, and a plate of cheese and crackers. Robbie stood at the stove, stirring a boiling pot of pasta.

"I hope you like spaghetti and meatballs," he said. "Because that's what we're having."

"I love spaghetti and meatballs." I helped myself to a cracker with goat cheese.

Clutching a big wooden spoon, Robbie poured some wine into two glasses. He lifted his, clinked it against mine, and said, "Cheers."

"Cheers." I took a sip. For some reason I thought of Communion wine.

Robbie's cell phone rang. He frowned at the screen, then took the call, waving the spoon at me. "One second. Doyle? Yeah. Nah, man, I can't. Not tonight. I'm busy. None of your business.

I'm not telling. I won't say if you're right or wrong. Think whatever you want, man. Okay. Check me at the theater tomorrow night. Yeah. 'K-bye."

"Doyle," he said as he pushed buttons on his phone, turning it off.

"Graduate school stuff?" I asked.

He laughed. "Yeah, grad school stuff." He gave the pasta another stir, then poured it into a colander in the sink. "Dinner is almost ready."

The funny baby-voice on the iPod was growing on me. "Who is this singing?"

"Blossom Dearie. She was a cool old lady." He tossed me a CD with a picture of a blond woman on the front. While I studied it, he made up a plate of spaghetti and meatballs for me. "Would you like salad? I can make a salad."

"Do *you* want a salad?" I asked.

"I could live without it. But if you want one, I can whip it up easy."

I didn't want salad. I felt like gorging on decadent delicious things and not bothering with fiber and vitamins and health. I wondered what was for dessert.

"Don't make a salad," I said.

He grinned and offered me a basket of garlic bread. I took a piece. It was warm and slick with butter. We started to eat. We didn't talk. I didn't know what to talk about. I looked around the tiny apartment, at the drawings on the wall that were probably done by his friends, the framed poster from *Rushmore*, and the toy robot on the windowsill.

"Tell me a story," I said to Robbie. "Something that happened when you were a little boy."

"Hmm. Okay." He ate some spaghetti and thought of a story. "When I was twelve, my mother finally let me walk to school by myself. It was only three blocks away, but until then she always walked there with me."

"What neighborhood did you live in?"

"Greenwich Village. It is not the least bit dangerous, as New York neighborhoods go. It's nothing like West Baltimore or even this neighborhood. But when I was little it wasn't quite as fancy as it is now."

He paused to take a sip of bubbly water.

"So there I am, I'm twelve, I'm walking to school alone for the first time, and this woman runs out of an apartment building, screaming and covered in blood. I can't understand what she's saying except for 'Help me! Help me!' I froze on the sidewalk. I was completely wigged out."

"Did she kill somebody?"

"I didn't know. I ran to the newsstand on the corner and told the guy to call the police. A police car arrived and they took the woman inside the building. They told me to go on to school. I couldn't just stand there so I went to school. I got in trouble for being late, and they called my mother to tell her. She was really mad. My first day walking to school alone and I get there late."

"Parents fixate on the least important things! So did you ever find out about the lady?"

"It was on the news that night. Turns out she was from Indonesia and had been brought here as a domestic slave. They made her work day and night, fed her gruel, and never let her leave the house. She got fed up and tried to kill the couple who were holding her captive with a carving knife. But she only managed to chop off her mistress's hand."

"Ew!" I reflexively grabbed my own hand to make sure it was still there.

"I know. After that, my mother didn't let me walk to school alone anymore. I wasn't allowed to go anywhere alone for another year."

"But that's ridiculous," I said. "That Indonesian woman was no danger to you."

"I tried to tell Mom that, but the screaming and blood freaked her out."

"What happened to the slave?"

"She was sent back to Indonesia and her captors were put in jail."

"Wow."

"Yeah."

"That's one of those stories that makes you wonder what's really going on in your neighbors' houses. Are they secretly hiding domestic slaves in their attics? Do they live in a maze of old newspapers they refuse to throw away? Are they working on an invention that will solve the mysteries of time travel?"

Robbie laughed. "See that window right there? Fifth floor, third from left?" He pointed to one of the glowing windows across the courtyard. The light was on but the shade was drawn.

"Yeah?"

"There's a girl in there who puts on a gypsy costume and dances around." He stood up and whirled around the kitchen, waving his arms. "Late at night, every once in a while. She keeps her shades closed except when she's doing her gypsy dance."

"Is she casting a spell?"

Robbie shrugged. "I don't know what she's doing. But she sure seems to want people to see her in that costume." He reached over to the stove for a pot. "More meatballs?"

"Just one more, please. They're delicious."

"Thank you." He spooned more sauce onto my spaghetti. "I also make a great shrimp risotto. Dad's recipe." He passed me more garlic bread. "Your turn to tell a story."

"Okay." I decided to tell him a story I'd never told anyone else. "One time Daddy-o decided to take St. John and Sully sailing for the weekend. They were going to sail all around the Chesapeake and fish and sleep on the boat. Jane and Sassy and I protested — it wasn't fair. We wanted to go. But there wasn't room for all of us on the boat, and anyway, it was supposed to be a father-son thing. This was before Takey was born.

"So Ginger said we girls could have our own fun weekend without them, and she took us to New York. We'd get a suite in the Pierre, she said, and go to shows — especially the kind of girly, cheesy musicals Daddy-o won't go to, like *Wicked* — and shop and eat out and ride in a carriage through Central Park . . . the works. Daddy-o and the boys would be jealous."

"The Pierre," Robbie said. "Wow — you're really rich, aren't you?"

"Um — not really . . . but in a way. It's a long story." I felt embarrassed. Don't hold it against him, Almighty.

"I'm sorry. It sounds like a fun weekend."

"That's what we thought. We took the train up to New York and checked into the Pierre. We had a beautiful suite overlooking the park and tickets to see *Wicked* that night. We got dressed up and went to the show and it was great. Afterward we went out for a late supper and Ginger said we could order whatever we wanted, so I ordered lobster. Ginger ordered garlic shrimp. She said she could be as stinky-breathed as she wanted that weekend since Daddy-o wasn't around. But then she didn't eat it. She didn't eat anything."

I ate the last bite of my garlic bread.

"Sassy and Jane and I chattered about the show and how we couldn't wait to watch *The Wizard of Oz* again now that we knew the real story behind the Wicked Witch of the West. Everything seemed wonderful. But near the end of dinner I realized that Ginger had been pretty quiet. I glanced at her and caught her staring at the next table with the saddest look on her face."

"What was at the next table?"

"Just some old married couple. I don't know if something about them made her sad or if she just happened to be staring sadly in their direction. It's weird for Ginger to look sad like that, though. She's usually very cool and unflappable."

Robbie offered me more garlic bread. "I don't care if your breath is stinky."

"Thanks." I took some, because he was eating it too, so we'd both be stinky. If it came to that. "We went back to the hotel and went to bed. I got up in the middle of the night to go to the bathroom and saw Ginger sitting in the living room, and she was crying."

"Oh. Poor Ginger."

"You don't understand — that's *so* not like her, at all. I asked her what the matter was, and she said, 'I'm sorry, honey, but I think we have to go home.' And I said, 'Why?' and she said, 'I just miss your father too much.'"

"Wow. That's kind of romantic."

"I didn't think so. I was ten at the time, and I was pissed that we had to go home before our big weekend was over. But I was scared too, because she was so miserable she looked sick. This weepy, pale person wasn't the Ginger I knew. She called Daddy-o, and he and the boys came home early too. She ruined everybody's weekend because she couldn't stand to spend one night without Daddy-o. I know it doesn't sound like a big deal but the whole thing shocked me. I realized my parents had never spent a night apart for as long as I could remember. They act all blasé about their marriage but they're actually completely dependent on each other."

"My mother would probably say that wasn't too healthy."

"I'm sure it isn't. It made me think of my parents in a new way. A new, kind of pathetic way. It was the first time I thought of Ginger as . . . well, *needy*."

"I think you're being too hard on her," Robbie said. "Your parents love each other. That's good."

"I guess. But it's not one hundred percent good."

I took a breath and stared at my plate, which had somehow been cleaned. When did I eat all that spaghetti?

Then I looked up at Robbie. He was waiting to hear why Ginger and Daddy-o loving each other wasn't one hundred percent good.

"Because they love each other more than they love us," I said.

"That can't be true."

"Yes it can." I drank some water. Time to change the subject, quick. "Whew. I just talked your ear off."

"That's okay. I talked yours off first."

"Both of our stories happened in New York."

"Stuff's always happening there. You should go back sometime."

"I will."

We sat in silence for a minute. It was a comfortable silence. I thought about what had just happened. I had blabbed to him a stupid story about my family. I had blabbed without self-consciousness. It was almost like talking to one of my sisters. And he seemed completely into it.

I looked at his hair, his liquid brown eyes, his smooth skin with its ever-changing happy expressions, his dimpled cherry grin. *That's it*, I thought. *I'm in love.*

"What's for dessert?" I said.

"Norrie, I think I'm in love with you," he said.

We stared at each other across the table in a strange, full-bellied, ecstatic moment of communion. Then he stood up, and I stood up, and he reached for me and pulled me to him.

We kissed until I thought I would lose consciousness. And I did lose consciousness in a way. I didn't faint or pass out, but my mind drifted away into another world where it sat numb and unthinking, put on mothballs until later, when I would need it.

I will now draw a curtain across this scene. I think this is about as far as a girl and her grandmother should go when discussing matters of the heart. But there is one little coda I want to add.

Late in the night I woke to find myself in a loft bed, the ceiling only a few feet above my head. Robbie lay next to me, snoring softly, one arm flopped over my belly.

I gently moved his arm and slid off the loft bed. The apartment was dark. The candles had burned to stubs, but light came in through the window. I put on Robbie's T-shirt and sat at the kitchen table and looked out.

The moon was full and shining in a clear, cold sky, beaming its light into Robbie's kitchen. Across the courtyard, a checkerboard of windows glowed even though it was two o'clock in the morning. The shade was open in the gypsy girl's apartment, and I saw her, dressed in a head scarf and shawl and long, bright skirt, whirling and twirling and singing. I looked into the other windows. A stocky young man climbed into a loft bed like Robbie's, and a gray cat jumped up next to him and rubbed her fur against his cheek. The guy nuzzled her. They rubbed their noses together, then settled down for the night. The gypsy girl whirled and danced. All was well in the hive of students.

■ ■ ■

When I got home after breakfast the next morning, the house was quiet. Ginger and Daddy-o and Jane were still sleeping, and Miss Maura was cleaning up the kitchen. I heard TV noises coming from the den, and looked in. Sassy was on the couch watching cartoons with Takey, her arm over his shoulder, his hand on her leg. They didn't notice me. They were both mesmerized by the show, with that TV zombie look on their faces, unselfconscious, cherry Popsicles melting in their hands. In that pose Sassy looked like a little kid, unaware of the way her left foot bounced off the end of the ottoman or the sticky Popsicle juice dripped down her fingers.

I felt old suddenly. Or maybe not old, but mature. I felt happy and sad. I touched my face, my bony new cheeks.

Everything was different now.

THIRTEEN

✉ ✉ ✉

YOU INVITED SASSY, AND ONLY SASSY, FOR TEA THAT WEEK.
Ginger, Jane, and I got the message: You were mad at us. I don't
know what Ginger did to upset you, but I figured some of the
rumors about me had gotten back to you. As for Jane, her crimes
were no mystery: the *Sun* had just published the story about her
blog and all the scandalous family secrets, and then she was suspended from school for blasphemy. She expected trouble — no,
she *wanted* trouble.

I came home from school and then realized I'd forgotten to get
tampons, so I asked Jane if she wanted to drive to Roland
Pharmacy with me. She was restless from being stuck at home
all day so she said yes. It started raining. We drove to the pharmacy accompanied by the slap of the wipers, the swish of the
water under our tires, and the smell of wet wool.

I pulled up in front of the pharmacy. "Come in or wait in
the car?"

"Wait in the car," Jane said. "Get me a Mounds bar."

I picked up a box of tampons and stopped to scan the magazine rack for a second. I heard a familiar voice say, "I'm picking
up a prescription for my mother." Brooks Overbeck propped his

elbows on the pharmacy counter, handing a prescription slip to the pharmacist.

"It'll be ready in just a minute, son," the pharmacist said.

Brooks turned and leaned against the counter to wait, surveying the after-school activity in the store. His eyes brushed past the middle school girls giggling over greeting cards and a woman studying moisturizers until they reached the magazine rack and caught me staring at him. As he ambled over, I casually held the box of tampons behind my back.

"Hey, Norrie, what d'ya know?"

"Hi, Brooks."

He pulled a cream-colored envelope from his jacket pocket. "Got this in the mail today. You'll be getting my official reply in writing, of course, once my mother shows me the proper way to write it, but off the record the answer is 'Yeah, baby!'"

"Answer?" I didn't know what he was talking about. "Answer to what?"

"You're a cool one." He tapped the envelope against his palm. "Always were, weren't you?"

"Cool? Me? No, I'm not cool at all." I shifted the box of tampons to the crook of my arm — let him see them, I didn't care anymore — and snatched the envelope out of his hand. It was thick, creamy Downs' stock, addressed to him, and the return address was mine. But the handwriting — thin, scratchy, yet forceful — was unmistakably yours, Almighty.

"I was hoping you'd ask me," Brooks said. "I got a few other invitations too, but I was waiting for yours."

I opened the card. *Mr. and Mrs. Alphonse Sullivan III request the pleasure of your company at the presentation of their daughter, Louisa Norris, at the Bachelors Cotillon, Saturday, December 21 . . .*

This might surprise you, Almighty, but I don't like it when people take actions in my name without my permission. My first thought was: *How dare she?*

My mind raced furiously, but I didn't know what to say to Brooks. This wasn't his fault.

"Overbeck," the pharmacist called.

"I've got to go," Brooks said. "I'll be in touch. *Ciao!*"

He returned to the counter for his mother's medicine. I grabbed a Mounds for Jane and paid the cashier. Then I ran out to the car.

"Did you see anybody in there?" Jane asked, because we almost always see somebody we know at Roland Pharmacy.

"Brooks," I said. "And you'll never believe what Almighty did."

"Oh, I'll believe it," Jane said. "There's nothing you can tell me about Almighty that will surprise me."

"You're lucky, then," I said. "Because she sure shocked the hell out of me."

And it wasn't going to be the last time, was it?

■   ■   ■

"Ginger!" I yelled when I got home. I threw my coat down at the foot of the stairs. Jane gleefully hovered nearby, ready for a dustup. "Ginger!"

It was strange that she wasn't in the sunroom with a cup of tea, talking on the phone with one of her friends. I don't know why I yelled for her. I wanted her to fight for me — for my right to choose my own escorts, to live my own life. But of course Ginger was probably in on the whole thing, wasn't she?

At last she appeared at the top of the stairs, looking rattled. She had her glasses on — her big bug-eye glasses — and her hair was half-teased on one side and flat on the other. She was wearing her flowered silk pajamas. Obviously something was wrong.

"Stop yelling and come upstairs, girls. Something's happened."

Jane and I looked at each other. Jane was anticipating something juicy. Most of her facial expressions contain an element of satanic glee.

We went into Ginger's room and found Sassy facedown on the bed, sobbing. Takey patted her clumsily on the head.

"What happened?" I asked.

"Wallace is dead," Ginger said.

"What?" Jane cried.

Ginger shook her head and sat down next to Sassy, rubbing her back. "Sassy found him. She was leaving Almighty's and saw Wallace in his car. Dead."

"Just sitting there?" I asked.

"With his eyes open," Takey reported.

Sassy lifted her wet, rosy face and nodded.

"Oh! Creepy," I said.

Jane and I curled up on the bed with the others. "Poor Sass," Jane said.

"It was awful." Sassy sobbed harder.

"How did it happen?" I asked.

"We're not sure," Ginger said. "Your father's at the hospital now, with Almighty. I'll bet it was a heart attack. What if it had happened while he was driving? He might have hit someone."

Sassy cried even harder, then bolted up. "I can't stand it! It's too awful!" She jumped off the bed and ran out of the room. A second later we heard her bedroom door slam.

"Why is she so upset?" Jane asked. "I mean, I know she just saw her first dead body, but she's acting like she killed the guy herself."

"He was always kind of a stiff," Ginger said.

I sighed. They were heartless. We all were.

The phone rang. Ginger reached over to get it. From the way she talked to the person on the other end I could tell it was Daddy-o.

"He's on his way home," she said, hanging up. "The doctors said it was a stroke. The funeral is on Friday."

"Poor Wallace," I said.

■   ■   ■

Having St. John and Sully home felt like a holiday, and Jane and Takey and I had trouble suppressing our happiness at seeing them in our time of mourning. Only Sassy grieved consistently. She sat quietly with us, listening to St. John's and Sully's stories of adventures in the wider world, wearing black at all times — she'd even dug up black pajamas somewhere — and bursting into tears over nothing. She was sadder than anyone else in the family, but that wasn't so strange, for Sassy.

On Friday we all dressed up in our black clothes and piled into a limo that took us to the cathedral.

I couldn't see your face very well through your lace veil. It was hard to tell exactly what you were feeling. I think you loved Wallace, but who knows what secrets you keep locked up in your heart?

I tried to stop Takey from pretending to shoot the mourners while we walked up the aisle, but he only listens to Miss Maura. Brooks was already seated with Carrie and his parents and Mamie. He nodded at me as I slid into our pew.

I stared at Wallace's body, all waxy-looking in his coffin, and it gave my heart a little pang, but I couldn't cry. I wanted to cry. It would have felt right. People around me were sniffling and wiping their eyes. Sassy wept and trembled through the whole mass. Not hard-hearted Jane, of course. Ginger was crying, but who knows over what. Maybe she'd lost an earring.

The sight of Daddy-o quietly weeping got to me. Daddy-o doesn't fake tears. Wallace wasn't his father, and if you think about it, Daddy-o has been to a lot of funerals for your husbands. Maybe he was remembering his real father. Or maybe he's just tenderhearted. Sassy got her tender heart from him.

Finally the ceremony ended and we filed out of the cathedral row by row. I felt tired. The faces in the pews blurred until, in the very last row, one face jumped out at me. Robbie. He looked at me so sweetly that I burst into tears at last.

"Oh, Norrie!" Sassy draped her arms around my waist and clung to me as we walked. That was all that kept me from rushing into Robbie's arms. The flow of people pushed us past him and out of the church.

I hadn't told him about the funeral; he must have seen the announcement in the newspaper. I longed to be with him, but I had to go to the luncheon. I don't know why the sight of his face set me off like that, but in the limo, all the way to Gilded Elms, I hid my face in a handkerchief and cried. And then I worried: What if I was turning out like Ginger? What if I couldn't be happy unless I was with Robbie, the way Ginger can't be happy without Daddy-o?

FOURTEEN

✉   ✉   ✉

THE NIGHT AFTER WALLACE'S FUNERAL, WE SETTLED AT THE
kitchen table for a quiet supper with Miss Maura. Sassy said she
didn't feel well and went upstairs to her room. The rest of us
fixed turkey sandwiches and ate them with glasses of milk, and
gossiped about who had said what at the post-funeral luncheon.

"Brooks Overbeck told me he's already bought a white tie and
tails getup for the Cotillon," Sully said.

"Good for him."

Sully and St. John exchanged a glance. In all the fuss around
the funeral I hadn't forgotten about Brooks and the Cotillon, but
it didn't feel right to talk about something so frivolous while
wearing mourning clothes.

"I'm going upstairs for a smoke," Jane announced. "And I don't
care who knows about it," she added to Miss Maura's raised
finger, poised for scolding.

"I'll go with you." I got up from the table, my sandwich half-
eaten. "To make sure you don't burn my room down."

Jane and I went upstairs to the Tower. Jane cracked a window and lit one of her cloves. I collapsed on my bed.

"So what made you cry?" Jane asked. "I mean, at the end of the funeral. Why were you really crying?"

"What kind of question is that? It was a funeral. Everybody was crying. Except you, of course."

"I know you think I'm mean. You weren't crying over Wallace. I'm sad about him. I really am. And I'm sad for Sassy that she found him dead. It seems to have broken something inside her."

"I wish she'd talk about it," I said.

The door pushed open — no one ever bothers to knock in this family — and Sully and St. John came in.

"The place looks like crap without my posters," Sully said. "Looks like a girl's room."

"It's my room now." I wasn't in the mood.

"It is and will always be my room, officially," St. John said. "I'm only lending it to you squibs."

St. John stretched his long self across the foot of the bed while Sully settled in the armchair by the window. They both looked at Jane.

"What?" she said. "I'm smoking. Deal with it."

"We need to have a talk with Norrie," St. John said.

"So talk."

"Get out of here, you feel me, shorty?" Sully said.

Jane stubbed out her cigarette. "Shut up, Sully. You and your dumb college slang."

"Oooh, Jane said 'shut up,'" Sully said.

Jane sashayed to the door. "Kiss my skinny white heinie."

"Oooh, Jane said 'heinie,'" Sully crooned. "Everybody in this house talks so twentieth century."

"Including you," St. John said. "When you're not trying to sound like a drug dealer on *The Wire*."

Which *is* how Sully talks when you're not around, Almighty, so forgive the swears. I cut some of them but for others there's just no substitute word that gives the same meaning.

Jane left, grumbling and slamming the door behind her. I sat up and propped myself against the pillows.

"We heard about this older dude you're with, N," Sully said. "Not cool."

"Sully, I thought you were going to let me do the talking," St. John said.

"Knock yourself out," Sully said.

"Daddy-o told us, Norrie. He's trying to pretend he's not worried, but you know he is. How old is this guy, twenty-five?"

"Yeah. So?"

"That's four years older than me," St. John said. "He's too old for you."

"You don't know what guys are like, Norrie," Sully said. "I hate to break it to you, but we're shitheads."

I looked to St. John for confirmation. Sully might be a shithead, but St. John?

He nodded solemnly. "Not always, but we can be. Some guys are. And usually the guys who go after the young girls are not the best kind."

"But you don't know Robbie," I said. "He's not like that. He doesn't go after young girls. All his ex-girlfriends are his age. This is just . . . an accident."

Sully sprang up. "Oh no. You're pregnant?"

"No," I said. "Not that kind of accident. I mean, it just happened. I know the timing's not perfect, but I can't help that. I met the love of my life now. I'd rather have met him later, in my twenties, but I didn't. It's fate. There's nothing I can do about it."

"Fate? Oh no, don't give me that," St. John said. "Whenever girls talk about fate it means trouble."

"Yeah, fate boys are always the real assholes," Sully said. "That's how girls justify their assholosity — 'I can't help it if he's a creep, it's fate!' Don't go falling in love, Norrie. It's all a big lie."

"Like you know," I said. "When have you ever been in love?"

"Norrie, listen to me," Sully said. "There's this guy in my frat, he's a senior. Every year when the new freshmen arrive he goes through the directory and finds the cutest girls. He picks them off, one by one. He invites them to a party, gets them drunk, has his way with them, and then checks them off his list. He even keeps a big chart with their pictures on the wall of his room. After he gets one, he draws a red X through her face. Then he goes around telling everybody that he's seen her naked and she's fat."

"So? All that proves is that your frat is full of creeps," I said.

"That's only one example," Sully said. "I could give you dozens of others, even worse."

"How do you know this guy Robbie's not seeing three other girls at the same time?" St. John asked.

"Well . . . I guess I don't know, for sure."

"He could be up to all kinds of things and you'd never know about it," Sully said.

"You haven't even met him," I said. "Why don't you at least meet him before you decide he's the devil incarnate?"

Sully laughed. "Ha! He'll never want to meet us. Your older brothers? He'd be scared shitless."

I didn't like to admit it to myself, but they had put some doubts in my mind. What did I know about Robbie, really? I only saw him once or twice a week. What was he doing with the rest of his time? Did he dangle me on a string while seeing other girls on the side? How would I ever know?

"What about Brooks?" I said. "He's a guy too. How do you know he's not just as bad as those guys in your frat?"

"He could be," Sully said. "But he would never be a jerk to you, because you're too connected. He knows that whatever happens between you will get back to Almighty and Mamie, and he wouldn't risk that."

"So the only reason I can trust him is because he's afraid of pissing off the family?" This was a troubling way of looking at love. I didn't like thinking about Brooks as a coward any more than I liked thinking of Robbie as a predator.

"What about you?" I asked. "Are you an asshole too? St. John?"

"Nah, not me," St. John said. "Sully is, though."

"I am not," Sully said. "I'm a nice guy. I can't help it if girls throw themselves at me. What am I supposed to do, resist?"

"Yes, that's exactly what you're supposed to do," St. John said.

"Dude, I'm only human," Sully said.

"You know what? I don't trust either of you," I said. But they're my brothers, and they were only trying to protect me. If I couldn't trust them, who could I trust?

FIFTEEN

⊠   ⊠   ⊠

A FEW DAYS AFTER WALLACE'S FUNERAL, I GOT A SYMPATHY
note in the mail from Robbie. It said:

Dear Norrie,

*I'm sorry about your grandfather's death. You looked so sad at the
funeral. I hope you don't mind that I crashed it, but I wanted to be
there in case you needed me. I saw that you have a lot of support
from your family, though, especially your sisters. I don't want to
disturb your family at a time like this, but if you want to call me,
I'm here. Waiting. Dial away. Or text or whatever.*

*Hope to see you in class on Tuesday, though I wouldn't blame
you if you cut it. There are times when speed reading doesn't seem
very important. Most of the time, actually. But I met you because
of speed reading, so I consider it a core requirement of any academic
program. It sure would be nice to see your ever-changing face.*

Robbie

"He didn't sign it 'Love,'" Jane pointed out, not helpfully.

"He didn't have to," Sassy said. "Just the fact that he sent the
note shows his love."

"You should show it to Almighty and Ginger," Jane said. "They'd be so pleased to see a young man who actually communicates by U.S. mail instead of texting. The etiquette of bygone days and all that. I don't see any notes from Brooks lying around."

"His father sent one," I said. "From the whole Overbeck clan."

"Still," Jane said.

"Yeah, still," Sassy said.

■　■　■

I went to Speed Reading on Tuesday night. How could I not? I was dying to see Robbie. I wanted to see how I'd feel about him now that he was probably a predatory jerk, according to Sully and St. John.

I got to class a little late and slid into the back row, right next to him. He inspected my face for traces of sadness. I'm sure he found some there. He laid one hand over mine and turned his attention to the teacher, who was discussing skimming techniques.

I hate skimming, I wrote on his notebook.

Me too, he wrote back. *If it's worth reading, I want to read every single word.*

The moment I was in his presence I knew Sully and St. John were wrong. Maybe I was naive. Maybe I was kidding myself. But I decided if I was going to get hurt, then I was going to get hurt. How else would I figure out how to tell the difference between a good guy and a jerk? My instincts shouted that Robbie was a good guy, and if my instincts were that wrong, I had a lot to learn.

After class, Robbie took my hand and we walked across campus to a café. "I have to tell you something," I said over mint tea.

"What, girl of mine?"

"There's this thing coming up, in a few weeks, called the Bachelors Cotillon. Have you ever heard of it?"

Robbie shook his head. "Is it a debutante ball?"

"Yes," I said. "I'm supposed to go. With my dad, and my brother, and this guy named Brooks. My grandmother will be very upset if I don't go. And ever since Wallace died, she's been even touchier than usual. I just thought you should know."

"When is it?"

"December twenty-first."

"The shortest day of the year."

"And the longest night."

"I hope you have a good time."

"I won't. Don't worry, I won't."

"No, I want you to."

"You don't understand," I said. "This boy Brooks . . . he's, like, picked out for me."

"Does he like you?"

"I don't know. It's hard to tell. He's very dutiful. He knows he's supposed to like me so he acts like he likes me. Maybe he really does."

"Do you like him?"

"He's nice," I said. "But I don't like him the way I like you."

"That's good to know."

"But I'm a dutiful person too," I said. "I guess that's why I'm going to the ball in the first place."

"There's nothing wrong with keeping your family happy, as long as you're happy too."

"That's the thing," I said. "I feel so funny lately. Restless and impatient and crazy and pissed off. I want to *run away*. Just leave and go go go go go — with you. Anywhere with you, anywhere there are no cotillons and no bossy grandmothers and no school uniforms or nuns or hockey games or lacrosse players or good girls or bad girls. Just us."

His mouth flatlined, his face neutral. "Yeah. That's crazy. You can't do that."

"You wouldn't run away with me?"

"I don't want to run away. I like it here. Besides, I've got a thesis to write."

See how responsible he is?

But my heart cracked, a hairline fracture. I was disappointed. More than disappointed. I'd expected him to say he'd go anywhere, do anything, as long as he could be with me. But instead, he's practical. He likes it here. He wants to get his degree.

He's grown up.

Two can play that game, I thought. *I'll be grown up too.* "All right. I'll do what I have to do and you can do what you have to do. Right now I have to go home, do some homework, and go to bed. Well, good night."

I hurried out of the café. I was tempted to look back to see if he was following me or at least watching me. But I didn't, because I knew it would ruin the effect of my dramatic exit. Still, I listened for footsteps as I walked to the car. At last, at the car, I turned around. No one was following me.

SIXTEEN

⊠ ⊠ ⊠

SULLY WENT BACK TO DARTMOUTH AND ST. JOHN WENT BACK
to New York, and things started to settle down again. You didn't
invite anyone to tea that week. We assumed you were sad and
missed Wallace. Sassy was still shaken up by his death. She went
to school and hockey practice, and once a week she went downtown to tutor the student she was working with, but the rest of
the time she stayed shut up in her room. She didn't come up to the
Tower for sessions with me and Jane, even when I invited her.

A week went by and I didn't hear from Robbie. So when it
was time to go for the final fitting of my Cotillon dress, I went
along quietly. It was Ginger's idea to invite Claire and her mother
along with us. She thought that might perk me up, I guess.

I was checking my phone for messages from Robbie the whole
time we were in the Seville Shop. You had no idea. In the dressing room, before I tried on my dress — no messages. After I put
on the dress and zipped it halfway up — no messages.

I stepped out of the fitting room and stood on the platform
before the three-sided mirror. Diane zipped me the rest of the
way up. I furtively checked my phone again — no messages.

I stood very still while Diane pinned and unpinned the silk at my waist. I've never stood so still in my life. My core had turned to stone. I felt like a ballerina in a little girl's jewelry box, the kind that spins around while a music box plays the Sugar Plum Fairy theme from *The Nutcracker*. I couldn't move if I'd wanted to, not unless somebody wound up the music box and made me spin.

"Are you happy with the length, hon?" Diane asked. "I could shorten the hem a little if you think you might trip over it."

I shook my head. "The length is perfect. Thank you, Diane. I'm very happy with it."

Back into the dressing room to take the dress off. No messages from Robbie. Nothing.

Why wasn't he calling? Had I done something to scare him away?

I heard Sully's voice in my head: *Told you — he's an asshole.*

He's not, I replied. *He's not.*

When the fitting was over and we all stopped at Petit Louis for lunch, finally my phone beeped. I had a message. I know how you hate texting at the table so I tried to be as inconspicuous as I could, but I just had to see who the message was from.

It was from Shea. She wrote: N I have 2 talk 2 u important.

"Who is it?" Claire snatched the phone from me. "What could she have to say that's so important?" The next thing I knew, Claire's thumbs were flying over the keypad.

"Claire, what are you doing?"

"I put her in her place. You're too polite."

I took back my phone but all it said was MESSAGE SENT.

"What did you say?"

"I told her to leave you alone. I said you don't want to talk to her. She's got nerve."

"Claire!"

"What? It's not like you're friends with her, right? That's what you keep saying. . . ."

I started texting Shea but you caught me with the phone.

"Norrie, put that contraption away this minute. For heaven's sake, we're in the middle of lunch."

I put away my phone. I tried texting Shea later to explain what had happened, but she didn't respond. Whatever Claire wrote her must have really hurt her feelings.

What was so important that she had to tell me?

"Forget about it," Claire said. "She was just trying to stir up some drama."

Meanwhile, I still heard nothing from Robbie.

I refused to make the first move. I had my pride. If he didn't like me anymore, he didn't like me anymore. There was nothing I could do about it. Maybe my brothers were right. Maybe everyone was right. He was a bad choice for me. I was too young, and he was too old, and lots of girls liked him and he was probably keeping us all dangling like puppets.

But I knew that wasn't true. He was a good man. He was mine. I felt it.

Dear Almighty, I don't know any other way to explain my actions.

I knew my duty and I had no intention of shirking it. I planned to go to the Cotillon. I had every intention of being the best debutante I could.

I know it didn't turn out that way. But I want you to know that I tried.

SEVENTEEN

COTILLON DAY: THE PHONE KEPT RINGING. THE DOORBELL KEPT ringing. Miss Maura was running around clucking like a chicken, and the house was an asylum. Every time the doorbell rang more flowers arrived. Daddy-o struggled to get into his tailcoat, and Ginger spent the day with her hair in curlers, while Takey and a playdate held a water gun turf war with the entire downstairs at stake.

Amid all this furious activity, I sat on my bed in the Tower and stared out the window. It was a frigid, cloudy day, and the bare trees scraped the pewter sky. My dress hung on the closet door. I had already been to Carl's and had my hair and nails done. I heard the bells ringing and the doors slamming and the frantic people of the household shouting. Ginger buzzed me several times from her room but I ignored it. I was just trying to breathe.

Jane and Sassy knocked on the door, which was ajar.

"You knocked," I said. "That's unprecedented."

"You should see all the flowers downstairs," Sassy said. "The whole living room smells like perfume. And Daddy-o bought you a special present — in a blue Tiffany's box!"

"She doesn't look very excited about her big night, does she, Sass?" Jane said.

"Don't talk about me as if I'm not here," I said.

Sassy curled up next to me like a kitten. She wrapped her arms around my waist and lay her head in my lap. For some reason this made tears spring to my eyes. I stroked her hair.

"I kind of get why you can't back out now," Jane said. "But think of it this way, Nor — it's only one night. And then it's over. It's not like you're getting married."

"And it won't be too unpleasant," Sassy said. "Not like going to jail or boot camp or SAT prep. You'll wear your beautiful white dress and eat crab imperial and drink champagne, and dance with Daddy-o and Sully and Brooks, and curtsy . . ."

"And then it's done," Jane repeated. "Brooks will probably try to kiss you, but you can always say you're getting a cold sore."

Jane is disgusting but she makes me laugh.

"Then tomorrow you can call Robbie and tell him that the Cotillon is over and everything can go back the way it was," Sassy said.

I teared up again. "I don't think that will happen. I haven't heard a word from Robbie for two weeks. I think he thinks I care more about money than I care about him."

"But that's not true at all!" Sassy said. "Doesn't he know you the least little bit?"

"He doesn't want me anymore," I said. "Ball or no ball. There's no other explanation."

"Then you should forget about him, Norrie," Jane said. "Who is he? Just some guy. Some stupid grad student — in *film*. Please.

What is that? It's not like he's saving the world or reforming society or anything."

"He's a good person," I said. "I know I met him too early, but I had such a strong feeling . . ." Sassy squeezed my waist. "I guess I was wrong."

Jane and Sassy helped me dress. I checked my phone every ten minutes for a message from Robbie, but nothing came. How could he give up on me so quickly? He'd just vanished. Something was wrong.

I put on my pearl earrings, and Sassy pinned a white gardenia in my hair. "There," she said. "You're all ready."

"I'm not doing this next year," Jane said. "But if Almighty finds some diabolical way to force me, then I'm going Goth." (You've been warned.)

The Ginger signal buzzed again.

"She won't stop until you go downstairs and see what she wants," Jane said.

"Why can't she ever come up here herself?" I grumbled.

"You're lucky she doesn't," Jane said, lighting up a cigarette. "Think about it."

"I guess it's time to go." I pulled on my long white gloves and picked up my silver clutch purse. The three of us paraded down the stairs, passing Ginger's room on the second floor. She sat at her dressing table in a white slip, pawing through her jewelry box. "Are you ready?" I asked her.

"Not even remotely," Ginger said. "Which earrings should I wear — the diamonds or the rubies?" She held one of each up to her ears for us to inspect.

"Rubies." I helped her fasten her bracelet.

"Tell your father I'll be down in a minute. It's an utter lie but tell him anyway."

The living room was flooded with flowers. The scent was almost overpowering. I stopped to read the cards that came with them, congratulating me and my parents on my debut. A huge arrangement from the Overbecks, of course, and an even bigger one from you. Thank you for the beautiful flowers, by the way.

In spite of the fact that it was the darkest day of December, all the flowers were in light springy colors like white and yellow and pale blue — all except one bouquet of a dozen blood-red roses.

I slipped the card from its envelope. They were from Robbie.

Dearest Norrie,

I don't know why you are ignoring me, but I'm going to ignore the fact that you're ignoring me and take one last stab at reaching you. You talked about running away, and I brought up my thesis! What an idiot! Run away with me tonight. I'll be waiting for you at Penn Station. We can take the train to New York. After that, whatever happens, happens. What do you say?

Either way, I'll be waiting.

Your Robbie.

My insides, which had felt sluggish all day, immediately woke up. What did he mean, I was ignoring him? When had he tried to reach me?

I thought of Shea and her mysterious text. Had Robbie seen her somewhere and asked her to give me a message?

Could she have gotten angry at Claire's text and taken some kind of revenge on me? Like telling Robbie not to contact me?

Anyway, he'd reached me now. I slipped the note into my purse.

■　■　■

The hotel dressing suite stank of hair spray. You were waiting for us with the chattering girls and their mothers, but you sat apart, watching. Your diamond brooch was the biggest jewel in the room — it lasered blinding beams of light like apon, and seemed to create a kind of force field around you.

Claire dropped her brush and ran to me. "Thank God you're here. You've got to save me from Lily! She's being such a bitch. She said she saw my dress on sale at Wal-Mart."

She clutched at my hands. I tried to shake her off. I wasn't in the mood for debutante dramatics. "Don't listen to her. She's obviously making that up."

"I know, but now my dress looks cheap to me. Why didn't I see how hideous it was when I bought it? For the rest of my life I'll be remembered as the deb in the Wal-Mart dress."

"You're crazy," I said. "No one is going to remember any of this for the rest of their lives."

"Moron, people post their deb pictures online and they stay there forever," Claire said.

Mrs. Shriver clapped her hands for attention. "Hello, girls and chaperones! Are you ready for your big night?"

"Yeah!" the crowd of demure debutantes screamed.

She went over the evening's procedure one last time: Receiving Line, Cocktails and Hors d'oeuvres, Introduction of Cotillon Members, Presentation of the Debutantes — walk to the center of the ballroom floor with your father, curtsy, and get escorted off the floor by the young man you've chosen for your escort. Then Dinner and Dancing. Line up from smallest to tallest and march into the ballroom. We'd all practiced it. We were ready.

The girls and their mothers cheered and clapped. Mothers kissed their daughters while the daughters flinched. I heard more than one girl snap at her mother, "You're smudging my makeup!"

I found a patch of space in front of a communal mirror and stationed myself there for one last check. I looked pale except for my cheeks, which were pink with rouge. I opened my purse and took out my lipstick. There was Robbie's note, glowing like plutonium, chiding me.

He'll be waiting at the train station, I thought. All I had to do was show up, and we could run away from all these flowers and swishing satin dresses, the perfume and hair spray and the fusty old dances that whirled girls around in the same patterns year after year.

I took my place in line with the other girls. You stopped to kiss me on your way out to the ballroom. I looked you right in the eye — remember? And you said something that surprised me:

"My dear sweet granddaughter, you've inherited my eyes."

You'd never said anything like that to me before.

The suite door opened and we paraded into the ballroom to the sound of the orchestra. Ginger and I joined the receiving line and waited to greet the bachelors as they entered the ballroom. Daddy-o wore his top hat and kissed me with wet eyes. Sully pinched my waist and whispered, "Welcome to hell, little sis," then laughed to show he was just kidding, sort of. Brooks's parents heartily wished me well, and Mamie said, "Any family would be thrilled to have you, thrilled!" Last came Brooks, who kissed my hand and said with mock formality, "Good evening, Miss Sullivan."

When the line broke up for cocktails and hors d'oeuvres, my stomach felt knotty and I couldn't eat. I sipped ginger ale and tried to make small talk with the overdressed old ladies and oddly flirtatious, red-faced men. Every time I opened my mouth, my brain chanted, *Robbie, Robbie, Robbie,* like a drumbeat. Soon it began to drown out the conversation, drown out the music, drown out everything until I was afraid I'd lose my mind right there at the ball.

Brooks was not to blame for anything that happened that night. He was a perfect gentleman. He took my arm and walked me around the room as if he sensed that I needed to calm down. "Have you practiced your curtsy? I've heard the judges are taking off points if your nose doesn't touch the floor."

I pretended to laugh. I thought his joke was funny; I just wasn't in a laughy mood.

"I'm very intimidated by those navy guys." He whooshed me past a row of cadets from the Naval Academy. "Can you imagine the discipline it takes to keep those white uniforms clean?"

My mouth said, "No," but my brain said, *Robbie, Robbie, Robbie.*

I glanced at Brooks's watch. 8:35. I wondered when Robbie would get to the train station. I pictured him standing by the gigantic Christmas tree, people whizzing past him, a spot of stillness in a blur of holiday travelers.

"Would you like some champagne?"

"Not now, thanks," I said. My head was already fuzzy, and I needed it clear. I felt bad for being such a drip but I couldn't help it.

Mrs. Shriver threaded through the room, quietly tapping each girl on the elbow and whispering that it was time for our presentation. We disappeared one by one, lining up behind a large screen at one end of the ballroom. I spotted Daddy-o in line with the other fathers, waiting to present us. He winked at me and I gave him a little wave.

"Take your seats, please," a man said. "Everyone, please take your seats."

Chairs scraped and glasses clinked as the guests found their places at the tables surrounding the dance floor. The orchestra went quiet, and a hush fell on the room. Mr. Ferguson greeted everyone and talked about the charity the ball would benefit. I tuned him out and searched my purse for a pen. I found a tiny pencil, the kind you use for keeping score in miniature golf, tucked away in a fold at the bottom. My heart was speeding, rushing all the blood from my head and around my limbs like a car on a racetrack, making me dizzy. But I was thinking clearly. The whole room around me blurred but the voice in my head was clear as pool water: *Robbie, Robbie, Robbie.*

I slipped Robbie's letter out of its envelope and tucked it back in my purse. Then I scribbled a note on the empty envelope. I dropped the pencil into my bag, clicked it shut, and gripped the envelope in one of my gloved hands.

The orchestra started playing "Stardust." Mr. Ferguson began to read the names: "Mr. John Preston Ames and his daughter,

Caroline Leslie Ames." Caroline Ames took her father's arm and made her entrance and curtsied. I watched her father walk to his table while her younger escort, a college boy, led her to the side of the dance floor to wait for the first dance.

"Dr. Thomas Cochran and his daughter, Mary Elizabeth Cochran."

I inched closer to the front of the line. Was I really going to do this? I wasn't sure I had the courage. The girl I used to be might daydream about running away, but in the end she would have chickened out. She would let herself be swept along with what was easiest, what caused the least trouble, what everyone expected her to do.

I felt different now. But was I really?

"Mr. Martin Mothersbaugh and his daughter, Claire Barton Mothersbaugh."

I leaned forward to watch Claire stride into the ballroom on her father's arm, beaming at the applause. I caught a glimpse of you reigning over the proceedings, front and center with Mamie, grimly clapping for each new girl.

And there on the dance floor stood Brooks, eagerly waiting his turn among the line of bachelor escorts. Could I really do this to him? Would he ever forgive me?

Did I really care?

"Dr. Philip Riggs and his daughter, Marissa Leah Riggs."

I was very close now. Only two girls in front of me. Daddy-o rubbed his palms together in nervous, delighted anticipation. Poor Daddy-o. He's such a darling, as Ginger would say. I hated hurting him most of all. But I believed that, when it was all over, deep down he'd secretly side with me. He wants me to be happy.

"Mr. Andrew Morton Stewart and his niece, Amalie Caton Stewart."

I was next. I stepped forward, took Daddy-o's arm, and slipped the pencil-scribbled note into the pocket of his trousers, under the pretext of brushing away a bit of lint.

"Ready, dear daughter?"

"I'm ready."

Mr. Ferguson announced us — "Mr. Alphonse Sullivan III and his daughter, Louisa Norris Sullivan" — and we stepped out into the spotlight. A flash from your brooch blinded me for a second. Daddy-o kissed me and stepped aside as I collapsed into a deep curtsy. I nearly lost my balance, but saved myself at the last minute, and rose.

Brooks stepped forward to take my hand and lead me away. The old Norrie would have gone compliantly with him. But the new Norrie surged forward and took over.

With one apologetic glance at Brooks I broke free and ran. I ran down the aisle that separated the rows of round tables to the ballroom door. Behind me I heard the startled, delayed gasps of surprise and confusion. I didn't stop to look back. I pushed out the door and ran down the stairs, all thirteen stories. I ran through the lobby crowded with holiday partyers, ran past the liveried doorman and the idling limos, out into the cold December air.

I had no coat, hadn't thought of getting it, didn't have time. It didn't matter. I turned onto Charles Street and ran north to Penn Station.

While I ran, I thought, *What if Robbie isn't there? What if he's given up on me, not having heard a word from me for weeks? What if he is the jerk Sully said he'd be, a liar, and never planned to wait for me at all? What if he's hiding, waiting to see if I'll come, only to sneak away laughing at my hopeless gullibility?*

It was too late to worry about that now. I had ruined my debut. I had humiliated my family and friends. I left nothing but scorched earth behind me. If Robbie wasn't there, I had nothing to go back to.

Or maybe I did, but I didn't want to.

I paused at the threshold of the station to catch my breath. The cold air burned my throat.

Robbie stood by the Christmas tree, just as I'd imagined. His face lit up when he saw me. He held out his arms. I ran to him.

All explanations would come later. The train arrived, we boarded it, and rode out of town through the night.

■   ■   ■

That's the whole story.

I'm sorry I embarrassed you and Daddy-o and everyone. But I must confess: Those three days in New York were so wonderful, I can't bear to think I might have missed them. Don't punish everyone else for my crimes. Please, please forgive me. And please don't cut us out of the will. I don't care about the money so much for myself, but Ginger and Daddy-o won't know how to get by. And what kind of life will poor Takey have?

I'm asking your understanding . . . and once you understand, I know you'll forgive me.

Sincerely and dutifully,

your granddaughter,

Louisa Norris Sullivan

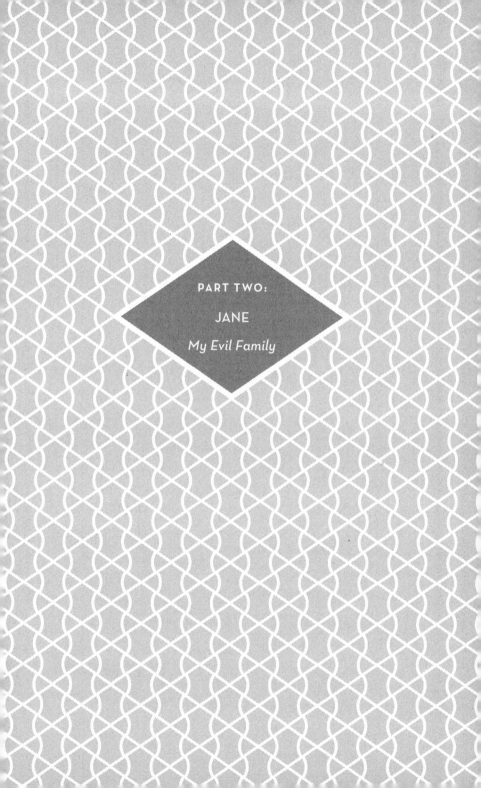

PART TWO:

JANE

My Evil Family

Dear Almighty,

You want a confession? Here you go:
www.myevilfamily.com
There you'll find all the evidence you need, complete and unedited. I left everything in. You're not going to like a lot of it, but that's the way the tea biscuit crumbles. This is a confession, so I have to be honest no matter who it hurts — right?

You've already read most of the blog entries, I hear. I'm attaching some explanation so you'll understand what was going through my mind when I wrote them. If that makes it easier for you to forgive me, great. If not, I guess we Sullivans will have to go on welfare or something. That ought to make you proud.

ONE

✉   ✉   ✉

myevilfamily.com

My Family Is Evil

Welcome to myevilfamily.com, a blog written by me, Jane Sullivan, to expose the sins of my family. We have committed a lot of sins over the centuries, so I'll start at the beginning and work my way up to now. Once I've covered everything my family has done wrong, maybe I'll move on to the crimes of other evil families I know.

On this blog, You, the World at Large, will learn the truth about the great and storied Sullivan family of Baltimore, Maryland. Maybe you've heard of my grandmother, Arden Louisa Norris Sullivan Weems Maguire Hightower Beckendorf, better known as "Almighty Lou." Why does she have so many names? Because she's been married five times. She's never been divorced—she's a heavy-duty Catholic, so the very idea of divorce makes her shudder. No, her first four husbands died. Four of them. Died. Does this make anyone suspicious? Am I the only one asking questions here?

Almighty gives lots of money to the Baltimore Museum of Art and the Peabody Conservatory and lots of other schools and charities and foundations. Everybody says what a good person she is. I'm not saying she's not a good person. All I'm saying is, once you know the truth you can decide for yourself. It's easy to give money away when you have tons and tons of it.

So if you're curious to know the real story of the Sullivan family, read this blog.

JANE OUT

As you may or may not know, Almighty, I'm not the most popular girl at St. Maggie's these days. Something in my personality rubs people the wrong way. And that's okay with me.

Little tricks like the one I played at Matt Bowie's swim party in September don't help. But who can resist? Bibi D'Alessandro is such a tempting target. *You* may think Brooks Overbeck should be elected Mullah of Roland Park, but *I* can't stand the way everybody fawns over him — especially girls.

So I borrowed Brooks's phone and sent Bibi D'Alessandro a text from Brooks. Except Brooks didn't know anything about it. He was swimming at the time. I wrote UR SO HOT BB. COME

HERE & KISS ME RT NOW and pressed SEND. Then I tossed his phone back on his towel and closed my eyes and tried to look innocent.

My friend Bridget giggled and said, "You are so evil." (You remember Bridget, right? She came to my birthday party last summer. Choppy brown hair, freckles? You called her "Pig-nose"? Not to her piggy little face, of course.)

"I am not evil," I said without opening my eyes. "Bibi is."

Bridget and Sassy and I had tagged along with Norrie to Matt Bowie's party. Not because I wanted to see these people but it was hot and I felt like a swim. I love swimming next to a cemetery — it helps remind me not to drown.

Bibi was stretched out on Eliza Caton Bowie's tomb when she got the text. The tomb is the best spot for sunning because it's long and flat and the stone warms up in the sun. Most Hated Tasha Wallace lounged on the ground next to her like a good toady. I saw Bibi lift her phone and shade her eyes to read the screen. She passed the phone to Tasha. While Tasha deciphered the message, Bibi sat up and looked over toward the group of us on the pebbly shore of the reservoir.

Brooks had just walked out of the water, dripping. He shook his hair and toweled off and sat down with his friends, laughing about how Ryan Gornick can spit water between his front teeth with pinpoint accuracy. Bibi stood up, adjusted her bikini, and swaggered toward us through the crumbling headstones. Tasha climbed onto Eliza Bowie's tomb to watch.

Brooks lay back on his towel and closed his eyes. It was too perfect, almost as if he were Snow White waiting for someone to come wake him with a kiss. And Bibi would be his Princess Charming, whether he liked it or not.

"This is awesome," Bridget whispered.

Bibi stood over Brooks's prone body, casting a shadow across his face, but he didn't open his eyes. She straddled him, knelt, and planted her hands on either side of his shoulders. His eyes popped open. She bent down and kissed him very much *à la française*.

Brooks jerked up, startled, and yelped, "Hey! What — ?" It was an involuntary reaction. His forehead bumped Bibi's nose, hard. Her nose started bleeding.

Bibi jumped up, shaken, wiping her nose and staring at her bloody fingers in confusion. Ryan and the other guys whooped and laughed. Brooks rubbed his thin wet hair, a good-puppy look on his face. I don't know what everybody sees in him, but Bibi's nuts about him, and so is Norrie's friend Claire and a million other girls. I sometimes wondered (*used* to wonder; we have our answer now) if Norrie liked him too, though she wouldn't come out and say so. Even Bridget gets this goofy look on her face when he's around. She tries to hide it from me but I SEE ALL.

"Hey, Bibi, I'm sorry," Brooks said. He offered her a corner of his towel to wipe off her nose and lip, but that just smeared the blood all over her face. "I didn't know you were there. Uh, what were you doing on top of me like that anyway?"

"When are you going to figure it out, Overbeck?" Ryan said. "Chicks dig you."

"She was seized by an irresistible urge to have your babies," Davis said. "It's simple biology."

"She walked over here in an Overbeck trance," Ryan said. "Must have Overbeck babies . . . Must have Overbeck . . ."

Bibi glared at them. "You texted me. You told me —" She saw the blank look on Brooks's face and stopped. "What's going on here? Is someone playing a trick on me?" Everybody laughed as she glanced from face to face, paranoid. Well, not paranoid, I guess, since she wasn't imagining things. Someone *was* out to get her.

"Bibi, don't get upset," Brooks said. "You can kiss me any old time."

Brooks was trying to help her joke her way out of it, but Bibi is humor impaired — which makes her more fun to tease — and didn't see the exit he was pointing out to her. She ran back to Eliza Caton Bowie's tomb to clean up her face.

Brooks jumped to his feet and started over to help her. "Hey, look, I'm really sorry about your nose. Let me help you. . . ."

Norrie and Claire came out of the water in time to see Bibi running away and Brooks chasing after her, apologizing like crazy. "What was that all about?" Norrie asked.

I shrugged, all innocent. "You know Bibi." I twirled a finger next to my ear to indicate insanity.

"Not really," Norrie said. "She's your friend."

"She *was* my friend," I said.

"Whatever." Norrie settled down on her towel and closed her eyes. She was too busy with her very important senior year debutante stuff to care about the petty problems of little sisters like me.

TWO

⊠   ⊠   ⊠

myevilfamily.com

Evil Comes to America

My ancestor Francis Sullivan immigrated to Baltimore
from County Meath, Ireland, in 1847, during the
Great Famine. He was twenty-one and illiterate. Like
many Irish immigrants, he found work on the B&O
Railroad. Francis liked to drink a lot. So did most of
the other railroad men. It was starting to become a
problem—fights, broken marriages, the usual—so
some women and priests started an abstinence
movement called Society of the Divine Thirst. It was
kind of like Prohibition in the 1930s, except drinking
wasn't outlawed, just severely frowned upon.

Francis Sullivan and his drinking buddies were pres-
sured by the Society of the Divine Thirst to stay out
of the taverns and go to church instead. But the railroad workers really liked to drink. So Francis got an
idea: Why slave away on the railroad when you could

rake in the bucks quicker by opening a tavern? The problem was how to do it without pissing off all the wives and priests. So Francis opened a club in Fells Point. He called it the Circle of the Stout Heart and claimed it was a men's-only abstinence society. But it was really a secret pub, and the men said Francis served the best pint of stout in the city. They told their wives they were going to an abstinence meeting—sorry, honey, members only—and then drank like pigs. Or fish. Whatever it is that drinks a lot. The Stout Heart was a big success. Soon the Society of the Divine Thirst gave up on abstinence as a lost cause. Francis died a prosperous man. A tavern keeper.

That was the beginning of the Sullivan family fortune—a fortune built on lies and vice. Evil, if you will.

Daniel Sullivan, unlike his father, Francis, went to school. He was no dummy. When he grew up, indoor plumbing was just developing. Daniel saw a way to get even richer. The newfangled toilets were always getting clogged up. So Daniel invented the toilet plunger. At least, he patented it. His former best friend, Patrick Heath, claimed that Daniel stole the idea from him.

Whatever. Daniel got the patent, and Daniel got the money and to hell with his friend Patrick.

Now the Sullivans were really rich. Then Daniel married the daughter of a rich tobacco farmer and got even richer.

That's right. Tobacco.

It begins.

JANE OUT

Coming up: the Civil War. Wait till you read about the evil stuff my family did then!

COMMENTS:
bridget2nowhere: Um, I hate to point this out, Jane, but you smoke. So you really can't dis your ancestors for growing tobacco.
myevilfamily: Cloves! I smoke clove cigarettes.
bridget2nowhere: They still have tobacco in them.
myevilfamily: I never said I was perfect. Besides, I know it's bad and I'm going to quit soon. Anyway, look, I can't help it because obviously tobacco is in my genes.

"No one's going to read our blogs," Bridget said. "How will anyone even find them?"

Bridget and I were hanging in the second-floor bathroom, smoking clove cigarettes out the window. We were trying to turn it into a bad girls' bathroom that nice girls would be afraid to use, but so far we kept getting interrupted by ninth graders whose idea of bad was chewing gum.

"The truth always finds a way," I said as three Trident chompers finally finished reapplying their baby-blue eye shadow and flounced out of the bathroom. "Eventually, word will spread, and we'll be famous."

"Okay, but how long is that going to take?" Bridget can really be annoying. Whiny. And that turned-up nose of hers *can* look a little like a pig snout. I never said you were wrong about that, Almighty. "Maybe we should post on the school blog. That way everybody will see it."

I shook my head. Bridget never thinks things through. "That's no good because then the nuns can shut us down. This way we have our own independent blogs and no one can stop us from saying anything we want. This is supposed to be a free country, once you get out of the nuns' jurisdiction."

"You have so much more stuff to write about," Bridget whined again. She's my best friend kind of by default. Since the whole Bibi episode last year nobody else really wants to be friends with me. "Bootlegging and murders and feuds . . . My family's big secret is that my mother had our cat put to sleep. She claimed Pawl had gum cancer but it was really just because he wouldn't stop peeing on the living room rug."

"Tell it, sister!" I tried to encourage her.

"It's so lame."

"You're not digging deep enough," I said. "Your family has got to have better secrets than that. What about your dad's business trips? Who knows, maybe he's really visiting his secret other family."

She looked doubtful. "You think so?"

"Anything's possible."

Bridget's blog is called bridget2nowhere.com, which was starting to look like truth in advertising. I was determined that *my* blog would make a difference in the world. A big difference. Stamp out hypocrisy wherever you find it! That was my new motto. And guess what? I found out the biggest hypocrites live in big houses uptown. Which just happens to be where you live.

"We need to band together," I said. "To form an Anti-Popular Front. We will destroy everything."

"To the Anti-Popular Front!" Bridget shouted. We clashed our silver rings together. Mine has a skull and crossbones, and hers has a peace sign. We had already talked about things we could do to destroy everything — typical bullshit things like shaving our heads, getting nasty tattoos, piercing every pierceable place on our bodies, running away to New York or Portland, Oregon, and living on the streets, or squatting in an abandoned warehouse downtown. But kids have been doing those things for years, and what does it accomplish? Nothing. We decided that the most destructive thing we could do — what would upset the adults in our world the most — would be to tell secrets. All the family secrets we knew. And show everyone that the upstanding citizens they admire so much are, at best, lazy sybarites and, at worst, criminals. Criminals who never get caught, and if they do, never go to jail. We would take down society through our blogs.

So you see, it was nothing personal.

Bibi and Tasha came in then. Tasha pinched her nose and Bibi tried to wave away the clove smoke. "Ugh, really, Jane," Bibi said. "You can smell that all the way down the hall. Are you trying to get kicked out of school?"

"She'll never get kicked out," Tasha said, rubbing her thumb and forefingers together in a way that suggested money.

I knew what they were hinting: that I'm coddled at St. Maggie's because you are one of the school's most distinguished alumnae and largest donors. But if that's true, why is Sister Mary Joseph clearly out to get me? Why was I given three weeks detention last year for protesting the school musical? Was jumping onstage and doing a striptease in the middle of *Guys and Dolls* really so terrible? True, I wasn't technically in the play, but the girls who *were* in the play were stripping too. (They were chorus girls singing that "Take Back Your Mink" song.) Just because I actually made it all the way down to my underwear before being hauled offstage, I got punished. Which only underscores my point: The play is sexist and exploits women, and a girls' school, of all places, shouldn't condone it.

But nobody got my message about sexism. All they cared about was that I took off my clothes.

Bibi and Tasha each shut herself in a stall and started talking over the metal dividers as if that gave them some kind of Cone of Silence. "Anyway, tell everybody to come to my house at eight," Bibi said. "And if they want anything to drink, they have to bring it, because my parents don't have anything. And make sure they know I invited tons of boys."

They flushed simultaneously and emerged to wash their hands. "Having a party, Beebs?" I asked.

"What — did you hear that?" she said.

I tossed my ciggie in the sink. "Just dry your hands and get out." I tried to sound tough. "This is the bad girl bathroom."

Bibi and Tasha laughed as they left. No one was taking my bad girl bathroom idea seriously.

"When's her party?" I asked Bridget. "Have you heard anything?"

"Saturday."

"Screw them. We'll have our own bash at my house. Just the two of us. And it will be way cooler than some lame high school party."

"Yeah," Bridget said. She always says that. She's my yes-girl.

A yes-girl comes in handy once in a while.

THREE

✉   ✉   ✉

myevilfamily.com

The Wrong Side of the Civil War — That Would Be the Evil Side

Another branch of my family is the Norrises. They also came to Baltimore from Ireland. Wilbur Norris got rich by ripping off poor people. He bought their farmland cheap, then sold it to the B&O Railroad for a fortune. Soon he was on the board of directors of the railroad, raking it in.

It's pretty hard to get rich without ripping off somebody. That's the point I'm trying to get across here.

When the Civil War came, Wilbur Norris sided with the South. He didn't own slaves (but some of my ancestors probably did — nobody wants to talk about it, but they must have. Hello? Tobacco farm?), but he was really into business, and he had business interests in the South (based on slavery, no doubt).

I would like to pause here and point out that we are talking about the SLAVERY of human beings. What is more evil than slavery? Nothing, except maybe genocide.

Wilbur Norris built the house my evil family lives in now. His daughter, Evangeline, lived in the Tower Room, the very room my sister is sleeping in at this moment. My sister's name? Norrie—short for Norris. And the beat goes on. . . .

During the Civil War, Baltimore was occupied by Yankee soldiers, but the Confederate army was camped just outside the city in Anne Arundel County. The Confederate soldiers could see the light from my sister's Tower Room if they used a telescope. Evangeline had a crush on a boy who was spying for the Confederates. So this boy, Russell Pinkney, sneaked into Evangeline's tower at night and sent secret spy signals to the Confederate troops in Anne Arundel County. Eventually the Yankees caught him and put him in jail in Fort McHenry for a while, so he missed the last half of his senior year and graduated late. He's lucky that's the worst that happened to him.

My ancestor helped a Confederate spy. My house was used to advance the Confederate cause. Even the very house I live in has a history of evil. I can't

get away from it. I hope it's not somehow seeping
into my skin through evil air molecules.

Coming up: Evil? Welcome to the Twentieth Century

JANE OUT

COMMENTS:
Sully: Hey, Jane, wtf is this?
myevilfamily: It's the TRUTH, brother. Recognize it?

Every report card I ever got has some comment like, "Jane
has problems with authority." To which Daddy-o always says,
"That's my girl — stick it to the Man!" which is so embarrassing.
Ginger sighs and adds, "Darling, let me give you a little tip: Fake
obedience until you graduate. Just keep your mouth shut and
pretend to go along with whatever the nuns say. That way you
don't waste a lot of precious time in detention and what have
you. After that, you can be as rebellious as your little heart
desires. Okay?"

I understand where Ginger is coming from — undermine the
system from within — but I just can't do it. The trouble started in
second grade, when I had my First Communion. Sister Madeleine
told us that once we took Communion, Jesus would live in our
hearts. I was really dreading the day Jesus moved into my body,
no matter how wonderful everyone said he was. I took the whole
thing too literally, I guess. But as soon as that wafer dissolved in
my mouth, I felt it. He was in there somewhere, floating in my

stomach, moving through my bloodstream on the way to my heart. It made me very uncomfortable. Since that day, whenever Jesus is mentioned, I feel that weird discomfort. It's like I have to clear my throat. That's a big handicap when you go to a Catholic school, because, as you know, Jesus's name comes up a lot, especially in Religion class.

Last year I had Sister Apollonia for Religion. (Do you remember your saints, Almighty? Saint Apollonia, patron saint of dentists, had all her teeth knocked out by a persecutor when she refused to renounce her Christian faith.) Sister Apollonia wears a little gold tooth on a chain around her neck in honor of her patron saint. She's a sweet, smiley nun whose religious focus is mostly on how much Jesus loves the little children. She also believes in giving out candy during class. Maybe that's her way of helping out the local dentists. She and I got along just fine.

This year I have Sister Mary Joseph for Religion. Right away I could tell she was going to become my archenemy. She has a stony face with a mean squint; Clint Eastwood in a wimple. She trained that squint on me and decided I was trouble from the get-go.

We started the year learning about the lives of the saints. "The saints teach us lessons about God," Sister Mary Joseph lectured. "Their suffering shows us what God wants us to strive for. Every generation has its own saints, with its own message from God. Yes, Mary Pat?"

"Why does God kill so many of his saints?"

"He doesn't kill them, he martyrs them. To make us pay attention," Sister M-J said.

Sister Mary Joseph told us we had to memorize a hundred saints and what they stood for by the end of the month. I kind of like the whole saint thing, because it's basically magic. My favorite part is learning which saints to pray to in which situations, from St. Matthew (patron saint of accountants, bookkeepers, and security guards) to St. Germaine Cousin (unattractive people).

A really cool one is St. Uncumber. She didn't want to marry the King of Sicily, so she prayed to God to let her keep her virginity. Presto, the next morning, she woke up with a beard and mustache. Virginity saved. She is the patroness of unhappy wives who want to get rid of their husbands.

I have a feeling Sister Mary Joseph would pray to St. Uncumber if she was ever in any danger of getting married. But the Clint Squint negates any need for miracles.

My patron saint is Joan of Arc: partly because we have the same name (close enough), but mostly because she is the patron saint of people who oppose authority. She was executed for heresy by the church. They retried her and found her innocent, but that was twenty-five years too late. She was safely dead by then and couldn't cause any more trouble.

"Tonight's homework has two parts," Sister Mary Joseph announced. "First — choose your patron saint. It doesn't have to be the saint whose name you share, but the saint you admire the most. Write a page on why you admire that saint and draw an icon for him or her, complete with symbols that saint represents. Part Two: Who are our twenty-first-century saints? Think of someone from the last fifty years or so whom you admire and think deserves sainthood. Write a page arguing for his or her canonization and draw an icon for him or her as well. This project is due next week. Any questions?"

I raised my hand.

"Yes, Jane?"

"Does the Church ever make mistakes? I mean, like, can the Pope ever be wrong?"

Laser squint. "What does that have to do with the lives of the saints?"

"Well, if Joan of Arc was a saint, why did the Church burn her for heresy?" I asked. "A bunch of priests and bishops said she disobeyed religious laws. Then later they changed their minds and made her a saint. So somebody in the Church must have made a mistake, right?"

"Catholic theology is very complicated," Sister Mary Joseph snapped.

"So if they could make a mistake then, they could make mistakes now," I continued without being called on. Sister M-J ignored me.

"Any *relevant* questions? Bibi?"

"Does the twenty-first-century saint have to be a real person, or can we make one up?"

Bibi's lame question didn't get the Squint. "I suppose you could describe an ideal modern person to be nominated for sainthood if you like. Anything else? Tasha?"

"Can we nominate you for sainthood, Sister Mary Joseph?"

Sister Mary Joseph's idea of a smile: The line of her thin lips stretched slightly outward. "That's very kind of you, Tasha, but I must humbly ask that you leave that decision up to the Vatican."

I must humbly ask . . . I wanted to puke. Sister Mary Joseph would have killed to be a saint, I knew she would. I wanted to nominate Tasha as the patron saint of sucking up, apple polishing, ass kissing, and best-friend stealing.

I raised my hand. There was something I'd always wondered and had never asked a nun before. Sister Mary Joseph reluctantly called on me.

"Sister, did you ever wish you could be a priest instead of a nun?"

Sister M-J gritted her teeth. "Stop wasting class time with these silly questions, Jane. Men are priests and women are nuns. You might as well ask if I ever thought of becoming a man."

"They have an operation for that now," I said. Even the prissiest girls in the class laughed.

"Jane Sullivan, if you're planning to spend the rest of the year with this attitude, you might as well walk out of this classroom right now and never come back. What will it be?"

Before I had the chance to answer, the bell rang. Everyone bolted to their feet.

"Any other br-r-r-rilliant questions?" Sister M-J trilled. "No? Class dismissed."

I was the first one to the door.

■　■　■

I took my drawing paper and pens upstairs to Norrie's room, the Tower of Evil. I like to have an occasional smoke while I work. At first she tried to say "No smoking in my room," but I countered with "Sully always let me," and she dropped it. She had just inherited the room from Sully and I guess she didn't feel complete ownership over it yet. It drives Norrie crazy when I smoke, which makes it more fun for me.

I was working on my icon for Joan of Arc. I drew her tied to a stake, staring at the sky, waiting for God to save her. Which he wasn't going to do.

She was such a badass. She wasn't one of those passive victim saints who just suffered — getting raped, beheaded, eyes gouged out, all that. She was a girl of action. She fought to change the world against crazy odds. She was seventeen years old — my age, Norrie's age, Hannah Montana's age — when she grabbed a sword and led grown men into battle against the English. In 1429. That's a badass.

When they were deciding whether or not to make her a saint (400 years after she died), some anti-Joan Church people said she shouldn't be a saint because she wasn't a martyr — because she didn't want to die. She wanted to live and she came right out and said so. I don't care if she was an actual saint or not. To me, that's a technicality. The fact that she wanted to live instead of voluntarily jumping into the fire (like the tooth queen, St. Apollonia) only makes me admire her more.

She was passionate. She said what she thought. She held nothing back. That's what made her great.

Norrie got up and looked over my shoulder. "Is Bridget doing St. Brigid?"

"Of course," I said, coloring the flames orange. "Even though St. Brigid was a lame-o."

"Milkmaids, cows, and illegitimate children. What's not to like?"

"You mean there are children whose parents aren't married?" I said sarcastically. "How is that possible? I thought you had to get married before the stork started dropping off babies."

"I like St. Brigid," Norrie said.

"You would."

"She was pretty."

"Exactly." St. Brigid's father tried to marry her to a young bard but she wanted to keep her virginity, so she prayed to God to take her beauty away. (Much like St. Uncumber. So many of the female saints were obsessed with their virginity.) The prayer was answered, though her beauty returned after she took her vows and became a nun. Why? What good did it do her then? So she'd look good in her stained-glass saint pictures? Everybody likes the pretty saints the best.

"I doubt St. Joan wore that much eyeliner," Norrie said.

"Fuck off."

"If you're going to barge in on me and use my room as a smokatorium, then you'll have to take my opinions along with it."

"Fine. I'll go back to my room," I said, but I didn't move. We were quiet for a while. She went back to reading in her window seat.

"Why are you going out with Brooks this weekend?" I asked.

She put down her book. "I don't know. Why shouldn't I?"

"Do you like him?"

She shrugged.

"See, that's not a good answer."

"Yes, I like him," she said. "Don't you like him?"

He's a nice boy if you like dull conformist milquetoasts — which, strangely, a lot of girls do. I know you like him, Almighty, and I don't mean to criticize your taste. I'm just saying.

"I know why you're really going out with him," I said. "Because Almighty wants you to."

"No I'm not," she said. "I'm going out with him because I want to see what it's like to go out with Brooks Overbeck."

What could I say to that? We were quiet again for a while. Sassy came in.

"What are you guys doing?"

"Nothing," Norrie said.

Sassy draped herself across the bed. She likes to lie down whenever possible. She gets that from Ginger. Ever notice how many daybeds and chaise longues we have in our house? That's so Ginger can get horizontal whenever the urge strikes her.

"I didn't see you and Lula at hockey practice today," Norrie said to Sassy.

"JV doesn't start until next week," Sassy said.

"So you're not even going to try for varsity? Some sophomores make it every year."

Sassy shrugged. "I'm not that great at hockey."

"Hockey is the dumbest game ever invented," I said. "And lacrosse is the second dumbest."

"You'd be good if you practiced harder, Jane," Norrie said. She is such a tool of the establishment.

Sassy stared at the ceiling.

"What's the matter, Sass?" Norrie asked. "You tired?"

"Yeah," Sassy said. "And I just got hit by a car."

"What?" Norrie jumped off the window seat and dove onto the bed.

"She's kidding." I joined them on the bed. "She must be kidding. Look at her. Does she look like someone who's been hit by a car?"

"I was, though." Sassy rubbed her eyes. "On Northway. A car backed out of a driveway and bumped into me. I'm okay, though." She absently touched her thigh. There was a small bruise there the size of a quarter.

Norrie freaked out. "Are you sure? Don't you want to see a doctor or something to make sure you don't have a concussion? Maybe you have internal injuries."

"I didn't hit my head," Sassy said. "Really, I'm okay. She didn't hit me very hard."

"Who hit you?" I asked. "Was it Mrs. Vreeland?" Mrs. Vreeland lives around the corner on Northway. Sometimes, when we were little and playing with other kids in the neighborhood, we ran through her yard as a shortcut. She called the police on us every time. I hate Mrs. Vreeland.

"No. Some lady I didn't know."

"But you're sure you're not hurt?" Now Norrie was shaking Sassy's arms and legs, checking for broken bones. Sassy lay limp as a rag doll. "Did you tell Ginger and Daddy-o?"

"No. What could they do?"

"I don't know," Norrie said. "But, I mean, they're our parents. . . ."

We all burst out laughing. Ginger and Daddy-o are not exactly helpful during emergencies. Remember when Takey was two and he fell off your piano stool and broke his nose? Daddy-o couldn't remember the number for 911. And Ginger — when one of us complains of being sick, she says drily, "I'll start making funeral arrangements."

"Really, Norrie, I promise I'm not hurt." Sassy sat up and made a muscle to prove it.

"Okay." Norrie leaned back against her headboard and propped her feet on Sassy's legs, pretending not to be worried anymore. "Maybe you should make Sassy one of your saints," she said to me. "She can get hit by a car without getting hurt. She's indestructible."

"Saints aren't indestructible," I said. "Haven't you ever looked at the windows in church? The saints are always getting shot by arrows or beheaded or burned to death. That's what makes them saints. You're thinking of a superhero, not a saint."

"All right then, maybe she's an angel," Norrie said. "They can't die, right? 'Cause they're already dead?"

"You mean like ghosts?"

"No, I mean like angels."

"Stop it, you guys," Sassy said. "I'm not a saint or an angel. I'm just lucky. Really, really lucky."

"Yeah, keep telling yourself that," I said. I got off the bed and went back to the desk to work on St. Joan's flames. I wanted to make them hotter.

FOUR

⊠   ⊠   ⊠

myevilfamily.com

100% True! Not made up! No lies!

How Lou Became Almighty

Now we come to the story of my grandmother, the
Almighty Louisa Norris Sullivan etc., etc. Her father
built Gilded Elms, where she grew up as the pam-
pered, adored, and strong-willed daughter of a
diplomat, and where she still lives. She inherited the
house after her parents died and she moved in as a
young bride with her husband, Alphonse Sullivan, Jr.,
a diplomat like her father.

As a girl, Almighty's best friend was Mary Margaret
Rennert, known as Mamie or Mame. Mamie's father,
James Rennert, owned a newspaper. Together
Mamie and Almighty Lou ruled St. Maggie's School.
They had the best parties. They rode horses and
swigged champagne and jumped into fountains in

their fancy clothes. They were famous for crashing stag parties at the Maryland Club wearing only bathing suits under their fur coats.

Almighty had lots of beaux (that's what she still calls her boyfriends), but her favorite was Junius Overbeck. He escorted her to the Bachelors Cotillon and she expected him to propose to her later that year. But at the Cotillon, Junius did something taboo—he danced the final dance with Mamie, not Almighty Lou. How could he not know that would piss off Almighty? And you don't want to piss off Almighty.

After the ball, all the young people went to the country club to dance the night away, and Junius couldn't take his eyes off Mame—even though he was supposed to be Almighty's date. Junius and Mame left the club together at dawn, and a week later Mame's parents announced her engagement to Junius Overbeck.

You might as well have dropped a nuclear bomb on Baltimore, Almighty was so mad. Almighty's best friend had stolen her beau at the Cotillon, an unforgivable crime. She stopped speaking to Mame and vowed revenge.

From that day on, Almighty made it her life's work to thwart Mame in everything she did. She and she alone would rule Baltimore society. And Mamie Rennert Overbeck would be relegated to the sidelines.

Tune in next time to find out more. This ancient feud has repercussions that still echo through the generations!

JANE OUT

COMMENTS:

bridget2nowhere: Isn't your grandmother going to get mad when she reads this?

myevilfamily: She doesn't read blogs.

bridget2nowhere: Still. Somebody might tell her about it.

myevilfamily: I hope they do.

Sully: Jane, Almighty's going to slit your throat and drink your blood out of her best Waterford crystal.

myevilfamily: I'm glad to see you can get the Internet way up there in New Hampshire.

Sully: STFU. My frat bros think your blog is hilarious. They think you're making this shit up.

myevilfamily: Can't they read my new slogan? 100% true! I thought Dartmouth guys were supposed to be literate.

"Norrie's going to the Holman dance with Brooks this Friday," I shouted to Bridget in the lunchroom. "You know — BROOKS OVERBECK!"

I had to shout because the lunchroom is like an echo chamber in hell — screechingly noisy. Boys are loud, but girls' voices with no bass line to counterbalance them are earsplitting. So it wasn't really my fault if Bibi happened to overhear my little announcement. I didn't shout it on purpose just because she was sitting at the table behind me, I swear.

■ ■ ■

I got a D on my St. Joan icon and an F on my twenty-first-century icon, St. Lux Interior. Sister Mary Joseph didn't like that I drew a speech bubble with "I'm a badass" coming out of Joan's mouth. She said I could redo St. Joan if I wanted to try to make up the grade. Also, if I wanted to erase Lux Interior's F (she's never heard of the Cramps! The inventors of horror-punk! What do they teach in those convents anyway?), I could write a history of Catholicism in Maryland. Like that was going to happen.

■ ■ ■

Bridget came over that Saturday night for a sleepover. Ginger and Daddy-o had gone out and Miss Maura had the night off so Sassy was having a Wii burp-off with Takey in the den. Norrie was out on a date with Robbie, though I didn't know he was Robbie at the time, like THE Robbie. I just thought of him as some guy in her Speed Reading class that she was acting all mysterious about.

Bridget and I took advantage of Norrie's absence to use her room as a tattoo parlor. Everything is always more fun in the Tower Room; maybe it's the atmosphere of Evil.

We sketched out what kind of tattoos we wanted. Don't worry, they weren't real tats — we drew them on with felt-tip pens. But for at least as long as we didn't wash — and I planned not to wash for as long as I could get away with it — we would look like badass girls with forbidden tattoos.

I was going to do Bridget's and she was going to do mine. At first I thought of making Bridget copy my St. Joan icon onto my back, but she isn't that great an artist and I was afraid she'd screw it up. "Stick with something simple," I told her, because I didn't want to spend all night drawing on her.

She toyed with a cow and a milk pail for St. Brigid but I convinced her that there could not be a lamer idea for a tattoo than a cow. Besides, I can't draw cows. So she chose a shamrock (also lame, but I didn't say so because it's easy to draw), and I chose a skull and crossbones — the universal symbol of danger, poison, and pirates.

I did Bridget first. I took an emerald-green felt-tip and practiced making shamrocks on a piece of paper until she was satisfied. Then she pulled off her sock and I drew a shamrock on her ankle.

"My turn," I said. "Use black. The darkest black pen in there."

While Bridget sorted through pens, I pulled my hair into a high ponytail to get it out of the way. I wanted the tattoo on the back of my neck. I bent my head down and she got to work.

The pen felt cool and ticklish on my skin, especially when it touched my spine. "Why are you taking so long?" I asked.

"I'm being careful. Don't you want me to do a good job?"

"Yes. Please do a good job."

"Okay, then shut up."

"You're not allowed to say shut up in our house."

"Fuck off."

"That you're allowed to say."

Sorry if that offended you, Almighty, but I'm only quoting Bridget.

Bridget pressed hard on the pen while she filled in the outline. A few more endless minutes spent bent over, and she was done. My head felt heavy as I lifted it. "How does it look?"

"Heinous. Look in the mirror."

I went to Norrie's dresser and tried to see the back of my neck in the mirror, but it was impossible. Stupid, I thought. Why did I decide to put the tattoo someplace where I couldn't see it?

"Here." Bridget gave me Norrie's hand mirror. I held it up the way they do at the hair salon so you can see the back of your fabulous new do. There it was. Inky black and evil-looking: the skull and crossbones.

"Doesn't it look cool?" Bridget tugged up one leg of her jeans to get another peek at her shamrock.

"I wish it was a real tattoo," I said. "I won't wash the back of my neck for a long time."

"It could still smear." Bridget's tattoo had already smeared slightly.

"I'll be careful." I really liked it. I thought, *When I turn eighteen and graduate from St. Maggie's Reformatory I am definitely going to get a real tattoo.*

■   ■   ■

"What's that thing on the back of your neck?" Norrie asked at breakfast the next morning. "You've got some kind of black splotch."

Sassy pulled my hair aside for a better look. "Is it real?"

"Of course it's real," I said.

"But it's not permanent," Bridget added. "It's just felt-tip."

"You drew fake tats with felt-tip?" Norrie said. "That's mature."

Sassy let my hair drop. "I'm glad it's not real. It's scary-looking."

"It's supposed to be scary-looking."

"Your hair covers it pretty well," Norrie said. "The nuns might not even notice it."

"Look at mine." Bridget lifted her ankle to show off her sham-rock just as Miss Maura came into the breakfast nook with a plate of eggs.

"No feet on the table," Miss Maura said.

"Will you draw a tattoo on me?" Takey asked me.

"Sure. What do you want?"

"A gun."

"No guns. I'll do almost anything else."

Takey made a pistol with his right hand, aimed it at me, and shot. "Ka-ping! You're dead."

Miss Maura shook her head and clucked back to the kitchen.

"I'll draw you a goldfish," I offered him. "I'll make him look just like Bubbles."

Takey shot me again, right between the eyes, before say-ing, "Okay."

■ ■ ■

At school on Monday, I was trying to make the bad girl bathroom badder by covering the stalls with graffiti when Bibi and
Tasha came in. I tucked my feet up on the toilet seat so they
wouldn't see me.

"You had him," Bibi was saying to Tasha. "If Shea hadn't
shown up, he would have been yours."

"Okay, but what does that say about him?" Tasha said. "Given
the choice between me and Shea, he picks Shea?"

"It's not that he *picked* Shea," Bibi said. "He just knew what
she'd do and what you wouldn't do, and he was in the mood for
some action that night. I guess."

"Still, it makes me wonder what kind of guy he is," Tasha said.
"How did Shea end up at your house anyway? You didn't invite
her, did you?"

"Fuck no," Bibi said. (Again, just quoting.) "Somebody
brought her."

"Somebody always brings her."

They were quiet for a second. I stayed perfectly still.

"Hey," Bibi said. "Is anybody in here?"

I held my breath.

"That stall door is closed," Tasha said. "I don't see any feet,
but . . ." She pushed on the door of my stall. I'd locked it. She
pushed on it again. I shut my eyes. When I opened them, Tasha's
head was blinking at me from under the stall door.

"Jane, are you spying on us?"

"It's Jane?" Bibi said. "Come out of there. We won't bite." I heard her snap her teeth together a few times. They laughed. I scribbled *B.B. + TASHA 4EVER* on the stall wall before I came out.

"I wasn't spying," I said. "Can't a girl get some privacy around here?"

"I heard your sister left Ryan Gornick's party with Shea on Friday night," Bibi said.

"I don't know who she left with," I said. "She went with Brooks. You like him, don't you?"

"No," Bibi said unconvincingly. "I'm just letting you know: People are starting to talk about your sister and Shea in the same breath. Like they're the same kind of person. Which would be a slutty person."

"Slut schmut," I said. "Nobody cares."

"Brooks does."

"You're just jealous because Brooks likes Norrie and not you," I said.

"I don't think he does like Norrie," Bibi said. "I think his grandmother is making him pretend to like her."

"Oh yeah? Well, maybe my grandmother is making Norrie pretend she likes Brooks."

"They let their grandmothers tell them who to date?" Tasha said. "What century is this?"

"Exactly," Bibi said.

"I totally agree," I said.

"Then we're all in agreement," Tasha said.

"I guess so," I said.

"All right then," Bibi said. "See you in Religion. I look forward to watching Sister M-J eviscerate you."

"So do I," I said. "I enjoy pain."

"You are so full of it," Bibi said.

I miss being friends with Bibi. I really do. But if I said so out loud, she'd never believe me.

FIVE

⊠　⊠　·　⊠

myevilfamily.com

100% True! Not made up! No lies!

Almighty vs. Mame: Socialite Smackdown

And so the great feud began. Mamie's wedding to
Junius Overbeck was the social event of the year.
Almighty was invited but refused to go. No, she had
a better idea. A lovely, wicked idea.

Almighty threw a party of her own the same day as
Mamie's wedding. But this was no ordinary party. It
was an irresistible invitation. A reception at Gilded
Elms with none other than the Duke and Duchess of
Windsor. You know, Edward, Prince William's great-
great uncle? The guy who abdicated the British
throne so he could marry his true love? Who just
happened to be a Baltimore girl, Wallis Warfield
Simpson, and an old girlfriend of Almighty's father.
Wallis hadn't been to town in ages, so her return was

a huge deal. Almighty begged her father to arrange the visit, and he couldn't resist spoiling his precious princess, Lou. With a snap of his fingers it was done.

Poor Mamie's wedding was ruined. No one wanted to go to an ordinary old wedding when they could meet British royalty. Even Mamie's own parents ducked out early for a chance to see Wallis and the former King of England close-up.

Mamie pretended it didn't bother her. She and Junius went on their honeymoon to Bermuda and came back happy and tan. But when Mame became chair of the Junior Assembly, which ran all the big social events in town, she left Almighty Lou's name off every invitation list. The Feud was on.

"I'll show Mame who runs this town," Almighty said, her fist clenched in rage. And she plotted her next act of revenge.

Stay tuned.

JANE OUT

By the way, there is no God. I have proof! But I'm saving it for the right moment.

COMMENTS:

Sully: Dudette, where did you hear this shit? Did Almighty tell you or are you making it up?

myevilfamily: I'm not making it up. I pieced it together from stories I've heard over the years. I did research too. A lot of this was covered in the newspaper.

Sully: I can't decide if it's embarrassing or not.

myevilfamily: It doesn't matter if it's embarrassing. It's the TRUTH.

St. John: There are no truths, only moments of clarity passing for answers. — Montaigne

---

I don't know if you're aware of this, Almighty, but every Tuesday at tea you like to pick on one of us. That Tuesday you decided to pick on me. Here's how I saw it. If you want to tell your side, feel free to write a rebuttal.

It started with, "Jane, what is the matter with your hair?" and went downhill from there. "It looks like a big, lank pile of worms."

"Thank you," I said. I'd actually tried to avoid being picked on by wearing a turtleneck so you wouldn't see my tattoo, but that strategy didn't work.

"She hasn't washed it," Norrie explained.

You poured yourself a cup of tea. "Why on earth not? You've got dishwater hair as it is. You've got to keep it clean so it shines, at least."

"Her hair is perfectly hideous," Ginger said. "I keep trying to get her to highlight it, but she doesn't believe in chemicals. Can you imagine? What kind of life would we have without chemicals?"

So I don't have beautiful blond hair like my sisters. So what. It all depends on how you look at it. You can call it dishwater, or you can call it "Proletariat Blond."

Anyway, blonds are everywhere. St. Maggie's is packed with blonds, natural and not. Why should I look like everybody else? I tried dying my hair black once, but it looked stupid on me because my eyebrows aren't dark enough. And then when Bridget tried to darken my eyebrows with a pencil, I looked like Colin Farrell.

"I still don't understand," you said. "Jane, why haven't you washed your hair?"

Silence. Norrie and Sassy loyally refused to tell on me. I didn't want to wash off my tattoo; that was the reason. I'd tried that dry shampoo stuff but all it did was make my hair clumpy and hard to comb.

"Why does she do anything?" Ginger drawled. "It's beyond our comprehension, Almighty. Best not to ask."

"I don't accept that," you said. "I want an answer."

"Don't worry, I'll wash it soon." I picked up my knife and buttered a scone. You glared at my hands and gave one of your mighty dragon's breath exhales.

"Jane Sullivan, you are sixteen years old, a full-grown young lady. Haven't you learned to hold a knife properly by this time?"

I stopped and looked at the knife in my hand. I have to say I still don't get it. You're always after me about my knife. What am I doing wrong?

"Ginger, how could you have let this go on so long? She's clutching that knife like a murderer. What are you going to do, stab the scone to death? This way." For the thousandth time you demonstrated the proper way to hold a knife.

"I don't see the difference," I said.

"Honestly. Thumb here, forefinger here. Rest the end against your knuckles, not your palm."

I adjusted my knife until you were satisfied. "Practice at home until you get it right," you said. "No man will ever marry a girl who holds her knife like that."

Like any boy notices how a girl holds her cutlery. I was afraid to look at Norrie or Sassy because we might all burst out laughing. I mean, come *on*, Almighty. You think Wallace married you for your table manners?

Speaking of Wallace: Just then he saw us through the glass door, gave us his little two-finger salute, and stepped inside to say hello, saving us from any more crazy cutlery talk.

"Having a nice tea today, ladies?" He carried a pot of orangey-yellow flowers. "I brought you some chrysanthemums to brighten up your table."

"Thank you, dear." You cleared away an empty plate to make room for the flowers. "Jane . . ."

Once again you fixated on the knife in my hand. I'm sorry I waved it in your face and pretended to threaten you, but you drove me to it. "You'll marry me, by God, if I have to force you to the altar at knifepoint!"

Norrie and Sassy and Ginger dissolved laughing. Wallace just looked confused. You rang for Bernice and got up from the table. "When you so-called *ladies* come back next week, I hope we can have a civilized tea. And Jane, I hope your hair will not look like an animal died on your head." You clicked your tongue and Buffalo Bill trotted at your heels as you disappeared into your enormous house.

Here's what happened after you left:

Bernice appeared to clear the table. "What did you all do to her? She had steam coming out her ears."

"Jane threatened her with a knife," Ginger replied.

"That'll do it," Bernice said.

Looking back, I guess you didn't miss much. When you leave the room, Almighty, you take the drama with you; I'll give you that.

SIX

⊠　　⊠　　⊠

myevilfamily.com

The Black Widow

Almighty was born with lots of money. I've already
told you some of the evil ways her ancestors earned
it. But she has even more money now. How did she
get it? By marrying people.

My grandmother has been married five times. Her
first husband, Alphonse Sullivan, Jr., my grandfather,
was rich like her. But he died of a heart attack when
he was 43. People said he worked too hard. My
father was ten years old at the time. Almighty inherited Al Jr.'s share of his family's money, of course.
Cha-ching.

Once the proper mourning period was over,
Almighty had no trouble finding new beaux, as she
so delicately puts it. Within two years she had
remarried. Her second husband, Geoffrey Weems,

was an investment banker. He worked too hard too, I guess, because he died a year later at 54, also from a heart attack. Double cha-ching!

Next she married Leo Maguire, who owned a shoe factory. You might not think a person could get rich from making shoes, but Leo did. He was very rich. And when he died five years after the wedding (cancer), Almighty inherited the shoe factory. Triple cha-ching!!!

At this point she wasn't just rich, she was filthy rich. Husband Number 4, Bertram Hightower, wasn't rich, so she must have loved him, though looking at his picture it's hard to see why (he was a total horse-face). His family had been rich once, but by the time Almighty came along they were just snooty. Bert's family owned a horse farm but they couldn't afford to keep it anymore, so Almighty took it over and now it's hers. She has a whole stable of beautiful thorough-bred horses to ride. That marriage lasted a good twelve years. It was really sad when Bertram died in a riding accident. Sad, and *not suspicious at all.*

After Bertram died, Almighty stayed single for a while. Then, at age 70, she decided to get married one more time. Husband Number 5 is Wallace Beckendorf. He's bald and quiet and he owns a nursery. He spends a lot of time tending Almighty's giant gardens, even though she has a gardener. He just likes being outside with the plants. We like him. He's very nice. We were hoping his mild demeanor would rub off on our grandmother, but no. Oh well. You can't have everything.

If anybody feels like investigating the circumstances of some of the deaths of Almighty's late husbands, be my guest. I'd do it myself, but I'm too busy getting brainwashed by religion.

While Almighty was busy getting married and widowed, The Feud between her and Mamie went on and on. If Mame donated a gym to St. Maggie's, Almighty donated an auditorium. When the mayor named Almighty head of the City Arts Commission, Mame accused Almighty of bribing every politician in the state to get it. After which, Almighty made a point of cutting off funding for Mame's pet project, Tin Ear Alley, a summer camp for underprivileged kids who suffer from that dreaded handicap, a lack of musical ability. Back and forth, back and forth. If Almighty invited you to a party and you went to Mame's instead, you went on her blacklist, never to be invited to anything again, unless you came crawling back to her on your knees and begged — and then only maybe.

Finally, ten years ago, after decades of scrapping over their little patch of Baltimore society, the source of their rivalry, Junius Overbeck, died. At his monster funeral, which filled the new cathedral, Almighty Lou made a big show of sympathy for Mame in her grief. I was there—I saw the whole thing. (Yes, I was only six, but I remember it.) Playing the magnanimous one, Almighty publicly called for an end to The Feud. It was time, she declared, for her and Mame to be friends and allies once more. "Together the two of us can do more good for the city than either of us ever could alone," Almighty declared at Junius's wake. "My dear Mame, let us put aside our long-held differences and declare a truce. I miss you, my old partner in crime."

Everyone clapped and had tears in their eyes. It was such a touching moment. The ancient Feud at an end at last. Or was it?

I have to say, I know my grandmother, and she does not give up that easily. My theory: After Junius died, she saw weakness in her victim and pounced. She saw a way to get Mame where it would really hurt her, get her good, once and for all. Would you like to know what it is? Maybe I'll tell you my theory sometime.

Next time: My mother. Did she drive her therapist to suicide? And why does she hate the word "heinie" so much?

JANE OUT

COMMENTS:

myevilfamily: Comments? Anyone? Too scared, eh?

"You washed your hair," Sassy said. "Thank God. You were beginning to smell bad."

"I was not." I'd finally given in and washed my hair. The girls at school had started holding their noses when they saw me. I figured a week with a skull and crossbones on my neck was long enough to make a statement. But I was still careful to wash around it on my neck area. "Is it still there?"

Sassy brushed my hair aside to check the back of my neck. "It's still there. It hasn't even smudged."

"Really? That's funny." I picked up Norrie's hand mirror and checked for myself. There was the fake tattoo, clear and dark as the day Bridget drew it. "The pen said 'washable ink.' What a lie."

"But aren't you glad it didn't wash off?" Sassy asked.

"Yeah," I said. "I'm just surprised. Bridget's shamrock bit the dust days ago."

"She's probably cleaner than you."

"Bite me."

"Maybe you left the ink on so long it sank into your skin and dyed it."

We were lounging around in Norrie's room on a Saturday night in November. It was very late. I was thinking about how next year Norrie would go to college and the Tower would be mine at last. Norrie was out somewhere with Robbie. I thought about what Bibi had said about her and Shea being lumped together. Not that I cared what Bibi thought but I didn't like her bad-mouthing Norrie.

"Sass, do you think going out with Robbie makes Norrie a slut?"

"No," she said. "Norrie loves him. There's nothing slutty about that."

"I wish Bibi D'Alessandro would shut up about it."

"Jane —"

I rolled my eyes. "Next year, when this room is mine, no one's going to be allowed in here."

"That's not fair," Sassy said. "The others always let us come in here. It's our playroom."

"Too bad. That's all coming to an end when the Reign of Jane begins. Don't worry — you'll only have to suffer through the Reign of Jane for one year, then you can take over and do whatever you want to the place. Cover it in unicorns and rainbows for all I care. It'll be just you and Takey then."

"That's going to be lonely," she said.

"Yeah, in a way. But think of all the privacy you'll have. And Ginger and Daddy-o's undivided attention." That made us laugh.

I opened Norrie's laptop and checked my e-mail. I found an interesting message from someone named Delphine Burrell.

Dear Jane Sullivan,

I've recently stumbled across your blog, myevilfamily.com, and enjoy it very much. In fact, I think many citizens of Baltimore would enjoy reading your thoughts on our city's history. May I interview you for a story for our paper's Metro section? I'd like to talk about your blog and your feelings about your family's history.

Thanks!

Delphine Burrell

Features Reporter

The *Baltimore Sun*

Hmm. Very interesting. The *Sun* wanted to do a story on me and my family. My *evil* family.

Should I do it?

"Any news?" Sassy asked.

"No." I logged off and shut the laptop. It was better not to mention the *Sun* to Sassy. She'd find out about it soon enough. Everyone would.

Outside, a car door slammed shut. I looked out the window.

"Norrie's home." I lit a ciggie so she would be greeted with the warm smell of clove as soon as she walked in. Oh, how she loves that.

"Jane, she'll kick us out."

"No she won't. She always says she will but she never does."

A few minutes later Norrie burst into the room. "I thought I'd find you in here." She was glaring at me.

"What? What did I do?"

"I'll show you what you did." She opened her laptop and it purred to life. She punched a few keys and myevilfamily.com appeared on the screen.

"What the fuck, Jane?" (Quoting! Quoting!) "You're blogging all our family secrets? And I had to find out at a party from a total stranger?"

"A total stranger reads my blog?" I said. "Wow. Who was it?"

"What difference does it make? Why are you doing this? And why didn't you tell me?" She turned to Sassy. "Did you know about this?"

"No," Sassy said. "Let me see."

Sassy started reading the blog posts. Norrie snatched the cig out of my hand and tossed it out the window. This was all very dramatic and exciting.

"I didn't think anybody would read it," I said. "Outside the family. I was going to tell you about it, but I was afraid you'd try and stop me, and I won't be stopped. The world needs to know the truth."

"The truth?" Norrie said. "This is just a bunch of old family stories. Who knows if there's any truth to any of them?" She sat down on the bed. "Why are you writing all those mean things about Almighty? She's going to kill you."

"If she finds out about it."

"*When* she finds out about it."

I knew then if I talked to the reporter from the *Sun*, you would definitely find out about it.

"I'm like Joan of Arc," I said. "Everyone thought she was crazy, but she had vision. She was only trying to do what was right."

"Jane, she burned to death. Think about it."

"I know," I said. "But that won't happen to me. Almighty wouldn't burn me at the stake. Even she's not *that* evil." (You're not — are you? Just kidding.)

Norrie sighed. "Jane, why are you doing this to us?"

I tried to explain to her why I did it. Here's what I said. Maybe it will help you understand.

"Whenever you read about Almighty in the newspaper, they always talk about how great it is that she gives money to schools and supports charity and has such a nice house and a colorful life and a distinguished family history. They make her — all of us — sound so glamorous. And I just thought some-body should tell the other side of it. To balance things out. That's all I'm trying to do."

"So you won't stop?"

I shook my head. "First Amendment. You can't stop me."

"Just don't ever write about me. If you do, I swear, I'll never speak to you again."

I didn't promise her one way or the other. A truth-teller can't make those kinds of promises.

SEVEN

✉   ✉   ✉

myevilfamily.com

How to Drive Your Therapist to Suicide

Just for fun, let's talk about another member of my family for a change. How about . . . oh . . . um . . . my mother?

My mother, Virginia Wells Sullivan. We call her Ginger, 'cause she hates to be called "Mom." According to her, just hearing the word "mom" ages a woman twenty years. And it's not very chic. So Ginger it is.

Ginger's got plenty of secrets I could spill — just as one example, did you know she uses a face cream with rabbit pee in it to keep her skin smooth?

Here's a typical Ginger day:

7:30 am: Lift sleep mask and crack one eye open to make sure Miss Maura has Daddy-o and kids ready for school and work. Confirm that all is under control. Go back to sleep.

10:00 am: Wake up to find Miss Maura delivering coffee, toast, grapefruit, and the paper in bed. But no time to dillydally! Must shower and get ready to meet Casey Stewart at Petit Louis for lunch.

12:30 pm: Lunch and gossip with Casey, followed by shopping at Cross Keys or Nordstrom or hair/nails/spa/dermatologist appointment.

3:00 pm (if Wednesday): Annoying interruption of a perfectly pleasant day for therapy with Dr. Melanie Viorst. Talk about how disappointing the children are. No matter how much one tries to teach them properly, they continue to speak as if raised in a trailer park. They use the most hateful words—"heinie," "wiener," "booger," and so on—just to upset their mother. Ask Dr. Viorst to please stop probing into why those words are so upsetting. Can't she see it's a simple matter of taste? Speaking of taste, revisit fear of mayonnaise—it's a disgusting concoction, what on earth IS mayonnaise anyway?—and how impossible it is to avoid mayonnaise in one's daily life when one is surrounded by WASPs and extremely WASPy Catholics. Mayonnaise is in EVERYTHING, you can't get away from it, it is so nauseating. . . . How does Dr. Viorst think one stays so reed thin? If one doesn't eat mayonnaise, one can hardly eat anything at all.

Weep decorously so Dr. Viorst can see that in spite of all appearances to the contrary, you hurt deeply inside.

4:30 pm: Home. Have a quick cocktail while greeting children and asking how school was. Whatever the children say (even if it's "I just got suspended for blasphemy"), answer, "Marvelous!"

6:00 pm: Daddy-o home from work. More cocktails and dressing for dinner.

7:30 pm: Out for the evening.

As you can imagine, discussing this frivolous life in therapy and CRYING over it could drive a psychiatrist to drink. Or worse.

One Wednesday, Ginger appeared at the North Baltimore Professional Center promptly at 3:00 for her regular appointment with Dr. Viorst. She sat in the waiting room and opened the *New Yorker*. She stared at the closed door of Dr. Viorst's office. Dr. Viorst did not appear. This was odd.

After half an hour, Ginger knocked on the office door. No response. She tried to open it. It was locked. Ginger shrugged and went home.

That evening Ginger got a call from someone she didn't know, saying that Dr. Viorst would no longer be seeing her. When Ginger asked why, the caller explained that Dr. Viorst had killed herself. "How dreadful," Ginger said to the caller.

Ginger hung up the phone and announced to her family, who were all seated together at dinner, that she always knew Dr. Viorst was crazy — even crazier than Ginger was — and what a relief not to have to try to think up problems to tell her therapist and cry over every week. Now that Wednesdays at 3:00 were free, she thought she might take up tennis again.

Oh, Ginger. Don't ever change.

JANE OUT

P.S. Does anybody know how to get ink off your skin? I've tried everything.

COMMENTS:
St. John: Did it ever occur to you that Ginger might be covering up a lot of pain with that brittle act of hers?

myevilfamily: What's your point?

Sassy: Ginger's right. Mayonnaise is totally gross.

Sully: I remember the night she found out about Dr. Viorst and she was REALLY upset. Remember? She was kind of in shock and she drank a LOT.

St. John: I hate to say this about my own little sister, but if our family is evil, the most evil member is you. And anyway, evil is a relative term. If you say there is no God, then you can't call people evil. Without God, there is no evil. Without heaven, there can be no hell.

myevilfamily: Oh, St. John, why don't you let your head explode and get it over with?

St. John: You're just trying to get a response from someone—ANY response.

myevilfamily: Heinie heinie heinie!

Sully: Here's some truth for you: Four years ago Jane Sullivan was the world's biggest Hannah Montana fan! Ha!

myevilfamily: I was all of nine. So was every other nine-year-old girl on earth.

Sully: You were twelve. And you were her #1 fan. So suck it.

"Jane, look at this." Bridget led me into the last stall in the bad girl bathroom. Someone had taken my cue and started scribbling graffiti on the walls. Except this wasn't the graffiti I'd been hoping for:

GIRLS WHO GIVE BJS TO PERVY OLD GUYS:
Shea D.

Norrie S.

Jane S??? (Maybe next year)

"Do you think Bibi wrote this?" Bridget asked.

"I don't know." To be honest, I don't think Bibi would stoop so low. She hates me, not Norrie. The whole *Guys and Dolls* debacle, etc. Unless she was jealous of Norrie because of Brooks.

Bibi and Tasha happened to walk in and catch us studying the stall wall. Bibi and I always did have the same pee schedule.

"Give it up, Jane," Bibi said. "This is not now and never will be a bad girl bathroom, no matter how much you vandalize it."

"I'm not vandalizing it." I showed her the graffiti. She and Tasha poked their heads into the stall to read it. Tasha nodded. "Yeah, I heard that."

"You heard what?"

"That Norrie was at this party with Shea and a bunch of older guys, and Shea was in the bathroom giving blow jobs to everybody."

"So? That doesn't mean Norrie was doing that."

"But Norrie was there. So maybe she was."

"That is so stupid," I said. "It isn't logical —"

"People have been texting about it since yesterday." Bibi scrolled through her phone, then showed me a bunch of texts with the letters *NS* and *SD* and *BJ*. "I haven't passed them on to anyone . . . well, except for Brooks. I thought he should know what kind of girl he's taking to the Cotillon."

"You're passing those ridiculous rumors to Brooks?" I was fuming. "You know they're not true."

Bibi shrugged. "All I know is what my cell phone tells me. Besides, Brooks was bound to hear it from somebody."

"He knows better than to believe that," I said. "He knows what Norrie's really like."

"Then Norrie has nothing to worry about," Bibi said.

"What about your blog?" Tasha said. "You're trashing your own family. What's the difference between that and texting?"

"You're spreading lies," I said. "I'm telling the truth. That's the difference."

"Strikes me as a pretty thin line," Bibi said.

■ ■ ■

I know you've seen this article, Almighty, but here's an extra copy for your scrapbook.

I must confess that when I first read the article I felt a great sense of satisfaction. My blog had made the front page of the Metro Section. The front page!

Now I'll really get some attention, I thought.

I didn't think about the rest of the family and what might happen because of my zeal to tell the truth. Not yet.

THE *BALTIMORE SUN*

Granddaughter of Social Lioness Reveals Family Secrets on Blog

BY DELPHINE BURRELL

MRS. LOUISA BECKENDORF — full name Arden Louisa Norris Sullivan Weems Maguire Hightower Beckendorf — is a philanthropist, city leader, social arbiter, and grande dame of such power that she is locally known as "Almighty Lou." Since making her debut at the Bachelors Cotillon in 1947, she has been the most influential hostess at the top of Baltimore society. She sits on the boards of numerous charities and arts institutions, and started a fad for wearing orange feathers in the 1970s. She has a wing named after her at the Baltimore Museum of Art. It is said that anyone who wishes to be invited to the most exclusive social events in town must get — and stay — on Mrs. Beckendorf's good side.

But now the fearsome and influential "Almighty Lou" may be cut down to size by her own granddaughter.

Jane Sullivan, 16, a junior at St. Margaret's Preparatory School and one of Mrs. Beckendorf's six grandchildren, has started a website called myevilfamily.com. The site is essentially a blog detailing the sordid history of the Sullivan and Norris families, from the origins of their great fortune to the petty social feud between Mrs. Beckendorf and her chief rival, Mrs. Margaret "Mame" Overbeck, to the mysterious suicide of her mother's psychotherapist. According to Jane Sullivan, Mrs. Beckendorf never forgave Mrs. Overbeck for stealing Junius Overbeck out from under her nose. Even now, when the two women claim to have patched up their differences, Jane suggests that her grandmother is plotting a devious revenge against Mrs. Overbeck.

This information is being gobbled up like candy by certain segments of Baltimore society — those who live and attend the posh private schools in the north of the city. "Almighty Lou has held power over us for so long that we love to finally see a crack in her perfect facade," said one Guilford doyenne who declined to speak on the record. "This is just too delicious."

"I'm only telling the truth," Jane Sullivan said when asked why she was airing her family's dirty laundry in public. "People look up to my grandmother because she's rich. Well, if they knew how rich people got that way, maybe they wouldn't look up to them so much. Destroy all evil! Destroy everything!"

Ms. Sullivan said she will continue to write about her family until all their secrets have been revealed. "I'm glad the *Sun* is publicizing my blog," she added. "That way everyone will know the truth. Power to the people!"

"Almighty Lou is going to wring that brat's neck," said a Roland Park resident who refused to give her name for fear of retribution. "There goes her inheritance."

Mrs. Beckendorf could not be reached for comment.

EIGHT

⊠   ⊠   ⊠

myevilfamily.com

Almighty's Evil Plan

Some people—not that many anymore, but some—
are fascinated by the Bachelors Cotillon, what it
means, and how the girls who are invited are
selected. Almighty Lou has a lot to say about who
she thinks is "good enough" to be a debutante. Even
though she herself is rich, she doesn't place much
emphasis on money. No, this is Baltimore, where
family and background are everything. Anybody can
get money. Connections are helpful, and, if neces-
sary, blackmail works too.

Even if you are poor(ish), you can be a debutante if
you come from an old Baltimore family and go to one
of the private schools. Wallis Warfield Simpson, the
famous Baltimore debutante who married the King
of England and became the Duchess of Windsor, had
so little money she had to wear homemade dresses

sewn by her aunt, but she was a Warfield, and that was good enough.

This system is breaking down now, in the 21st century. Outside of Baltimore (especially in "vulgar" New York), money means everything, and that value system has infiltrated our provincial little city. Also, what's family? The so-called "old families" are pretty watered down at this point. Society is a lot more fluid and in some ways more democratic.

But not the Cotillon. It is sticking to the old ways for as long as it can.

Why would anybody care about all this? Plenty of people don't. But I know why Almighty cares. One reason anyway. She can use things like the Cotillon to control people. And the person she wants to get to the most? Mamie Overbeck.

Here's my theory: Almighty still hasn't forgiven Mame for stealing Junius from her in 1947. She's been harboring that grudge for all these years, cultivating it and watching it grow. . . . And when she saw her granddaughter, Norrie, and Mame's grandson, Brooks, playing together as children, she got an idea.

If you read *Great Expectations* or saw one of the movie versions, you might remember Miss Havisham. As a young woman she was ditched at the altar, and now she hates men. She adopts a beautiful girl named Estella and raises her to be coldhearted. Then, as an experiment, she invites a poor young boy named Pip to play with Estella. Miss Havisham knows that Pip will fall in love with Estella and that she will break his heart. Which is pretty much what happens. Miss Havisham has raised Estella to be her revenge against men.

I think Almighty is pulling a Miss Havisham — using Norrie. She knows Brooks likes Norrie, and she is forcing them to go to the Cotillon — the scene of Almighty's own humiliation — together. But she also knows — everybody knows — that Norrie has fallen in love with someone else. So she is bound to break Brooks's heart. But still Almighty insists they go to the Cotillon together.

Mame loves her grandson Brooks and doesn't want to see him hurt. Almighty can hurt her through Brooks, using Norrie. It's diabolical.

And that is my theory.

Come on, admit it, Almighty. I was right, wasn't I?

■ ■ ■

You may not have realized it, but Norrie, Sassy, and I were eavesdropping at the top of the stairs when you came over to tear Ginger and Daddy-o a new one about that article in the *Sun*. We heard the whole thing. You were roaring mad. You know how sometimes you draw a frown on your face with lipstick when you're angry? Well, we have a name for it: Mr. Yuck. And you were sporting Mr. Yuck that day.

I'm going to re-create the scene for you, in case you're curious about how it looked from my point of view. Sometimes I wonder if you realize how scary you can be, Almighty.

"This is your fault," you yelled. "You're terrible parents! You're not even parents — you're glorified babysitters!"

"Marvelous to see you as always, Almighty," Ginger said.

You'd brought Buffalo Bill with you as usual, and he was sniffing around the bottom of the stairs.

"You brought up a godless hell-raiser! At *least* one that I know about. I have never in my life felt so betrayed by a member of my own family. Alphonse, what do you have to say?"

I could hear the shrug in Daddy-o's voice. "I'm sorry, Mother, but Jane is old enough to have her opinions. What can we do to stop her?"

"Plenty! Send her away to boarding school, for starters. A very strict convent-style school, far away, maybe Switzerland. They'll discipline her if you can't, and she won't be here in town publishing nasty lies about her grandmother in the newspaper."

"Nobody reads the newspaper anymore," Ginger said. "If we ignore it, this whole thing will go away."

"That is exactly the kind of lenient attitude that got us here in the first place. One daughter running around with some grown man from New York, another one hell-bent on destroying the whole family, and who knows what Sassy's up to. . . ."

I almost laughed, but Norrie put a finger to her lips and scowled like she'd kill me if I made a sound. At the mention of her name, Sassy squeezed my knee and looked nervous. "What? You've got nothing to worry about," I whispered. And yet she looked worried.

Downstairs, Takey wandered over to Buffalo Bill. He had a squirt gun in his holster and started tugging on the dog's tail.

"They've got your incorrigible spirit in them, Mother," Daddy-o said. "Can't blame them for being Sullivans." He made a weak attempt to laugh. *La di dah, isn't being a Sullivan such care-free fun?*

But you weren't falling for that. You didn't yell, but we could hear the uncoiled fury in your voice. "A Sullivan does not disgrace her family. Your daughter has severely misbehaved. Grow a spine and punish her. I'd like to punish that reporter too, and whatever moron is editing the *Sun* these days. Whatever happened to journalistic standards? They wouldn't have dared to print such trash in the old days; they knew they'd have me to answer to."

"Well, Mother, you can sue them for libel if they printed anything untrue," Daddy-o said. "But I don't think they did."

Sassy pinched me. "Ginger and Daddy-o are on your side," she whispered.

"A lot of good that will do me."

"Take away her computer," you suggested.

"She needs it for school," Ginger said.

"Do something!" you said. "She's spreading lies about our family all over the world. I won't have it! Where is she? I want to have a talk with her."

Norrie and Sassy gripped my arms. "Uh-oh."

"We'll talk to her," Ginger said. "You'll see her at tea on Tuesday."

Thanks, Ginge. But it wasn't enough to save me.

Meanwhile, Takey unholstered his squirt gun and shot Buffalo Bill with water, right between the eyes. Bill whimpered and ran off.

We could hear you stomping around like a bull. "Takey! Leave that poor dog alone! I'll go up and drag Jane out of her room myself if I have to. These girls of yours are causing nothing but trouble!"

The three of us sprang to our feet and scrambled upstairs to Norrie's room. Norrie locked the door. We sat on her bed, biting our nails as if waiting for a killer in a hockey mask to burst in.

"Jane Dorsey!" you roared. You can really be loud when you want to be. "Come out this instant! Jane Dorsey Sullivan!"

"What would Joan of Arc do?" Sassy asked.

"She'd face her persecutors," I said. "She'd refuse to back down." I stood up, straightened my school uniform, which I hadn't had time to take off yet, and marched to the door. "On to the inquisition." I opened the door. There you were. Your tiny body blocked my way out. "Hello, Almighty. Looking for me?"

"You know damn well I'm looking for you. Come with me, young lady." You glanced into the room and added, "You two, don't think you're off the hook. If I hear a breath of scandal about either of you . . ."

Then you led me downstairs to my room and shut the door. "Sit down."

I sat at my desk. "Would you like a chair, Almighty?"

"No. Now you listen to me. You will shut down that clog or whatever you call it, and shut it down now. You will erase all traces of it, except for this — you will publish a disclaimer saying that you made up everything you wrote about our family. The history, everything. I don't care if it's true or not, you'll do it. And you will call that reporter and tell her you were playing a prank on her and deny everything she printed. My lawyer will be in touch with her to demand a retraction. Is that clear?"

I shook with anger and fear so hard I clenched my teeth to keep them from rattling. Put yourself in my place. How dare you demand that I lie and say that everything I wrote — all that TRUTH — was a lie?

Uh, that's what I was thinking at the time. Now, of course, I'm totally sorry about it and agree that it's all my fault.

"Jane, do you hear me?"

"Yes," I said. "I hear you. But I won't do it."

"Oh yes you will."

"Oh no I won't."

"Don't play stubborn with me. I invented that game."

"I know. It's in my blood. I can hold out as long as you can."

"No you can't," you said. "Because I have power. And you don't."

"Try me."

"I will. Disobey me at your peril, young lady."

"Come on. What can you do to me?"

"You insolent brat! I can ruin your life. You wait and see."

"I can't wait. I want you to ruin my life. I hate my life! I want to destroy everything!"

"You're doing a lovely job of it." You threw open the door and stormed out. I heard you march downstairs and through the living room. "I'm holding you two responsible!" you shouted at Ginger and Daddy-o. "Bill, come!" The front door slammed shut.

"Okeydokey," Daddy-o drawled now that you were gone. "By the way, Mother, what time should we come for dinner on Sunday?"

"I wish she wouldn't make such a fuss. So the kids are hellions. I don't understand what she expects *us* to do about it."

I heard ice rattling in glasses. "I suppose one of us had better talk to Jane."

I went downstairs to save them the trouble of finding me.

"There you are, darling. What did Almighty say?"

"She said I have to stop blogging forever and take back everything I already wrote, or else."

"Or else what?"

I shrugged. "She wasn't specific. Something bad will happen."

"Darling, do you really think this blog of yours is worth all this fuss?" Ginger said. "I mean, it's just a lot of silly family gossip. Why do you care?"

"It's the truth," I said.

"So what?" Ginger said. Then she paused, as if something had just occurred to her. "You didn't write anything about me, did you?"

"Oh, so it's okay as long as it's not about you?" I said.

"Lovebite, of course she did," Daddy-o said. "Didn't you see that bit about your therapist committing suicide?" He waved the newspaper. "It's buried in here somewhere."

Ginger went pale. "I haven't had time to read the article carefully." She snatched the paper from Daddy-o and skimmed until she got to the part about her.

I have to admit, at the moment I kind of wished I could melt into the carpet and drain away into the sewer, never to be seen again. Ginger put down the paper and took a sip of her vodka.

"There was a time when psychotherapy was considered a private matter."

"It's not like you don't talk about it," I said. "You told Mr. Sonnenshein at the pharmacy every detail. The cashier at Eddie's too."

Ginger rarely loses her temper, but I was pushing it. You should have seen her, Almighty — you would have been proud.

She slammed her drink on the side table. "Listen, Jane Dorsey, I've had enough of your silliness. I know you're trying to stir up trouble and you probably love all this attention in some kind of fucked-up way, but it's time to stop. Now."

"Where'd you get that theory?" I said. "Your therapist?"

Daddy-o tried to hide his whole head in the newspaper. Ginger pressed her lips together and glared at me until she looked a lot like Sister Mary Joseph.

"I don't want to lose my composure," Ginger said. "So you had better go to your room now."

"Let me just get a snack first —"

"Go to your room NOW!"

I scurried to the stairs involuntarily. I didn't mean to obey her but she scared me. Ginger hardly ever gets mad.

Still, I couldn't resist taking one last jab at her.

"Heinie!" I yelped as I started upstairs. It was the worst word I could think of, the word Ginger hates most in the world.

Ginger's face reddened over her freckles. "Stop it!"

"Heinie heinie heinie! Wiener! Booger! Shut up!"

She swayed, nauseated by my vulgar language. "Are you quite finished?"

"Mayonnaise!" We glared at each other. I felt tired. It washed over me suddenly, draining me of energy. I'd had enough conflict for one day.

"Now I'm finished," I said.

■　■　■

That fight was the beginning of a bad mood that lasted for days. The bad mood seeped into everything I did. And Sister Mary Joseph didn't help.

"The most important element of love is . . . what? Mary Pat?"

"Obedience," the obedient Mary Pat said.

"Correct. Love is obedient and long-suffering, just like Jesus on the cross. And disobedience invites the devil into your life."

I hate this kind of talk SO MUCH. It makes my blood boil. Do these nuns really expect us to suffer like Jesus and never fight back? To never defend ourselves? How sick is that?

I raised my hand.

"Yes, Jane?"

"I don't understand. God spoke to St. Joan, and she obeyed. But that was her big mistake. She obeyed him right up until the end, and he didn't save her. Why? What is the difference between burning on a stake in a village square and burning in hell?"

"Burning in hell lasts for all eternity," Sister Mary Joseph said. "Joan suffered at the stake for a short time, but she was rewarded with an eternity in heaven."

"You don't know that. How do you really know that?"

"Jane, that is what is called faith."

"I call it stupidity —"

"God's mercy is mysterious to our weak human minds. St. Augustine said that we can't understand God any more than a hole on the beach can understand the ocean."

"That's a convenient excuse. You know what I think? I think that sounds like bullshit. I think maybe there is no God. NO — I take that back. I know it: There is no God. And if there is a God, I hate him."

The classroom fell silent. Outside in the school parking lot I heard a bus rumble to life. I was doomed and I knew it.

"Jane Sullivan, that is blasphemy," Sister Mary Joseph said. "Report to Sister Cecilia immediately."

Sister Cecilia is the principal. She is not as scary as Sister Mary Joseph. I left Religion class as fast as I could. I couldn't wait to get out of there. Even Bridget looked shocked.

I waited outside Sister Cecilia's office for a while. In the waiting area she has one of those pictures of Jesus where his eyes follow you all around the room. Creepy.

She let me into her office and closed the door. Even though she is a nun, Sister Cecilia has a worldly, sophisticated air about her. If she hadn't decided to be a Bride of Christ, she might have been a fund-raiser for a modern art museum or something like that.

"Sister Mary Joseph told me what you said in class. Jane, do you really believe there is no God?"

"No. I don't know." Sitting there across the desk from her, I suddenly felt like crying, but I didn't know why. It seemed like I wanted to get in trouble all the time but when trouble actually came I didn't like it. "What difference does it make whether I believe or not? If he exists, he'll still be there. If he doesn't, he'll never know I don't believe in him."

"I'm sending you home with a letter to your parents. Tell them to come in and talk to me soon. I'm suggesting you get some spiritual counseling."

"Great. That's just what I need."

"And I'm going to suspend you from school until after Christmas. Perhaps you need some time to think things over."

Suspension. For saying something in class. I didn't get suspended for stripping in front of the whole school, but for saying there is no God . . . well, at least they didn't kick me out altogether.

"I'm going easy on you, because I don't think you've committed true blasphemy."

"Yes, I have. I said —"

"Sister Mary Joseph told me what you said. But I don't think God is the one you are angry with."

"How would you know?"

"I don't know. I suspect. That's what I want you to think about while you are suspended." She tapped some papers on her desk. I noticed a copy of the *Sun* in one of the piles and realized she'd probably read the story about you and my blog.

"Stop fighting, Jane," she said. "Take mercy where you find it."

And with that I was dismissed. Sent home. Suspended.

I knew everybody in the family would be thrilled to hear it. Especially you.

NINE

⊠　　⊠　　⊠

myevilfamily.com

Farewell to Wallace

I'm going to lay off my evil family for once out of
respect for Wallace. He was Almighty's husband
and he died this week. The funeral was yesterday.
Everybody was sad and crying and the family is in
some kind of crisis, though I'm not sure what exactly
is going on. I don't know if Almighty is sad about it or
not. She's not easy to read. She doesn't look very
happy, though. I wonder if she'll get married for a
sixth time?

Then there's the fact that I was suspended from
school for blasphemy—also known as TELLING THE
TRUTH—which didn't make anybody too happy
either. And I kind of get the feeling Norrie and Sassy
are keeping secrets from me, but I can't be sure. If
they are, I wish they'd talk to me because we're

sisters and we support each other. Really, you can talk to me! As long as you don't mind hearing the TRUTH back from me.

Anyway, here's to Wallace. He was a good man. I wish I'd paid more attention to him before he died. It was all very unexpected.

Then today Takey's goldfish, Bubbles, died. It's November. Death is everywhere.

JANE OUT

My first week of suspension, I spent a lot of time alone in the house. I sat in Takey's room and stared at his talented goldfish, Bubbles. I was hoping to catch Bubbles practicing his tricks but he wouldn't do anything unless you dangled food in front of him. I'd never really been alone in the house before, not for long. It's pretty echoey when you're the only person in it.

Then Wallace died and that overshadowed any trouble I was in. I have to assume you were more upset about your husband dying than my suspension from school.

We were all kind of numb, except for Takey, who seemed confused, and Sassy, who couldn't stop crying. I don't know about you, but you looked grim. Your red lipstick slashed across your mouth — not a Mr. Yuck frown, just a straight, flat line. Do you do that on purpose to signal your feelings, like a mood ring?

Norrie and I tried to guess what your grim expression meant. Were you grieving? Depressed? Angry? Resigned to your fate as a five-time widow? Out to make somebody pay? We really couldn't tell.

I was torn between wanting to steer clear of you and feeling I should offer some sort of granddaughterly comfort, however lame. But you've always made a show of your independence, so I decided to steer clear. If you wanted your grandchildren to run up and hug you, you should have pinched our cheeks once in a while. Not that we would have enjoyed that. .

I felt sad for old Wallace. How can you not like a guy who · grows flowers? He was the only grandfather I ever really knew. But he was so quiet he seemed more like an extra arm attached to you than a grandfather.

At the end of the funeral service, Norrie — who'd been tense — suddenly burst into tears as we filed out of the cathedral. Between basket-case Sassy and now sobbing Norrie, I felt like the hard-hearted one. I felt sorry that I wasn't all wrecked over Wallace. But what could I do, fake it?

■   ■   ■

The day Wallace died, Sassy started crying and pretty much didn't stop. Her room is next to mine and I could hear her crying through the wall. The night after the funeral, I went in and found her facedown on her bed, sobbing.

I rubbed her back. "Why are you so upset about Wallace?" I truly wanted to understand. He was a nice man, and Sassy had been closer to him than the rest of us had been, but her reaction still struck me as extreme. "He was pretty old, you know."

That only made her cry harder. I didn't know what else to say to her. When I was five and my kindergarten teacher died, Miss Maura soothed me by telling me Ms. Seipp was looking down on me from heaven, and I shouldn't feel sad because she was blissfully happy. But I couldn't comfort Sassy with that, now that I'm on record as not believing in heaven. I'm beginning to see how useful the idea of heaven can be — even if it doesn't exist. Without heaven I had no words to say. And so she cried and cried and cried, and all I could do was rub her back while she soaked her pillow with tears.

Me being me, I couldn't resist taking a stab at it anyway. I can't stand it when she cries.

"Since there's no God, that means no devil either," I said. "So at least we know Wallace isn't in hell."

She kind of screamed into her pillow and pounded her fist on the bed.

"You're wrong about God." Sassy choked out the words. Her face was all red. "There is a God. There must be. Because He's made me unkillable for some reason."

"What?" It took a second for her words to sink in. "Hey, did you get hit by a car again?" I brushed her hair aside to check for head wounds. She didn't answer me. "Why would God make you unkillable and not Wallace?"

"I don't know!" she cried. "That's what's making me crazy."

"You're crazy all right," I joked, but she didn't laugh. She just kept on crying. I stayed with her until she cried herself to sleep, just like Takey used to do when he was a baby.

■ ■ ■

After Sassy fell asleep, I went downstairs to get a glass of milk. The house was quiet, but I saw a light on in Daddy-o's study and went in to say good night.

He sat at his desk, his back to the door, studying a picture with a magnifying glass and concentrating so hard he didn't hear me come in.

"What are you doing, Daddy-o?" I asked.

He turned and saw me and smiled. "Hi, Janie. Look — it's your favorite saint." He moved his chair aside so I could see the print he'd been studying: a young girl in armor — Joan of Arc — riding a white horse past a medieval city and carrying a pennant. Joan looked awfully calm and happy for someone riding into battle. Even the horse grinned with anticipation.

"It's a miniature from a manuscript dated around 1505," Daddy-o said.

I sat down in his St. John's College chair. The prints of medieval icons and framed family photos in his study are a funny combination. Next to a primitive etching of Mary and the baby Jesus is a color photo of the young Ginger holding baby Sully in a Louis Vuitton Snugli. Baby pictures, Halloween costumes, the eight of us lined up on the stairs like the Brady Bunch, and my favorite, a funny shot taken on Nantucket: six of us riding one tandem bike. Norrie's curled up in a basket in front, Daddy-o and Ginger are pedaling, St. John and Sully ride in child seats on the back, and I'm an eight-month-old fetus in Ginger's swollen belly.

Daddy-o put down his magnifying glass. It felt strange to

sit alone with him in a quiet house. That hadn't happened in a long time.

"Tough day, wasn't it, sweet pea?"

I nodded and sipped from my glass of milk.

"I know Almighty can be tough on you kids," Daddy-o said. "But her life isn't always easy. Imagine burying five husbands." He shook his head. "I'd be lost if your mother died. I really would."

I didn't know what to say. I'm not used to seeing Daddy-o get so emotional. His feelings for Ginger baffle me. What does she do for him? It's a mystery.

I love Ginger. If she died I'd be devastated, and yeah, I'd miss her. She can be pretty funny. But I wouldn't be *lost*. Ginger doesn't let us depend on her too much — that's Miss Maura's job. But that night I realized she makes an exception for Daddy-o. He really does depend on her for . . . something.

And now, Almighty, I will give you a little glimpse of how your son really feels about you.

"What about when Almighty dies," I asked. "Will you be sad?"

"She's my mother," Daddy-o said. "I'll grieve for her. I'll miss her. But I'll tell you a secret." His eyes fell on my glass of milk. I passed it to him and he took a swig. "I'm afraid of what will happen to the family when she dies. She's our anchor. I'm afraid we'll fall into . . . chaos."

"Chaos?" I didn't understand. He just shook his head like he didn't want to explain.

·

I thought about poor unkillable Sassy upstairs in her tormented sleep. "Maybe Almighty won't die. Maybe she's immortal."

"No," Daddy-o said. "If anyone could achieve immortality, it would be Almighty. But I wouldn't wish it on her. That would be a terrible curse."

"Why? Wouldn't it be great to know you could do anything you wanted with no consequences? You could jump out of airplanes without a parachute, swim far out into the ocean, eat ice cream for every meal. . . ."

"Yes, but how long would you enjoy those things?" Daddy-o said. "Your life would lose its meaning. That would be a tragedy." He polished off the rest of my milk and slammed the glass on his desk with an "Ahhh. How's your suspension going, Miss Blasphemy? Nice having a little break from school, isn't it?"

"It's fine," I said, though it was actually lonely and boring.

"I don't mind that you roughed up the nuns. That's pretty hard to resist," Daddy-o said. "And I like that you question authority. But you have to start asking yourself this: Is it worth it?"

"Sure it's worth it."

"So far, maybe. But remember St. Joan. She paid for her beliefs with her life. Are you willing to go that far?"

"I don't know."

"How far are you willing to go?"

"I don't mind being suspended. Beyond that . . . it depends."

"Good answer. A little advice: Choose your battles carefully. Something to think about. One more thing: I don't agree with you that there's no God. Want to hear how I've worked it out?"

"Okay." Ever notice how Daddy-o treats everything like it's a math problem?

"Well, if there's no God, then everything's allowed. Right? There's no right or wrong. No consequences to your actions. Like immortality: If there's no death, then you can do what you like. It's the same thing. No God means no death. But clearly death does exist. We were just at Wallace's funeral today. Since death exists, that must mean God exists. Hmm? Hmmm?"

He grinned triumphantly, but I was still skeptical.

"I'll have to think it over. You went too fast for me."

"You think it over upstairs in bed. Nothing like a good episte-mological puzzle to put you to sleep."

"All right." I got up to kiss him. "Good night, Daddy-o." I took one last look at the print he was studying and added, "Sleep tight, St. Joan."

■   ■   ■

A few days later I went into Takey's room to visit Bubbles and found him floating in his aquarium, dead. Takey was shooting him with a water pistol, pretending to have killed him. At least, I think he was pretending. It's hard for me to see how a goldfish could be killed by a water pistol.

"Should we give him a funeral?" I asked.

"No," Takey said. "I'm sick of funerals."

"Me too."

The next time I looked, Bubbles was gone. Miss Maura must have unceremoniously flushed him down the toilet. For the rest of the week I couldn't go to the bathroom without first checking to see if Bubbles wasn't somehow swimming in the bowl.

I don't agree with Daddy-o. Just because we can die doesn't mean there's a God. How can God let his creatures be flushed down the toilet? And that's not even the worst thing that happens on Earth.

TEN

⊠   ⊠   ⊠

myevilfamily.com

The Story of Norrie

She did it. She broke free. And in very dramatic fashion too. As you will soon be reading in the *Baltimore Sun*, Miss Louisa Norris Sullivan was presented to society last night at the Bachelors Cotillon in the Belvedere Hotel. However, as soon as she made her curtsy, she ran off, leaving her escort in the lurch, and met her true love at Penn Station. They jumped on the next train to New York and disappeared. Norrie thoughtfully left a note in Daddy-o's coat pocket, explaining that she'd be back before Christmas and not to worry. She called, too, as soon as she got to New York, reassuring us that everything was fine. It's just like a honeymoon.

I wonder if she'll forgive me for writing about all this . . . now that she knows what it feels like to rebel against your own family.

Way to go, Norrie! I'm proud of her. She has tempo-
rarily replaced me as Family Badass.

JANE OUT

COMMENTS:

Norrie: I told you not to blog about this. I hereby
officially declare — publicly, since you love the attention so much — that I am never speaking to you again.
myevilfamily: But I'm on YOUR side! I'm only trying
to defend you!
Norrie: Never. Again.

Was it worth it?

■   ■   ■

I have no idea what was in Norrie's mind the night of the
Cotillon, but there was something in the air. I felt restless. I
hadn't seen anyone from school since my suspension, not even
Bridget. I missed all the school holiday parties, the Christmas
Concert, and the Holiday Pageant. So when Bridget told me the
Bowies were having a "Screw the Cotillon" party, Sassy and I
fired up the Mercedes and drove out to the farm. We could see
the bonfire from the road almost a mile before we got there.

I met Bridget at the bonfire. We left Sassy roasting marshmallows and went inside the big house to see who was around. In
the living room this girl in Norrie's class, Shea Donovan, was sitting on a boy's lap, kissing him. Bridget stared at them, then
pretended not to look.

"Thank God you're here," she said. "This is worse than school. I never have anyone to talk to there, now that you're not around. And there's no one to talk to here either. I miss you so much."

I rubbed the back of my neck. "Is that tattoo still there?" I bent my head and lifted my hair to give her a good view. For weeks I'd been trying to wash it off. Sassy said it was still there. I tried to look in the mirror but it was hard for me to see it for myself.

"It's faded a little but it's totally still there," Bridget reported. "That is so weird. You should sue that marker company."

"I don't mind. I wanted a tattoo, remember?"

"Still, the pen said the ink was washable."

An icky smacking sound came from the couch where Shea and the boy she was making out with wrestled. Bridget and I looked at each other and wordlessly agreed it was time to leave the room. We wandered through the dining room into the kitchen, where some boys were raiding the fridge. Tasha and Bibi perched conspicuously on the kitchen island. Tasha was sobbing and Bibi was trying to comfort her.

I hadn't seen Tasha and Bibi in weeks. I assume that without me at school the bad girl bathroom has gone straight.

Bibi looked up and saw us. "Hey, stranger." She almost sounded friendly. I think she was panicking because she didn't know how to get Tasha to stop crying.

"What's the matter?" I asked.

"Tim Drucker gave us a ride to the party," Bibi explained. "He texted Tasha and asked her if we wanted to come with him. And she likes him, so she said yes and she was all excited —"

"Shut up, I was not," Tasha said through her tears.

"Yeah, okay. And you're crying for no reason. It's all right, you have nothing to be ashamed of." Bibi reached into her bag and pulled out another Kleenex.

Tasha took it and swabbed her face with it. "Tim kind of disappeared when we got here. So Bibi and I started playing Count to Shea —"

"It's a party game we made up," Bibi explained. "We bet how many minutes until Shea does something slutty. The winner gets ten dollars."

"I guessed fifteen minutes and Bibi guessed twenty. And ten minutes later we walked into the living room and there was Shea sucking Tim's face off." Tasha dissolved into tears again.

"Look at it this way." Bibi dug through her bag again, this time pulling out a ten-dollar bill. "You won the game!"

Tasha batted the money away. The whole scene was ridiculous. But I felt the stirrings of something strange and unfamiliar. I didn't care if Tim Drucker was making out with Shea or Tasha or half the boys' soccer team, but seeing Tasha cry like that, I couldn't help but feel sorry for her. A little. Especially because she and Bibi were being friendly to me.

"You know what we need to do?" Bibi said to Tasha, stuffing the ten-dollar bill into Tasha's fist. "We need to get the hell out of here. Are you going to the club, Jane?"

"I guess we could crash the party," I said. I did want to see how Norrie was doing. Who knows, maybe at that very moment she was giving you all the finger at the ball. I wasn't aware of that at the time, however. You can't hold Norrie's actions against me, Almighty. That wouldn't be fair.

"Great! We'll all go," Bibi said.

Bridget tugged on my sleeve. "She's just using you to get into the country club," she whispered.

"I know," I said. "I don't care."

And I didn't care. I'd been thinking about Bibi and Tasha and choosing your battles, and I was beginning to think that this one wasn't worth fighting. Maybe I'm outgrowing this kind of pettiness.

If only everything could resolve itself so easily.

■　■　■

Around midnight we all crammed into the car and I drove back into the city. Bridget played around with the radio and we sang along to every Christmas song that came on. The post-deb party was in full swing when we got to the club. Brooks was dancing with Claire Mothersbaugh. I looked around for Norrie but I didn't see her. By now you know why.

Claire saw us and ran over, breathless with the news. "Norrie ran away! Right in the middle of the Cotillon!"

"What?" Sassy cried. There was an immediate commotion. Everyone started talking and asking questions. I stood in the middle of the crowd and grinned. I couldn't stop grinning. It was such a strange feeling.

Norrie. Perfect Norrie. She revolted!

"Everything seemed okay, except she was weird in that way she's been weird lately," Claire said. "They presented each of us girls, said our names and everything, and Norrie did her curtsy. But before Brooks could take her hand she took off and ran! Everybody freaked. Your dad found a note in his pocket later. She ran off to New York with Robbie!"

"Is Norrie coming back?" Sassy asked me. "Is she gone forever?"

"She'll be back soon," I said, but then I thought, *Maybe she won't. What if she doesn't?*

No, I thought. *She's our sister. She has to come back.*

And to make sure she knew she was welcome, I decided to write about her heroic adventure on my blog. To show my support. Because Sassy and I might be the only ones on her side.

But I guess Norrie didn't see it that way. No one sees the blog my way. I'm misunderstood.

ELEVEN

✉   ✉   ✉

myevilfamily.com

Why Christmas Sucks

It just does. I don't feel like getting into it right now.

JANE OUT

I feel like I'm constantly apologizing. I'll be honest with you — I don't enjoy it.

Norrie came home from her New York adventure at noon on Christmas Eve, loaded down with presents. She shut herself up in her room to wrap them. Robbie had stayed in New York to spend the holidays with his parents. She seemed happy, except when I crossed her line of sight.

She came downstairs before dinner to put the presents under the tree. I hovered anxiously. She hadn't spoken to me yet, not really.

"You can stop hovering, Jane," she said. "I forgive you."

"You forgive me? For what?"

She threw a silver-wrapped box at my head. I ducked. "If you're going to have that attitude, I won't forgive you."

"Okay, okay. I'm sorry I splashed your private business all over the Internet."

"*Thank* you. Jesus."

"Are you sure you forgive me? Because you don't sound all that happy with me."

"I'm not happy with you, but I'll get over it, because it's Christmas, and we're family, and I love you. I forgive you, St. Joan, for taking the whole family up in flames with you."

"That doesn't sound very sincere."

"Fine. I give up."

I sank into the comfy yellow chair next to the end table with the candy dish on it, and reached for a cinnamon candy. It seemed right that I should feel something burning, even if it was only cinnamon in my mouth. A small fire glowed in the fireplace, and the smell of sugar cookies wafted in from the kitchen. Ginger and Miss Maura had decorated the house with holly and pine garlands and a big wreath on the front door. The mood wasn't quite festive, though. There was a lot of tension in the air. But at least there was a sense of activity, of things happening.

"Did you get me anything good for Christmas?" Norrie asked.

I got her a blue cardigan sweater. "Yeah, you'll definitely love it."

"Always so sure of everything." She looked me in the eye for the first time since she got back; her anger at me was ebbing. She can be motherly when she's in the right mood. I usually resent it, but lots of times her motherliness has kept us from clawing each other's eyes out.

It was four o'clock — only a couple of hours to kill before the big Christmas Eve party. Daddy-o had gone to the train station to pick up St. John. Sully was out doing last-minute shopping, and Ginger was resting upstairs on the chaise longue in her room. Sassy and Takey came in from the kitchen, where they'd been helping Miss Maura decorate the Christmas cookies. Takey had crumbs on his chin. He started crawling around under the tree, peering at the names on the packages.

He picked up a square box from Norrie and shook it. "Did you get me something in New York?" he asked her.

"Mm-hmm." She spread out her pile of packages so they wouldn't be all in one spot under the tree.

"Did Ginger and Daddy-o punish you for running away?" Takey asked.

"They haven't punished me yet," Norrie said. "I think they might leave it to Almighty."

Takey shuddered. You've got a reputation in our house, that's undeniable.

"Poor Norrie," Takey said. "I hope Almighty doesn't ruin your Christmas."

"She won't," Norrie said. "No one can ruin Christmas. Don't you remember *A Christmas Carol*? With Tiny Tim and 'God bless us, every one'? No matter what Mr. Scrooge did to that Cratchit family, he couldn't spoil their Christmas."

I hereby inform you that the Mr. Magoo version of Dickens's *Christmas Carol* is the official Sullivan Family Favorite Version, though I have a soft spot for the 1951 Alastair Sim one, and Sassy and Norrie love them all, even the Albert Finney version from the 1970s, which is a musical. I think I once heard you say you find the story insipid.

"So Almighty is like Scrooge?" Takey said it, not me.

I looked up from unwrapping another cinnamon candy. Sassy caught my eye, but Norrie made herself busy at the tree.

"No," she said. "Almighty is not like Scrooge. She loves Christmas. Remember last year at the pageant when she sang all those Christmas songs?"

Sassy had spent the whole morning getting ready for our pageant skit. We usually practice for weeks ahead of time, but this year's been so crazy . . . I suppose you could argue that I had a lot of time on my hands since I didn't have to go to school for the past month, but I was busy thinking about more important things like good and evil. At the last minute Sassy said she wanted to do the final scene from *The Winter's Tale*. I objected that it wasn't Christmasy enough and suggested reenacting a scene from *Rudolph the Red-Nosed Reindeer* instead. It's my life's ambition (so far thwarted) to play Herbie, the elf who wants to be a dentist. But, as you are well aware, Sassy went ahead with the Shakespeare and roped the rest of us into her little scheme. We all know the play because everyone in school reads it in tenth grade. Sassy made the minimal costumes and recruited us to take parts, promising cue cards so we wouldn't have to memorize our lines. As long as she made it that easy, I was willing to go along. We figured we'd go on last, right before you and Daddy-o do your piano cabaret thing.

She was determined to do *The Winter's Tale* and she wouldn't explain why. I sensed she was hiding something. Turns out I was right.

When did this family become such a hive of secrets? The more I try to blast the truth out of them, the more secretive they get.

■ ■ ■

Your Christmas Eve extravaganza was weak in the jolly department this year, Almighty. There was still the big greeting at the front door, Handel's *Messiah*, and the gigantic tree in the library; still the contingent of globe-trotting visitors from Africa and Russia and England, etc., in their wonderful clothes with nothing better to do for the holidays. But the Overbecks didn't show — no Mamie, no Brooks . . . did that have something to do with the Cotillon? And you wore black velvet instead of red, for Wallace. And when you greeted me with a Christmas kiss you whispered, "You're next" in my ear. I'm warning you right now: I'm not doing it. If you must have a debutante in the family, better start working on Sassy.

■ ■ ■

Going downstairs to the theater for the Christmas pageant usually lifts my spirits — I love the blue, red, and gold patterns painted on the walls and the silver curtain on the little stage. I love it when Daddy-o recites "'Twas the night before Christmas . . ." every year. It wouldn't be Christmas without that. Or without Ginger doing a tipsy "Blue Christmas," accompanied on the baby grand by St. John.

Then it was time for the annual skit by the Sullivan children. Remember that year Sassy, Norrie, and I sang "Sisters" from

White Christmas? With the feathers and everything? Everybody loved that. This year our costumes were easy — we just threw sheets over our clothes to make togas for a generic classical feel — except for Takey, who had to wear a wig and white makeup, and Sassy, whose wig looked a lot like your hair, in case you didn't notice. Considering we pulled it together in one day, I thought we did pretty well. But even though we'd rehearsed, I wasn't expecting Takey to do that little thing at the end — the thing that had everybody in tears. It was Sassy's idea — her special stage directions. I had nothing to do with it. And it wasn't in the original play — I checked.

It was nice of you to try to cheer everybody up afterward with your Christmas cabaret medley — good effort. Not sure it worked, though. Anyway, midnight mass is always good for a laugh, right?

■   ■   ■

You've probably waded through this long explanation thinking, *This is no confession. Jane isn't repentant at all.* That's understandable. But now we come to the part where everything changes, the part where I see the error of my ways and vow to mend them.

It happened, of all places, in the cathedral, Christmas Eve, at midnight mass.

Something in *The Winter's Tale* must have gotten to me, because I stepped inside the cathedral feeling solemn and almost . . . reverent. Usually I find the Christmas service so superficial, between the lip-glossy girls in their new Christmas jewelry and sweaters fresh out of the box, the priests in their weird medieval robes, and the cardinal's chummy chat about his last visit to Rome and His Holiness's health. Oh, Cardinal, we're so impressed that you're friends with the pope. Do you know Beyoncé too?

Then, down at the end of my row, I saw two people, a man and a woman in their thirties, nodding out. At first I wondered if they were asleep — it was midnight after all. But they sloped forward in slow motion, jerking slightly when their heads touched the pew in front of them, and I realized they were junkies. They didn't look homeless or anything like that — the man needed a haircut but he wasn't dirty, and the woman's tweed coat looked new.

What kind of person would get high and go to mass? Maybe they were hoping for an extra-transcendent experience. I kept glancing over at them to double-check, to make sure they weren't the Ghosts of Christmas Yet to Come in disguise. They woke briefly and smiled at each other with barely opened eyes.

Weren't they afraid someone would see them? Like, someone from their families? The woman could have gone to St. Maggie's. Maybe we know some of her relatives. It's possible.

Seeing those junkies made me gloomy. *I should pay attention to the mass*, I thought, and shut them out. I looked at the stained-glass windows and tried to remember the stories they told. There was St. Brigid of Kildare, the patron saint of good old Bridget to Nowhere. Bridget was probably somewhere in the cathedral with her family. So were Bibi and Tasha and Shea and Brooks . . .

On a window over the confessional, grouped with Lazarus and the Prodigal Son, was the image of Joan of Arc. She knelt before a glowing angel, receiving a message from God, not fighting but listening and obeying. Typical Church propaganda. But there on her knees, the way she bent forward . . . it echoed the nodding of the junkies. It sounds stupid, and I'm embarrassed to admit it — like I said, I was in a somber mood to start with — but I started to cry. I don't know why I was crying exactly. A lot of stuff was built up inside me and it decided to come out through my eyes.

The soprano singing "Ave Maria" from the balcony didn't help. All these images flashed through my mind, like watching the highlights reel of your life before you die: Takey's little gesture at the end of *The Winter's Tale*, Daddy-o reciting "A Visit from St. Nicholas," Norrie running up Charles Street in her white debutante dress, Sassy sobbing on her bed, Wallace in his coffin . . .

. . . me, half-dressed, getting dragged off the school stage during *Guys and Dolls*, and the hurt look on Bibi's face . . .

. . . and you, Almighty, singing Christmas songs in your black velvet dress. You and Mame and Bibi and me.

The bell tolled midnight. It was officially Christmas Day. Everyone stood to sing "Joy to the World." It was supposed to be a happy moment. But as I stood there singing in the cathedral where countless weddings and baptisms and funerals had been held — ceremonies for Ginger and Daddy-o and Wallace and all of us — while the junkies smiled dreamily and St. Joan gazed down on me from the stained-glass window . . . I felt the weight of history bearing down on me. Real history. The kind you can never fully know.

I got the family stories all wrong. I must have. Maybe someday somebody will write the story of my life and get it all wrong, and it will serve me right. Even I don't fully understand what I'm thinking or why I do the crazy things I do. How could anyone else?

I was arrogant, Almighty.

As the tears streamed down my face, Sassy took my hand, and my heart swelled big, like the Grinch's. At that moment I loved everyone in the church, everyone in the city, everyone in the world, even Sister Mary Joseph. Even tyrannical you. St. Augustine said that we can't understand God any more than a hole on the beach can understand the ocean. I was that hole, tiny, and the smaller I felt the more I filled up with love. I was afraid I'd explode. It hurt. Being filled with love sounds like a good thing, and it is, but that doesn't mean it doesn't hurt.

T W E L V E

✉ ✉ ✉

myevilfamily.com

The Truth About Me

It's Christmas Eve. Or actually, it's early early
Christmas morning. I just got back from midnight
mass. Anybody who knows me knows I'm not exactly
religious. I declared that there was no God in Religion
class. I was suspended from school for blasphemy.

But something happened to me while I was sitting in the
cathedral tonight. It wasn't a religious awakening or anything. But I realized that I've been hard on everybody
around me and easy on myself. And that isn't fair. So
here, in the spirit of Truth, is the Truth about me.

I'm more like Almighty than I want to admit. I'm
a LOT like her. It's scary.

I've been feuding with Bibi D'Alessandro all year. I
criticized her for being conformist and superficial.

I criticized her new best friend, Tasha, for being the tagalong beta to Bibi's alpha.

I was mad at her. Because I used to be Bibi's best friend. Until the Great Striptease.

Last year for the big spring musical our school did *Guys and Dolls*. Bibi got a great part — Miss Adelaide, the head chorus girl. I didn't get a part. I sing like a donkey. So I was on the stage crew.

On opening night, the play was going great. Bibi and the other chorus girls took the stage for their big number, "Take Back Your Mink." Where they do a kind of fake striptease. I don't know what came over me, but I was seized with the need to get on that stage. So I jumped onstage and stripped too. Only I wasn't wearing a special body stocking and corset like the other girls. I really stripped. It got a big cheer before I was hauled off the stage.

You'd think I would have been suspended for that, but I wasn't. Not that Bibi and her parents didn't try real hard to get me more than just detention for ruining Bibi's big number. They said the only reason I wasn't expelled was because Almighty has so much pull. They were probably right.

I didn't mean to hurt Bibi. I just saw an opportunity and couldn't resist. To make it up to her and show her I was sorry, I baked her some cookies and delivered them to her house before the show the next night. She ate the cookies. They had pine nuts in them. It turns out Bibi is allergic to pine nuts. I didn't know that. Nobody knew it, because she had never eaten pine nuts before.

Well, now we know.

Her face turned red and she was covered with hives. She couldn't go onstage. Her understudy had to play Miss Adelaide.

The show only played for two nights, and I'd ruined both of them for her. I never meant to. But I can see how she would be mad.

After that, she stopped being my friend. Tasha stepped in as New Best Friend. Bibi's parents won't even let me inside their house. They think I'm out to get their daughter. They think I'm evil.

And maybe I am. I come from an evil family, after all.

I didn't used to be an outcast. I used to be popular. But after the whole Bibi debacle, I was exiled. The only person who was willing to be friends with me was Bridget. I didn't care that much because I always had my brothers and sisters. But Sully's in college and St. John lives in New York, and Norrie is all preoccupied with her love life and Sassy is going through some kind of crazy existential crisis. That leaves Takey, but he doesn't really like me and keeps trying to shoot me.

The Bibi feud isn't the only evil thing I've done. I'm a very bad person. I'm selfish, and I'll do anything for attention, and I'm naturally mean to people. I use a fair amount of bad language. I don't try as hard as I could in school. I don't respect my parents as much as I should. I should probably be telling all this to a priest but I'm too lazy to say a bunch of Hail Marys. Besides, I don't believe in that.

I've got lots of other faults too, I'm just too sleepy to think of them now. But I will say, in my defense and in the spirit of Truth, that I'm fiercely loyal to the people I love (even if it doesn't seem that way) and I'll defend them to the death. So I do have at least one good quality.

And so, in the spirit of Christmas: If I hurt you or caused you any trouble, I beg your forgiveness. That goes for everyone, even you, Almighty.

Merry Christmas, everyone.

JANE OUT

COMMENTS:
bridget2nowhere: Merry Xmas to you too, bitch.

The next morning, I took a shower and scrubbed my neck extra hard. Then I checked the back of my neck with a hand mirror.

The skull-and-crossbones tattoo was gone. Finally.

Weird.

■ ■ ■

There it is, Almighty. The most contrite confession I could muster. If you read my last blog entry, you'll see I confessed before you even asked me to. And I mean every word of it.

Your move.

With love and reluctant admiration,

your granddaughter (and a Sullivan to the core),

Jane Dorsey Sullivan

PART THREE:

SASSY

The Winter's Tale

Dear Almighty,

I, Saskia Wells Sullivan, hereby confess to murder. I killed Wallace. I didn't mean to, but still his death was my fault. I admit it.

I don't want to go to jail, but I will if I have to. It's up to you.

I will accept any punishment you think is fair, but please spare the rest of the family. They don't deserve to lose their inheritance. Only I do.

I don't expect you to forgive the unforgivable. I only hope that by telling my story I can be redeemed.

So here it is: my honest, sincere, true, sad, heartbroken confession.

ONE

✉   ✉   ✉

MY LUCK CHANGED IN EARLY SEPTEMBER.

My friend Lula was showing me and Aisha her new house in Owings Mills. Her parents built it from scratch, which fascinated me since the only house I've ever lived in is our house, which is just *there* and has been there forever, take it or leave it. But Lula actually got to tell the architect what kind of room she wanted, which way the windows should face and what the closets should look like and where the reading nook should be. The house wasn't quite finished so the contractors were still puttering around in their muddy boots, their tools clanking against their belts.

We were wandering around the second floor. Lula had just showed us her parents' bedroom suite. I was opening doors and peeking into places while Lula and Aisha discussed the possible uses of her mother's dressing room. Scattered through the house were odd nooks for all kinds of strange purposes like laundry-folding and wine storage and scrapbooking.

I opened a door at the end of the hall and stared into total darkness. "What's in here?" I asked, and felt along the wall for a light switch. I couldn't find one, so I took a step into the room . . .

but my foot never touched the floor. It landed on nothing, just air, and I fell into the darkness. It was the scariest thing that had ever happened to me . . . up till then. A lot of scarier things have happened since.

For one endless second I wondered how far I would fall — I had no idea — and what it would feel like when I landed. What would I land on? Would it hurt? Would I break all my bones? Be impaled on a spike?

I seemed to be falling forever, into a bottomless pit.

And then I landed on my back, on something scratchy but cushiony. I took a moment to catch my breath. Lula was scream-ing. I could see her about ten feet above me, framed in the light from the doorway. Wherever I was, it was dark.

"I'm okay!" I called up without thinking. I wasn't sure I was okay, but I didn't feel any pain. I was lying on some prickly stuff. I felt my way to my feet. What was around me? Were there more holes in the floor to watch out for? I didn't want to fall again. I'd been lucky to have landed on whatever that prickly stuff was.

"Oh my God, Sassy!" Lula cried. "Can you get out of there?"

I reached for the door overhead but it was too high. I was stuck at the bottom of some kind of weird room, ten feet below the door. I wasn't hurt, except for the little prickly things stuck in my skin. "What is this stuff?" I asked. I felt disoriented and confused.

Aisha screamed for help. A worker appeared beside her. "What happened?" he said. "Someone fell down there?"

Lula pointed down at me hysterically. "Did you break anything?"

"I don't think so," I said. "Is there a light?"

"It hasn't been hooked up yet," the worker said. "I'll get a ladder. Be right back."

"What is this place?" I asked Lula.

"I don't know," Lula said. "But I don't like having it in my house. It's like a horror pit or something."

The worker returned. "Step back," he said. He set a ladder down on the floor and held it steady. "Climb on out of there."

I clutched the ladder and climbed out of the dark pit. Lula grabbed me. "Oh my God, Sassy, are you okay? What's this pink stuff stuck to your clothes?"

"We stored the extra fiberglass down there," the worker said. "Lucky for you." That's what had cushioned my fall. "How'd you manage to get stuck down there?"

"I opened the door and reached in to turn on the light," I explained. "And there was no floor!"

The worker laughed as if this were the craziest thing he'd ever heard. "Do you always walk into strange rooms without checking to see if there's a floor first?"

"Do you always build rooms with no floors in them?" I shot back. Who expects a room to have no floor in it? I felt outraged by his laughter. What I had done wasn't so foolish. In all my fifteen years I had never come across a floorless room before.

"You should put a warning sign on that door," Lula said. "It's dangerous."

"You're right," the worker said. "I'm sorry. We weren't expecting visitors today." But even though he said that, he didn't seem sorry. He seemed like he thought I was some kind of idiot. "Are you hurt, miss? Check all your bones. Any bruises? Do you need to go to the emergency room?"

I shook out my hands, my arms, my legs, but everything was fine, except for the prickly fiberglass in my skin and a quarter-sized bruise on my thigh. But that might have been there before; I couldn't remember. "No, I'm okay."

"Lucky girl."

He's right: I was lucky. That was the beginning of my strange period of luck. It lasted until it ran out.

■   ■   ■

"I still don't get it," Jane said. "Why didn't the room have a floor in it?"

"I don't know," I said. "Do I look different?"

We were camped on Norrie's bed, up in the Tower Room. I stretched out my neck to give them a clearer view of my face so they could tell me if they'd noticed any changes.

"No," Jane said. "You look dorky as ever."

"You've still got a little fiberglass in your hair." Norrie plucked at me like a mother chimp picking nits off her baby. "Why would you look different?"

"I feel different," I said. "Like something happened to me. Like maybe I fell through a hole in the space-time continuum or something."

They both laughed. I should have known they would. But I really did feel like something about me had changed. I had a rubbery, invincible feeling. Strong, like nothing could hurt me.

"Now that you say that, I do see something different about you," Jane said. "Your eyes are all crossed funny . . . and your

ears are growing . . . your giant nostrils are getting bigger . . .
Sassy, you're turning into a monster!"

"Ha-ha, so hilarious," I said. I'm self-conscious about my giant
flaring nostrils. Once, Sully said if I flapped them hard enough,
I could use them to fly.

We heard a thumping up the stairs and paused to see who
dared to come up and spy on us. Ginger hardly ever bothers, but
sometimes Miss Maura or Daddy-o tries to eavesdrop on us.

"Bare feet," Norrie said, cocking her ear. "It's only Takey." A
few seconds later Takey's chubby shadow darkened her doorway.
He pointed his Super Soaker at us.

"All right, you girls," he said in a low threatening voice.
"Everybody come downstairs with me. Do as I say and no one
gets hurt."

"Why should we?" Jane asked.

"Because if you don't, I'll blow you to kingdom come," he said,
still using his mean gangster voice.

"Bubbles has a new trick and he wants us to see it," I
translated.

"We've been practicing," Takey said. "Come downstairs."

We marched at squirt-gunpoint down to Takey's room where
his goldfish, Bubbles, lived in a big tank. Takey loved Bubbles.
Last year for his birthday I bought him a fish-training kit. It
came with a set of tiny hoops and poles and a little plastic basketball and basketball net, and some fish flakes and frozen
bloodworms as treats. Takey taught Bubbles to swim through the
hoops and long tubes, to limbo under a pole, to zigzag through
an obstacle course, and push a basketball into a basket with his

nose. Our big goal was to get him to jump through a hoop in the air, like a dolphin. Takey was hoping to show everyone this big trick at the Christmas Eve party.

I never realized before how smart fish are. Bubbles was just like a dog. He wanted food, and if you dangled food in front of him, he'd do anything within the power of his little fish body. It was fun to watch, but it made me sad too. There he was, trapped in his tank, with nothing better to do than entertain us in exchange for fish flakes. It was not much of a life.

"Let's see this miracle," Jane said.

Takey dropped his squirt gun and took a bow, like a magician. "For his first trick, Bubbles shoots a basketball."

"We've already seen that one," Jane said.

Norrie elbowed her in the ribs. "But we'd love to watch it again."

"Yes, we'd *love* to watch it again," Jane said.

The tiny basketball net was set up at one end of the tank. Takey held a bit of fish food on a stick at the surface of the water. Bubbles swam up and nibbled the food. Then Takey dropped the little plastic basketball into the water. Bubbles nosed the basketball down the tank toward the net. At the net, Takey waggled another bit of food at him and Bubbles pushed the ball into the basket.

"He shoots, he scores!" Takey cried. We clapped. He fed Bubbles more food as a reward.

"And now, for the most death-defying trick ever performed by a goldfish," Takey said. "The amazing Ring of Fire!"

We clapped again. Takey held up a small hoop decorated with plastic flames taken from Jane's old Hot Wheels set. Using clear nylon fishing line, he tied the hoop so it dangled just above the water in the middle of Bubbles's tank. He prepped the stick with plenty of food.

"Drumroll, please."

I rapped out a drumroll on the table. Takey held out some food, and Bubbles jumped out of the water to snatch it off the stick. Then Takey reloaded the food stick and held it through the hoop. Bubbles jumped up and, following the food, dove through the hoop. Norrie gasped and we all applauded vigorously.

"Ta-da!" Takey took a low bow. I squeezed him and gave him a kiss.

"You did it!"

"Thank you. Thank you." He solemnly fed Bubbles his reward.

"That fish is going to get fat," Jane said.

■ ■ ■

That night in bed I lay on my back and blinked in the darkness. A streetlight glowed through the crack in my curtains. The house made a low hum, the sound of its guts working — water running through the pipes as someone brushed her teeth or flushed the toilet, the purr of the dishwasher, the clicking of clocks. Outside in the yard, the last crickets of summer sang *good-bye, good-bye.* A car drove slowly down the street, its headlights bleaching the wall of my room.

Just beyond our little domain I could hear the traffic, the cars rushing down busier streets, zooming along the expressway toward the gigantic hive of the city — the buzzing, screaming, screeching, squalling city.

Then I heard sirens in the distance and a rumble in the sky, the city moving toward me, getting closer and louder, heading straight for my room. The rumble passed right over our roof, the *chop chop chop* sound of a helicopter grating through the air. I peeked through the curtain and saw a searchlight scour the yards and alleys behind the houses on our street. The noise faded and got loud again, circling the neighborhood. A police chopper. The sirens screamed up Charles Street, then disappeared. More sirens followed it. *Chop chop chop* overhead.

Our neighborhood was patrolled by police choppers all summer long, so I shouldn't have been surprised. Sometimes I think they're spying on us. But there seemed to be more sirens than usual, and that night I closed my eyes and wondered *What's going on out there?* just before I fell asleep.

TWO

⊠   ⊠   ⊠

WHEN I WENT DOWN TO THE KITCHEN FOR BREAKFAST THE
next morning, Miss Maura sat riveted to a breaking news story
on TV while Takey calmly slurped a bowl of Cheerios and looked
at a Casper comic book. I fixed myself a plate of eggs from the
pan warming on the stove and sat next to Miss Maura.

"What's going on? I heard sirens last night."

"Some nutjob's holding a bunch of people hostage at the
7-Eleven on York Road," Miss Maura reported. "He's been in a
standoff with the police all night. They don't know how many
people he's got in there with him. The whole street's closed off."
She shook her head, clucked, and sipped her coffee. "Imagine
being stuck in a 7-Eleven with a crazed killer all night."

"Morning, all." Daddy-o came in dressed for work in a striped
suit with a pale blue shirt and a bow tie. He poured himself some
coffee before he noticed me and Miss Maura glued to the TV.
"What's all the fuss?"

"Hostage situation," Miss Maura said. "7-Eleven. York Road."

We ride our bikes to the York Road 7-Eleven to get Slurpees
in the summer. Takey likes that old sign for the Swallow at the

Hollow, the one with the bird wearing a straw hat and a bow tie and drinking a beer. He thinks the bird looks like Daddy-o.

"Oh my." Daddy-o leaned over to watch the news. "Everything bad happens on poor old York Road."

"The hostages have been trapped inside the storage room in back of this 7-Eleven for almost ten hours now," the TV reporter told us. "Police say — wait —"

There was a commotion behind the reporter, and three hostages rushed out of the store with their hands in the air. The police grabbed them and pulled them away to safety.

"It looks like the gunman has released three hostages," the reporter said. "We don't know how many more people are left inside, but these hostages should be able to tell us more about who the others are, who the gunman is, and what exactly he wants."

Norrie walked in jingling her keys and headed straight for the coffee. "Come on, Sass. We've got to leave."

"Wait a second. I want to see this."

"Jane's all ready to go. I can't be late this morning — I've got a French test first period."

She dragged me out to the car, where I turned the radio to news. The just-escaped hostages had told the police what was going on inside the 7-Eleven. A crazy guy who used to work there had gone in with a gun and forced the clerk and the customers into the storage room. He wouldn't let them out to go to the bathroom or get water or anything. He pointed his gun at each of their heads and threatened to blow their brains out. He shot two people for no real reason, and the rest of them had to sit for hours right next to the dead, bleeding bodies. They didn't know what he wanted, just that he kept ranting about his girlfriend taking his baby away. The three hostages got away by tricking the gunman somehow, but they were worried about what he might do to the rest of the hostages now.

"Scary," Norrie said.

"How is this going to help that guy get his baby back?" Jane said. "Dude's not thinking things through."

I tried to imagine it. I tried to imagine how bad it felt to have your baby taken away, or what it felt like when someone held a gun to your head. But my mind couldn't hold on to those images for long. It wanted to drift toward happier thoughts.

Just as we turned into St. Maggie's drive the radio announcer reported that the gunman had burst out of the store waving his gun and threatening to shoot. The police gunned him down. Inside the store they found four dead people.

Jane switched off the radio. "Thanks, Sassy. I'm going to be scared to get a Slurpee now. And I love Slurpees."

"All you can think about is Slurpees?" Norrie said. "Five people just died."

"Yeah," I said.

"Cherry-red Slurpees," Jane said. "I won't be able to slurp one without thinking of blood."

"You're so disgusting," Norrie said.

"Yeah," I said. She's ruined Slurpees for me forever. I can't get that image out of my head — the Slurpee machine dripping blood. And cherry used to be my favorite flavor.

■   ■   ■

I had history first period that morning, which was unlucky, because we were studying slavery and the Civil War. Not that it wasn't interesting, but thinking about slavery reminded me of the 7-Eleven hostages, and I was having a hard time not thinking gruesome thoughts already. There's so much suffering in the world that I can't even fathom. Like, what would it really be like to be a slave? For your whole life? To live through beatings and losing the ones you love over and over again, and having no control over where or how you live . . . I think about these things sometimes, lying in bed at night. How would I act if I were in a concentration camp? Would I be selfish, or would I help others? How did it really feel not to have enough food to eat? How did it feel to be very sick and never get better? To have burns over half your body? To have soldiers ride through your town and kill everyone in sight?

How would I act? I didn't know. I couldn't imagine it. I *failed* to imagine it.

Nothing truly terrible had ever happened to me.

There was that time when I was four and I sliced open my upper arm on a sharp branch while climbing a tree and I had to have stitches. The nurse told me to clench my teeth together while the doctor sewed me up. It hurt. But then the nurse gave me a lollipop for being good, and everything was okay again. When I got home, Jane was jealous of my lollipop. I still have a little scar on the soft underpart of my arm.

How does that compare to feeling cold metal against your temple and hearing a click?

I'm a lucky girl. I know that. I'm so lucky I can fall down

black holes and not get hurt. I might be the luckiest girl in the whole world.

In history class that day, Sister Martha talked about Harriet Tubman and the Underground Railroad, people running from terror and risking their lives to help the slaves escape. If I had the chance, would I risk my life to help someone? How will I ever know unless I'm tested?

Later that day, I found an answer. I went to a Community Service Committee meeting, and the senior who ran the committee, Nancy Blalock, talked about the projects she had planned for the year. Most of it was the usual stuff — clothing drives, food drives, fund-raisers for a needy kids' summer camp. But one thing she said caught my attention. There was a tutoring center downtown for poor kids who were having trouble in school, and though it wasn't an official St. Maggie's activity, anyone who wanted to volunteer could. I joined the Community Service Committee and the first thing I did was volunteer to be a tutor.

"Why do you want to do that?" Lula asked me. "The tutoring center is probably some seedy place near the bus station, with fluorescent lighting and dirty bathrooms."

"How do you know?" I said.

She shrugged. "That's what every place downtown looks like."

"That's not true." Some of the girls at St. Maggie's are so ignorant it's embarrassing. And I say that even though Lula's my friend.

"Some little kid needs my help with her homework," I told Lula. That was my cover. I did want to help someone. But I also wanted a chance to go downtown and look around by myself.

She laughed. *"Your* help? You're terrible at homework! You're always getting your sisters to help *you."*

She's right, of course. I'm hardly the brainiac of the family. I probably wouldn't be much help to anyone. But I wanted to try.

I think you understand, Almighty. Once at tea you told us about when you were sixteen and worked as a candy striper in a hospital downtown. All you did was hand out magazines and clear away dinner trays, you said. But you must have volunteered for a reason. Maybe you had the same feeling I have — you wanted to help someone in some small way. You wanted to be useful and independent.

I don't want to waste my life as a rich, spoiled girl. Who knows how long I have before some weirdo takes me hostage in a convenience store and kills me? Tutoring was the only useful thing I could think of that would get me out of my snow globe of a life for a little while and into the real world, where I could really test my luck.

■ ■ ■

When I got home from school that day, I decided to walk over to York Road and see what was happening at the 7-Eleven. I didn't tell anyone where I was going. I thought I'd just step onto York Road and peer down the street in search of commotion.

I couldn't see the 7-Eleven from the corner of Northway and York, but I could see police lights flashing. I started walking up York and kept going until I got to the 7-Eleven.

The store was closed and cordoned off by yellow police tape. A few police cars were parked in the lot. A woman in a trench coat talked to a uniformed cop. A truck from Eyewitness News was parked on the street, but there was no reporter in sight. Maybe she was in the truck, resting or reapplying her makeup.

There was nothing to see, no bloodstains or anything like that, at least not on the outside. Through the broken plate-glass window I saw a big steel door behind the counter. Behind that door was the storeroom where the hostages had been held all night.

I bought a pack of gum at a newsstand across the street and headed home. I was walking down Northway when a car backed out of a driveway and hit me. That was the first time.

THREE

✉　✉　✉

I BOUNCED OFF THE TRUNK AND FELL TO THE SIDEWALK. THE car stopped and a woman got out, screaming and flapping her arms.

"Oh! Oh! Oh my God! Are you okay? Are you all right?"

I sat on the pavement in a placid stupor, stars dancing around my head, sparks shooting out from the wires above me. But everything was okay. Everything seemed okay.

I pushed myself to my feet and brushed off my knees. "I'm fine. Really. I'm fine." I had a little scrape on my elbow, but that was all.

She was upset, though. She seized my head in her hands and stared into my eyes, gasping with worry, and shook my hands, one at a time, to see if it hurt me.

"I'm okay. No big deal," I insisted.

She started crying. "I've never hit anyone before! I was so scared!"

"I know." I felt strange, like I did at Lula's house after falling into the room with no floor. Shaken up and disoriented. But this woman was more upset than I was. I tried to comfort her. "Don't worry. I'm not hurt. Everything's fine."

"Are you sure? Are you sure? Oh, thank God. Do you want me to take you to a doctor or something? Do you want me to drive you home?"

"No, I only live a few blocks away. I'll be okay."

"Please, let me drive you home," she said.

"I'm okay. Really. You can go on your way now."

"If you're sure —"

Her car was still running, and the exhaust fumes tickled my nose. I waved to her and started walking away so she would see that I wasn't hurt. She was free. Free to go on her way and continue her life as before, not having hurt a soul.

I looked back. She was sitting in her car, still watching me. I waved again.

When I got to my room, I checked myself for damage, even though I didn't feel anything. I had the scrape on my elbow, and that bruise on my thigh from before. That was all.

■　■　■

After school the next Monday afternoon, Norrie drove me downtown to the Fayette Street Learning Center for my first tutoring session. "I'll go hang at the Starbucks and be back to pick you up at five," she said. "I don't know if I can do this every Monday."

"Maybe next week I'll take the bus," I suggested.

"Yeah, right. Have fun."

I was serious about taking the bus, and she was serious about it probably not happening, but I don't see why. I'm fifteen, plenty old enough to take the bus by myself. When you were fifteen you were galloping around town like a wild pony — that's what you told us. But everybody seems to think it's not safe for me to take the bus alone.

The Fayette Street Learning Center is in a storefront not far from Lexington Market on the border between busy, commercial downtown and scary, deserted West Baltimore. I went inside and presented myself for duty.

"You're in tenth grade, right?" the man behind the reception desk said. He had a shaved head and wore a white shirt, a thin blue tie, and a diamond earring in one ear. His heavy plastic name tag said LARRY GANT. "You've been assigned to an elementary school student. We figure by tenth grade you should have elementary math down."

"Math?" I said. "I requested English. I specifically wrote on my application 'Anything but math.' I'm terrible at math."

Larry Gant nodded. "Sure, but we need math tutors, so you're tutoring math. You'll be working with a fifth grader named Cassandra Higgins. You can handle fifth-grade math, right? You're in tenth grade now! Way past that baby stuff."

I didn't appreciate his patronizing tone. When I said I was bad at math, I meant it. I feared for poor Cassandra Higgins.

"Will this involve fractions?" I asked.

"I believe so."

"I'm screwed."

"Nah. Come on. Just follow the book." He passed me a workbook — *Divide and Conquer: Math Adventures*, Teacher's Edition — and added, "The answers are in there. All you have to do is explain them."

That's what I was afraid of — trying to explain math to someone. It's supposed to be logical, but it seems to me you either get it or you don't. Why couldn't they have assigned me to tutor English? I prefer subjects where there's no right answer. Usually that means there's no *wrong* answer either.

"Cassandra's waiting for you in room six. Down the hall, make a left."

I walked down the hall — fluorescent lit, just as Lula had predicted — past classrooms and meeting rooms full of students and tutors studying at cubicles. I walked into an office divided into four sections, each with its own desk and two chairs. There was no one in the room except for a chubby-faced girl, about eleven, wearing red-framed glasses. Her hair was braided in a dozen or so neat cornrows anchored with red beads, and she wore a red T-shirt over blue jeans and Adidas. In front of her on the desk was the student edition of *Divide and Conquer*, a red spiral notebook, and a red pen.

I approached the desk. "Hi. I'm Sassy Sullivan."

"Sssassy Sssullivan?" She was not the first person to make fun of my super-sibilant name.

"Yesss," I said. "Sssassy Sssullivan. I sssuppossse you're Cassssandra Higginsss?"

"Yesss."

"Sassy and Cassie," I said. "Sounds like a show on the Disney Channel."

"No. It's Cassandra. No one calls me Cassie."

"Okay."

"Are you going to teach me math?"

"Um, yeah. I mean, not *teach*, exactly. But I can try to help you with your math homework."

"*Try* to help me?" She frowned. Her frowny face is intimidating for a fifth grader.

"That's all anyone can do, right?" I tried to turn her frown upside down with a smile, but it didn't work. It never does. I sat down at the desk. "So, what seems to be the problem?" *Dr. Sassy is here to cure your mathematical ailments.* "You've been in school for a few weeks now. Have you had any math tests yet?"

"Yeah," she said.

"So what grades did you get?"

"An F, and then a D."

"Great! That shows progress, right?"

"What did you get on your last math test?"

The memory of a red C-minus flashed before my eyes. Should I tell her? It might not inspire much confidence in my ability to help her. But then, I myself had no confidence in that, so maybe honesty was the best policy. Maybe she'd like me better if she thought we were both math morons together.

"This isn't about me."

"Hmmph. Heard that before."

"Okay, let's be honest here. I don't like math. You don't like math. But it's a part of our lives and we can't escape it. What subjects do you like?"

"Social studies. Language arts."

"Me too. I was hoping to tutor you in language arts, but I guess you don't need it."

"No, I don't. I need tutoring in math." She pushed her latest test, the one with the D, across the table to me. I stared at it. Fractions swam before my eyes, scrambling and unscrambling in an unnerving way. I struggled to think of something — anything — relevant to say.

"So, um, what's your teacher's name?"

"Ms. Frazier."

"Do you like her?"

"No."

Now we were getting somewhere. "Why not?"

"She's crazy. She has a fake foot, and when she's mad she pops it off her leg and says she's going to throw it at us."

"A fake foot? Like a prosthetic?"

"Yuh-huh. She waves it at us, shoe and all."

I laughed. "You're making that up."

"It's true." But she smiled in this cryptic way so I couldn't be sure.

"How'd she lose her foot?"

Cassandra shrugged. "She doesn't say. We're too scared to ask her."

"Well. How can anyone learn math under terrible conditions like that? Living in fear of being hit with a prosthetic foot?"

"That's what I say. But my moms doesn't buy it. Probably because my friend Keema manages to get A's on her tests somehow. Don't ask me how."

"My friend Lula can solve quadratic equations just by looking at them," I said. "It's like a superpower. But she's terrible at French. She can't pronounce *la jeune fille* to save her life. 'La june fee.' If you saw her in French class, you'd think she was retarded. But if you saw *me* in math, you'd think *I* was retarded."

Whoops. I'd said too much. Cassandra gave me a skeptical look, what Daddy-o calls "the hairy eyeball."

"Your math level is *retarded*, and you're going to tutor me?"

I showed her the teacher's edition Larry Gant had given me. "Look! I've got the answers. We can figure it out."

I wasn't ready to give up yet. If I couldn't help this girl — who, actually, didn't seem to need help with much other than math — then what good was I? Besides, I liked her.

Cassandra opened the book. "Does it say how to multiply fractions in there?"

I found the chapter on fractions and read it out loud. "Multiplying fractions is easy! First try canceling. Divide one factor of the numerator and one factor of the denominator by the same number." I looked at the first problem on Cassandra's test. "Did you cancel?"

"You tell me."

I had no idea. I kept reading. "Now multiply the numerators. Then multiply the denominators. Write the product of the numerators over the product of the denominators . . ." My eyes glazed over.

"The problem is the words they use — numerator and denominator," Cassandra said. "Why can't they just say 'the top number' and 'the bottom number'?"

"You're right. Why can't they?"

Larry Gant knocked on the door. "Okay, girls. Time's up for today. Cassandra's mom's here."

"Wow, we didn't get *anything* done," Cassandra said. I wish she hadn't said it in front of Larry.

"Sure we did," I said more brightly than I felt. "We got lots done for the first day. See you next week."

"Yeah. Okay."

After she left, I sat in the cubicle and flipped through *Divide and Conquer*. It was filled with cartoon illustrations of math concepts reenacted by a family of pencils. They weren't funny.

Norrie was waiting for me in the lobby. She took me to Lexington Market for a crab cake to celebrate my first day of tutoring. I ate the crab cake, even though I knew I didn't deserve it.

FOUR

✉ ✉ ✉

THE NEXT DAY WAS A TEA DAY. I REMEMBER A LOT OF TALK about Brooks Overbeck and Norrie and college applications and the Cotillon. I'm interested in those things, but I found myself tuning out. It was a cloudy afternoon but warm, and through the big glass doors that led to the terrace I could see Wallace outside helping Raul with the gardening. He wore blue overalls and a straw hat covering his bald, pink and white head. He spotted me and gave me his two-finger salute. I loved Wallace's salute — it was like a silent way of saying "Howdy, partner." I wanted to salute him back but I know that's not good table manners.

I'd never wanted to hurt Wallace — you know that. I loved him. He never forced the grandpa thing on us. I liked the way he stood quietly by your side, watching in admiration while you ran your fiefdom. I liked the way he insisted on referring to you as our "grandma," even though it doesn't suit you.

You were telling Norrie that you could pull some strings at Georgetown if she needed it, while outside, Wallace watered the rosebushes. The sun had come out and he wiped a bead of sweat off his large forehead. I offered to take him some iced tea, and you said I could be excused.

I went into the kitchen. Bernice was sitting at the table watching *The People's Court*. I poured the tea over ice and added a slice of lemon and a sprig of mint, no sugar. "Sweet tea is for Southerners," you always say. I guess that means we're not Southerners. But you also say, "Yankees brag too much," which implies we're not Yankees either. I don't know what we are. Our own breed, I guess.

"Tell Mr. Wallace I've got a chicken sandwich ready for him if he's hungry," Bernice said as I left the kitchen with the tea.

"Will do, Mildew." We both snickered. It's an old joke we kids have with Bernice. None of us liked your old secretary, Mildred — she was so bossy and stuck-up we called her "Mildew" behind her back. Bet you didn't know that. A little bonus confession for you.

Wallace was putting away the hose when I found him near the garden shed. "Is that iced tea for me? Well, thank you so much, honey." He took off his hat and took a long drink. "Had enough of that girl talk in there?"

I nodded. "It'll be terrible after Norrie and Jane leave for college and I'm the only one left to go to Tuesday Tea. Just me and Ginger. I'll have to put Takey in a dress and make him come too."

"I bet Takey looks pretty good in a dress."

"He does. Norrie and I made him wear all our favorite old dresses when he was littler. With lipstick. He looked like a doll. Jane even put her old tutu on him and taught him a ballet routine."

"Poor boy. Where were his big brothers when he needed them?"

"Sitting on the couch laughing at him," I said.

Wallace chuckled. "Well, your grandma has good reason to sit down and talk to you girls every week. She's preparing you to take her place in the world. She's an important woman, and someday you will be too."

"Just because I'm her granddaughter?"

"No, I think you'll be important in your own way. But being her granddaughter doesn't hurt. Want to help me put this garden hose away?"

I helped him carry the hose into the shed and rest it under the worktable. "Up to anything interesting? Aren't you getting your driver's license this year?"

"In February. I have my learner's permit."

"Good for you. You need someone to take you out driving, I'll be happy to do it."

"Thanks. Everybody else is always too busy."

"I'll bet they are. What else are you up to?"

"Well, I started tutoring at this place downtown," I told him. "They assigned me to a fifth grader. The only thing is, they want me to help her with math."

"Not your forte, eh? Stick with it. Maybe teaching math will help you understand it better."

"Anything's possible, I guess," I said.

Have you ever been inside the garden shed? Wallace and Raul decorated it like a clubhouse. Raul put pictures of his family on one wall, and Wallace tacked up a picture of a race car and an old photograph of you from your debutante days. I bet it's still in there, unless Raul took it down.

I heard someone calling my name. Jane stood on the terrace yelling, "Sassy! Vacation's over! Time to come back to your jail cell!"

"Guess you're wanted back at tea," Wallace said. "Thanks for the drink, Sassafras."

"You're welcome."

He gave me the two-finger salute, and I saluted him back before walking up to the house.

"I hope Wallace didn't bore you with too much of his plant talk," you said when I got back to the library and took my seat at the table.

"He never bores me," I replied.

"You're a saint," you said.

Don't worry, Almighty. I know you loved him. He knew it too.

FIVE

⊠　　⊠　　⊠

THE FIRST MONDAY IN OCTOBER, I DECIDED TO TAKE THE BUS downtown to tutoring. I braced myself for a storm of protest, but it turns out if you don't tell people what you're doing, they can't say no. Miss Maura thought Norrie was driving me downtown. I lied and told Norrie that I was getting a ride with Lula and her mother. Norrie said, "Cool," and forgot all about me. Ginger and Daddy-o barely know what I do all day, and as long as there's a breathing body in my bed every night they don't worry about it.

I walked to Charles Street and waited at the bus stop. When the bus came I took a seat and watched the buildings I'd known all my life pass by from a new perspective. Everything looks different from high up in a bus. It's kind of like watching a movie that's been filmed in your neighborhood; you recognize the houses but they look different somehow.

The bus took longer to get to Fayette Street than I thought. Cassandra was waiting for me in our cubicle. Another tutor-student pair worked in the cubicle behind her.

"Hey. Ms. Frazier throw any body parts at you lately?"

She didn't laugh. "Just sit down and help me." She dropped a workbook on the table with a few crinkled sheets of homework stuffed inside. "I've got to finish these problems tonight and we're having a quiz tomorrow. My mother said if I don't get at least a C in math this year, she's going to make me go to summer school."

"That would definitely suck." I opened the workbook and looked at the problems. Long division. I know how to do that. I don't always get the right answer, but I understand the basic concept.

"I've got a calculator at home," Cassandra said. "I don't see why I can't just use that. It always gives the right answer."

"You still have to learn how to do division on paper, or in your head," I said. "In case you find yourself on a desert island where there aren't any calculators."

"That's never going to happen. And anyway, why would I need to do long division on a desert island?"

"Well, what if there's some big catastrophe and there's no electricity and your calculator won't work? What then, huh?"

"Calculators use batteries, genius. I still don't see why I would stop in the middle of running for my life from a big catastrophe to do long division."

"Well, what if you're in a restaurant and you need to split the check?"

"While the world is falling apart all around me?"

I shrugged. "Long division wasn't my idea." I looked at her homework. "I think I see where the problem is. Decimals."

"I know that's the problem," she said. "I don't understand why they're always moving around the way they do. When the teacher makes those looping lines underneath them."

I always thought that was weird too. If you can move decimals around so easily, don't they *mean* anything? "I can't really explain it," I said. "You just have to do it."

Her look made me want to crawl under the desk.

"That's your lesson for the day? Just do it?"

"Um —" I looked at the test again. I remembered struggling with the same problems, and finally realizing that the best way to handle it was not to try to understand it — for some reason my brain doesn't want to understand it — but just to learn the procedure and follow it like a recipe or a formula. Wasn't that what math mostly was anyway — formulas? But how could I say this to Cassandra? A better tutor would be able to help her understand the thinking behind the recipe.

"Are you going to say something or you going to sit there like *Dawn of the Dead*?"

"*Dawn of the Dead* isn't a person," I said. "I used to think that too. I thought the movie was about a zombie named Dawn. But it's really about the morning after the *Night of the Living Dead* —"

"You're a tutor who knows more about zombies than you do about long division. Is that what you're trying to tell me?"

I wanted to cry. Tutoring was not working out. I wasn't helping anybody. I was just wasting Cassandra's time and probably turning her off of math forever.

I was an awful tutor. I glumly pondered this terrible reality as I walked the four blocks to the bus stop. It was getting dark, and it occurred to me that if I walked uptown a few blocks to the Walters', I might still catch Daddy-o and get a ride home with him.

I was crossing the street, deep in thought, when suddenly I found myself face-to-face with the metallic green hood of a Honda. I heard a screech of brakes as I landed on the street on my butt.

I sat on the asphalt in a daze. Someone ran over to me. "Miss? Honey? Are you okay?"

A small crowd gathered around me. A young man stared into my eyes. "Hello? Are you okay? Oh my God!" He pressed a cell phone to his ear as I blinked at him. "9-1-1! I need an ambulance!"

"I'm okay," I said. I started to stand up, but the young man and an older woman helped me to the curb and sat me down again. A police car drove up, lights flashing, siren wailing.

I started coming back to myself. I picked a piece of gravel off my palm. Just like the last time, the car had barely tapped me. I wasn't hurt, just a little confused.

Two police officers stood over me. The young man who'd helped me said, "It was an accident. I was making a right turn and I didn't see her —"

"It's true," said the older woman. "I saw the whole thing. The girl was crossing against the light."

One policeman talked to the young man and the witness while the policewoman asked me if I was hurt anywhere. She checked my arms and legs for broken bones and looked into my eyes with a flashlight. Then an ambulance arrived and a paramedic took over for the policewoman.

"I'm okay — really," I insisted. "I don't need an ambulance."

"Let me be the judge of that." The paramedic put me inside the ambulance and checked my arms and legs again. He pressed against my abdomen and asked me if it hurt. He stared into my eyes and asked if my head hurt.

"You look okay," he said. "But we'll take you to Mercy to make absolutely sure."

I had to go to the hospital? Ginger and Daddy-o would freak. "Really, I just want to go home," I said.

"It's policy. We have to do it. We'll try not to keep you too long."

The policewoman popped her head into the ambulance. "Can I get a statement from her now? Can she do that?"

The paramedic nodded. "Sure."

The policewoman asked me my name and address and to tell her what happened. I told her I had a tendency to space out while I walked and wasn't watching where I was going. She shook her head.

"Sweetheart, this is the big city. You've got to keep your head about you. Now, do you want to call your parents?"

"No," I said.

"Well, if you don't, I will," she said, handing me a phone.

"That's okay, I've got one." I took my phone out of my backpack and called Norrie. "Can you come pick me up from Mercy Hospital?"

"What? What happened?"

"Nothing," I said. "I got hit by a car again. But I'm fine. They're making me go to the emergency room just to make sure. But I'm perfectly okay."

"Oh my God! What's the matter with you? Why do you keep walking in front of cars?"

"I'm not doing it on purpose," I said.

"I'm going to call Daddy-o. He's already downtown. He'll be there faster."

"Please don't tell Daddy-o and Ginger," I said. I didn't want to upset anybody. Even then, before the big disaster, I knew I was somehow responsible for these accidents.

"Sassy, you got hit by a car! Your parents should know about it."

"Norrie, come on —"

"Sassy, no. I'm sorry. I'm calling Daddy-o right now." She hung up.

I sighed and made myself comfortable on the ambulance gurney. It was going to be a long night.

SIX

✉   ✉   ✉

I WAS STARVING WHEN DADDY-O AND I FINALLY GOT HOME from the hospital. Since my case was hardly critical, I had to wait three hours to see a doctor. Miss Maura had kept our suppers warm for us. Everybody fussed over me — even Ginger, in her way: She asked Miss Maura to get me some ice cream if I wanted it — but all I had to show for the accident was a plastic hospital bracelet and another bruise, this one on my left arm. The doctors had confirmed that I was otherwise unhurt.

"You've really got to get your head together, Sass," Jane said. We had gathered in Norrie's room late that night for a recap of the day. "Getting hit by two cars in one month — that's pathetic. I wonder what the record is?"

"What record?" Norrie said.

"Most times somebody's been hit by a car in a month," Jane said. "Or at all."

"I hope you're not trying to break some crazy record like that, Sassy," Norrie said. "You're not, are you?"

"No," I said. "But I do feel weird about something."

Norrie immediately put the back of her hand to my forehead.

"Weird? In what way? Do you think you have a concussion? Maybe the doctors missed it."

"Not like that," I said. "It's funny how things have been happening to me — accidents, I mean — and I don't get hurt. Falling down that hole in Lula's house, and getting hit by two cars . . . I kind of feel like my bones are made of rubber or something. Like I'm indestructible."

In bed, late at night, when I relived the accidents in my mind, I saw myself bouncing off cars unharmed like a cartoon character, some kind of indestructible rubber superhero. I saw my body bouncing off floors and hoods and windshields and bumpers like an eraser off a desk.

"Sassy, don't think that way," Norrie said. "You're not indestructible. You have to be careful."

"Here's what I want to know," Jane said. "Why do you keep walking in front of moving cars?"

"But what if I am?" I said. "What if I'm immortal?"

Jane laughed her annoying snort-laugh. She can be so smug. I'm sure she thought that if anyone in the family was immortal, it would be her.

Now that I'd said the words out loud, I couldn't get them out of my mind. I was immortal. Unkillable.

The thought terrified me. But I couldn't resist a moment of Jane-like bravado.

"Out of my way," I said. "I've got some death to defy."

SEVEN

⊠　　⊠　　⊠

"I GOT A C ON MY LAST MATH TEST," CASSANDRA ANNOUNCED the next week. "Not that you had anything to do with it. Just thought you might like to know."

She waved the test paper, with its big red C and a "neutral" face — Ms. Frazier had drawn a straight line where the smile or frown should have been.

"Cassandra, that's great!" I said. "Congratulations. How did you do it?"

She shrugged. "I don't know. A C isn't all that great."

"It's a lot better than an F."

"Yeah."

I opened the workbook, flipping through it without really knowing what I was looking at. "What lesson should we work on today?"

"Here's my homework for tomorrow." She passed me a paper covered with problems. Oh no. Fractions again.

"Are you all right?" Cassandra asked.

"Me? Sure. Why?"

"You got a big purple splotch on your arm."

"Oh. This." The bruise on my left forearm had spread in the week since the last car accident. I tugged the sleeve of my sweater over it. "It's nothing. Totally hideous, but not as bad as it looks."

"It's hideous all right. How did you get it? Somebody hit you?"

"Yeah," I said. "With his car."

"You got hit by a car? Why aren't you dead?"

I shrugged. "I don't know. It didn't hit me that hard. It's happened to me before, and I didn't get hurt then either."

"Whoa. You're lucky."

"I know." Should I tell her? I wondered. Should I tell Cassandra my theory? I was curious what she'd think, though deep down I knew what she'd think. She'd think what everyone else thought: that I was crazy.

But what the heck.

"I have this idea that I can't get hurt. Or killed, or anything like that. Like, maybe I'm immortal."

She pushed her red glasses up her nose like she wanted to make sure she was seeing me right, even though it was her ears, not her eyes, that were troubling her.

"Say that again?"

"I think something happened to me — it's a long story — that made me immortal."

"What happened? Did you get bit by a vampire?"

"No. But I keep getting hit by cars and just bouncing up like, 'Everything's okay.'"

She frowned. "I don't believe you."

"Maybe I'm not immortal, I don't know. I'm just saying it's weird, that's all."

"You're right that's weird. Spooky too. And I don't believe it. My mother told me everybody dies sometime. My granddad died last year. I saw his body at the funeral. He looked kind of like a big, wrinkly doll. And when nobody was looking, I touched his hand."

"What did it feel like?"

"Kind of waxy and cold. But I could tell he was dead for real, because that was his face and his hands all right, but you could see he wasn't in there anymore. And that's when my mother told me everybody has to die. Maybe not till you're really old like granddad, but still, that's a rule and that goes for everybody. And I don't see why God would make a special exception just for you."

"I'm not saying God made an exception for me." I'd never even thought about it that way. Did I sound that stuck-up? "I'm saying something happened to me, where I fell down this weird black hole and it changed my body somehow, and plunged me into some other world where cars hit me and I don't get hurt. Kind of like Spider-Man."

"You fell down a black hole? Into another world? Now you're just out-and-out lying to me."

"I know it sounds funny —"

"So do I live in this other world you fell into? And if I do, how come I'm not immortal?"

"Maybe you are. I don't know."

"Nobody is immortal. Somebody shoots you — you bleed. Maybe you die, maybe you don't, but you still hurt. My big brother got cut once, and he has a scar from here to here." She drew a line with her finger from her collarbone to below her ribs. "And the police shot his friend Kevin and he died. He didn't bounce up and say everything's cool. He died. What's wrong with you?"

I felt embarrassed. My immortality theory suddenly sounded so stupid. "You're right. I'm not immortal. How could that be? I just *feel* like nothing bad can happen to me. Like my bones are made of rubber and can't break, you know?"

She was shaking her head at me. "To get something like that, being unkillable, you've got to pay a price, right?" she said.

"Probably," I said. "Something like giving up your soul."

"Yeah, or maybe just causing a lot of bad stuff to happen all around you. Like, nothing ever touches *you personally*, but everybody around you suffers. You spread destruction wherever you go."

"Are you talking about me now, or just about some theoretical immortal person?"

"I'm talking about people who can't be killed. If they exist."

"Do you think they exist?"

She looked down at her math workbook. "You got a math problem that proves it?"

"No," I said. "Maybe we should get to work." I sighed. "I hate fractions."

"I hate them too."

"If we force ourselves to concentrate really hard, maybe we can figure this out," I said.

"Okay. It will be a relief after all this crazy talk."

I knew it sounded crazy. But it didn't *feel* crazy. It felt true.

EIGHT

⊠　　⊠　　⊠

THEN CAME THAT DAY. NO ONE WAS INVITED TO TEA BUT ME. IF the others had come with me, would things have turned out differently? I guess we'll never know.

I remember we talked about Norrie and Brooks. You said Norrie wasn't treating him well. "Teasing him, running hot and cold," you said. "Acting as if she doesn't know if she likes him or not —"

"Maybe she *doesn't* know," I said.

"Irrelevant! That's no way to behave. One should always act decisively, even if one hasn't made any actual decisions. To waffle and waver is unladylike and rude." You poured yourself some tea and splashed a drop of milk in the cup. "Have you met that young man she likes — Robertson, is it? I'm sure he's a lovely person but he's *far* too old for her. And Norrie says he's from New York. Well. You know I love to visit Manhattan but New York is not like Baltimore. *Anybody* can be from New York."

I sipped my tea and wished my sisters were with me. It was hard to keep up the conversation by myself. I was distracted.

I glanced out to the terrace. Across the lawn, Wallace emptied a bag of seed into a bird feeder.

"But Jane is even *worse*. Disgracing the family in public! In the newspaper! Why would she want to do that? I simply don't understand. What really troubles me is she's putting the family history in the worst possible light. There are different ways of looking at the past, you know."

I know. According to Jane, there's the way that makes you look good, and there's the truth.

Then you said something that still hurts when I remember it.

"But you, dear." You patted my hand. "You, at least, are a model grandchild."

Now you know the truth. You had me all wrong. I'm the worst grandchild of all.

Wallace pottered through the house in his socks, having left his muddy work boots at the back door. "Just wanted to say hello to you ladies before I go off to the garden center. Can I get you anything, Lou?"

"No, nothing, just get whatever you need. But check with Bernice before you go and see if she needs anything from Eddie's."

"Roger." He tossed me a little salute on his way out of the library. Wallace's last salute.

A few minutes later I left through the kitchen door. And here is exactly what happened next.

Wallace's old Cadillac rumbled in the garage, so I headed that way to say good-bye to him. I stepped onto the driveway. The car suddenly backed out.

The strange black magic in my blood drew the car toward my body, pulled it like a magnet.

The Cadillac hit me.

The car slammed to a stop. I bounced off as usual. My hands pushed me off the trunk and broke my fall to the ground. My left knuckles scraped the driveway, not deep enough to bleed.

"Don't worry, Wallace!" I called. "I'm fine!"

I rose to my feet and brushed myself off. I slapped the trunk of the car twice so Wallace would know I was okay. Then I walked around to the driver's window.

"Sorry about that, Wallace. I hope I didn't scare you."

I looked through the car window. Wallace's hands gripped the steering wheel at ten and two o'clock. His head was tilted back against the headrest. His eyes were open but blank, unblinking.

"Wallace?"

I knocked on the window. He didn't move. I opened the car door. His body slumped against me.

He was dead.

Wallace was dead. And I had killed him.

But you already knew that. You've known all along.

You were standing at the kitchen window, watching.

NINE

✉ ✉ ✉

WHEN I GOT HOME, I THREW MYSELF ON GINGER'S BED AND
cried. I couldn't tell her the real reason I was so upset. She
thought I was sad that Wallace had died, and I was. I was sad
and shocked. But I felt guilty too. I was afraid to say anything to
anyone about what had really happened. I was afraid no one
would understand, or believe me, or take it seriously. And then I
was afraid they *would* take it seriously.

You could have said something. But you didn't. I started
to wonder if you had seen anything at all. I don't wonder
anymore.

Ginger rubbed my back and tried to soothe me. "Poor darling.
Don't take it so hard. Wallace was old. Everybody has to die
sometime."

"The doctor said it was a stroke," Daddy-o told us. "Blood clot
straight to the heart, very sudden. Nothing anybody could have
done about it."

That was what everyone said: It was nobody's fault. But I
knew the truth. It was my fault. The shock of hitting me with his
car caused the stroke and killed him.

It was just like Cassandra had said. Immortality kept me safe from harm, but it was causing destruction all around me. Real destruction. Death.

■　■　■

That night I couldn't sleep. I lay in my bed, listening to the sounds of the traffic in the distance. A garbage truck rumbled down our street. No police choppers that night.

I replayed Wallace's death in my mind, over and over. In slow motion I saw the car back out of the garage. I saw myself walk across the driveway. I tried to stop myself from stepping onto the asphalt, but I couldn't control my legs. They kept walking. I tried to stop the car from backing up, but it kept going. I tried to make my body jump out of the way before being hit, but it stayed rooted to the ground.

I watched myself run to the car window. I tried to make Wallace laugh and give me one of his salutes, but he wouldn't cooperate. Every time I ran to the window, he was just the way I'd found him: frozen, hollow-eyed, dead.

■　■　■

At the funeral, you could hardly stand to look at me. It wasn't easy to see your eyes through the veil you wore, but I could tell — they pierced straight into my soul. You blamed me for shocking Wallace to death. You didn't say a word about it, which only made me feel worse. And then Takey kept shooting at people with his thumb and forefinger — *k-pew, k-pew* — and I couldn't get him to stop, and I was afraid you'd blame me for that too.

From my seat I could see Wallace's sharp, beaky nose poking out of his casket among the sprays of lilies. Father Burgess said, "Let us pray," and everyone knelt to pray for Wallace.

I tried to focus on the Father's eulogy, but my heart pumped heavily, flooding blood into my ears and eyes, blocking my senses. A few of the Father's words got through to me — eternal life, heaven, forgiveness, sin. *I have a kind of superpower,* I thought. *Eternal life. I am the one person on Earth who will never die.*

But then, why should I die? Why shouldn't I live forever? My life could be wild and fearless and exciting . . . like yours.

I thought far into the future of all the funerals to come. Yours and Ginger's and Daddy-o's someday. St. John and Sully and Norrie and Jane, even Takey . . . each of them, one by one, lying in Wallace's place like dolls in their caskets. They'll be old when they die, I hope, but it hardly matters. I'll be left all alone, to live out eternity with no one to love.

I started to cry. I wept as we filed past the casket to say our good-byes. Father Burgess patted my shoulder in consolation, and then I realized what I had to do. It was so obvious. I had to confess my sin.

After the funeral, we stepped out into the gray light to ride to the cemetery. As limo after limo pulled up and drove off I wondered, *What would happen if I threw myself in front of that car? What if I ran over to Charles Street and threw myself right into the traffic? What would happen this time? Would I come away without a scratch?*

■　■　■

The next day, I went to confession after school. I wondered what you had told Father Burgess about how Wallace had died. Maybe he already knew what I'd done.

I started with the easy stuff, confessing to taking the Lord's name in vain about a zillion times, to talking back to my mother only about a million times, to having impure thoughts once in a while, and to coveting some of my sisters' clothes. Finally I got to the real reason I was there.

"Father, I have one more sin to confess," I said. "The sin of murder."

There was silence behind the screen. I thought I heard a stifled chuckle, but that might have been him clearing his throat.

"Murder? That is serious. Please tell me what happened."

So I told him. I told him that I had somehow become invincible, that cars were always crashing into me but never really hurting me. "On the day Wallace died, he accidently hit me with his car . . . and I think he thought he hurt me. He didn't know I have this superpower where cars can't hurt me. And I think he felt so bad, or maybe so shocked, that it killed him. Which means *I* killed him."

"Hmmm." I could see the shadow of Father Burgess's finger tapping his chin as if he were thinking hard about this. "That is a strange set of circumstances. I'm glad you came to talk to me about this. You are carrying a number of misconceptions around in that head of yours."

And then he let me have it. Nicely, but he still tried to set me straight. First of all, he said, I'm not invincible — far from it — and I shouldn't go around thinking that way. I should be careful and try to avoid accidents at all times, because no matter what I think, I could be seriously hurt.

Secondly, he said, I am not guilty of murder. What had happened was an accident and not my fault. You and I both know that he's wrong.

I tried to get him to see the truth. "If it's not murder, how about manslaughter? Negligent homicide?"

"This isn't *Law and Order*, my dear," he said. "God doesn't plea-bargain."

"I'm not trying to plea-bargain," I said. "I'm trying to convince you of my guilt."

He said again that it was an accident, it wasn't my fault, Wallace would have had a stroke anyway, blah blah blah. Because he didn't believe I was invincible. He didn't take my confession seriously. And the proof was in the penance: only one Hail Mary. For the sin of pride, not for murder.

He let me off way too easy, I thought as I knelt at the altar of St. Joan and said my one required prayer. I knew what I had done was serious, and I couldn't rest until I had paid the price. I vowed to go out into the world and find a penance of my own, one that would fit my crime.

I didn't know then that you would offer me another chance to confess — or that you would punish everyone else along with me.

TEN

✉   ✉   ✉

A FEW DAYS LATER, AT HOCKEY PRACTICE, AISHA SMACKED THE ball toward the goal and it flew off course and hit me in the eye. I fell down. My eye really hurt. When the coach lifted my hand away from it, she said, "Ouch."

I was sent to the nurse, who put an ice pack on my face. My eye was black and blue, and it ached. It hurt way more than any of the bruises I got when I was hit by those cars. Which made me start to wonder: What if it was over? What if I'd lost my invincibility?

Perhaps that was my punishment for killing Wallace. But I couldn't be sure yet.

I eyed the passing cars on my way home from school. Would one of them jump the curb and go after me? Would this be the time I was finally killed?

I made it home safely enough. At the sight of my eye, Miss Maura handed me a package of frozen peas and made me hold it there until it defrosted, after which she would serve the peas for dinner.

I went upstairs, peas plastered to my face, to visit Takey and Bubbles. I knew Takey had been practicing a new trick with

Bubbles and I wanted to see how it was going. I found him sitting on the edge of his bed, staring at the fish tank.

"What's the matter?" I asked.

"I don't know," Takey said. "Bubbles won't do his trick."

I looked at the tank. Bubbles lay on his side, floating on the surface of the water.

"Oh no." I sat down next to Takey. "This looks bad."

The last thing we needed was another funeral, but when a goldfish dies you can't just flush him down the toilet.

Takey aimed his gun finger at Bubbles. "Get up, Bubbles, or I'll shoot. Ka-pow."

"Too late, Takey," I said. "He's already dead."

"Why?" Takey asked. "Did he have a stroke like Wallace?"

"I don't know," I said. "Maybe."

All those fish tricks down the drain. It would take forever to train a new goldfish to put on a show like Bubbles. Not only that, it was sad to see the little guy floating there, lifeless.

Takey aimed his finger gun at me. I obediently put my hands up. "Hey, I didn't kill him." I only confess to murders I actually committed.

"Why is your eye all black?" Takey asked.

"I lost my lucky force field."

"What?"

"I got hit by a hockey ball." And between that and the death of Bubbles, I knew something had changed. My luck had turned. Wallace's death had done it. Just like falling down a black hole into another dimension made me invincible, murdering my stepgrandfather made me vincible again.

That's what happens when you commit the worst sin in the world. You lose your chance at immortality.

It made sense to me at the time.

■ ■ ■

I was very careful on my way downtown to the Learning Center. Now that I knew I could get hurt if a hard object hit me, I felt skittish around cars. I stood shakily at every crosswalk in my bruise-hiding sunglasses, waiting for the light to change and then making sure all the cars were completely stopped before I stepped into the street. Once, a car turning left onto Charles whizzed by a little too close for comfort. I scooted out of the way and let out a scream. The other crosswalkers looked warily at me as if I were a crazy person.

I made it to the Learning Center without getting run over, but my neurotic carefulness had made me late. Cassandra was waiting for me in the study room. I sat down across the desk from her and took off my sunglasses.

"Whoa," she said. "What happened to you?"

"I killed my grandfather," I said. "Stepgrandfather."

"You killed him?" She looked surprised. I guess kids don't expect to hear that their math tutors are murderesses.

I nodded.

"I got your back," she said. "I won't tell anyone."

"It doesn't matter," I said. "Everybody already knows."

She squinted at me. "Then why aren't you in jail?"

"It was an accident. That's what everybody says."

"Sure it was." The squint hardened into a look that said, *White people are always getting away with murder.* Or maybe that was just my guilty conscience talking. "There's a cop on the beat where I live, whenever anything bad happens and the kid says, 'It was an accident,' he always says, 'No such thing as an accident,' Then he slaps on the cuffs."

"I know." I started to tear up a little. I really didn't want to cry in front of Cassandra. It seemed so unprofessional. "It's all about luck. Everything is about luck. I always felt very lucky. Then I fell down that black hole —"

Cassandra shook her head. "Don't start with that again."

"But then I killed a man. And ever since I became a murderess, my luck has changed. I am no longer immortal. Flying hockey balls can hurt me. Pet goldfish can die."

"I don't know why you're telling me all this," Cassandra said. "But I will say that if you kill somebody, you'll start to have bad luck. That makes sense to me."

A few tears leaked out of my eyes. I tried to wipe them away nonchalantly, but Cassandra saw them. She must have felt sorry for me. She patted my arm. "I know you didn't mean to kill anybody, Sassy. You're a good person inside. Even though you leave a trail of destruction wherever you go."

"Like a zombie." I sniffled.

"Yeah, a lot like a zombie." She crossed her eyes and held out her arms stiffly, zombie-style. "Brrra-a-ai-ins," she moaned. "Math tutor need brains."

I took a deep breath and tried to pull myself together. I was supposed to be there to help her, not pour out all my problems to her. Time to get to work. "How did you do on your math quiz last week?"

She pulled out a paper and laid it on the desk in front of me. B+.

"B-plus! That's fantastic!" I grabbed her hand and shook it. "How did you do that? You certainly didn't get any help from me."

"That's for sure. I don't know — I guess it's just starting to click in my head or something."

"Wow," I said. "Maybe I am still lucky in some ways. I'm lucky to be a tutor whose student is so smart she tutors herself."

"Damn right, you're lucky."

"Cassandra — if I'm not helping you, why do you still come?"

"Partly because my mother makes me. And partly because I like to hear your crazy stories. But it's mostly my mother."

I opened my backpack to get *Divide and Conquer*. I pulled it out with one of my schoolbooks and an old copy of the *Sun*, folded to the news story about Jane's blog and our evil family. The article was illustrated with a big picture of our house, tower and all.

Cassandra spotted the newspaper. "Can I see that?" She took the paper and stared at the picture of the house. "Is that where you live?" Her eyes widened. "It's a castle!"

From across the desk, upside down, our house looked unfamiliar. It's always just been home. But now that I saw it through Cassandra's eyes, I realized it is unusually big. And the tower does make it look kind of like a castle.

I blushed. What kind of family lives in a castle? Even our big family doesn't need all that room. It's obscene.

"I know," I said. "I'm ashamed of it."

"Ashamed? If I lived in a big house like that, I'd be proud."

Her saying that made me feel even more ashamed. I was ashamed to live in such a big house, and ashamed that I was so spoiled I wasn't even proud of it.

"Read the article," I said. "Read what it says about my family. Then you'll see why I'm ashamed."

Cassandra read the article carefully. When she was done she shook her head. "So? Everybody's family's got relatives who do bad things. But not everybody lives in a castle."

I wondered what Cassandra's house looked like. I wondered if she even lived in a house. Maybe she lives in an apartment. Will I ever see it? Probably not.

ELEVEN

⊠   ⊠   ⊠

ONE OF THE BOOKS WE READ IN ENGLISH THIS YEAR WAS
The Winter's Tale by William Shakespeare. Maybe you already
guessed that.

I was reading it in the cubicle before my next tutoring session
with Cassandra. She was a few minutes late, and when she came
in she asked me about the book.

"That's Hermione, the queen of Sicily." I pointed to the marble
statue on the cover. "This play is about a family feud. Leontes,
the King of Sicily, thinks his wife, Hermione, is cheating on him
with his best friend, so the friend runs from Sicily in fear for his
life. Leontes puts Hermione in jail for treason and orders their
baby daughter, Perdita, killed."

"That's cold," Cassandra said.

"Yes it is. It's so cold Hermione dies of heartbreak in the arms
of her friend Paulina."

Cassandra said, "And then her ghost comes back and
haunts him."

"No," I told her. "But that would be good. After Hermione
dies, Leontes finds out that he was wrong about his wife and his
friend. The knowledge of the terrible injustice he has done turns

his heart hard as stone. Then, years later, Perdita, the baby who was supposed to have been killed, miraculously reappears, all grown up and engaged to marry the son of Leontes's friend, whose name is Polixenes. Leontes and Polixenes end their feud. Leontes says, 'If only Hermione were alive to see this happy day.'"

"But she's not, and it's *all his fault*," Cassandra said. "What is it about this story that sounds so familiar?"

I ignored her taunt. "Paulina says that she has made a statue of Hermione so lifelike Leontes will think she is alive. She takes everybody to her country house to show them. When Paulina casts a spell over the statue, a miracle happens: The statue comes to life! Hermione is alive again and reunited with her husband and daughter. And Leontes is very sorry that he ever lost faith in her and in his friend."

"How does the statue come back to life?" Cassandra asked.

"Paulina casts a spell over it. She says, 'Music, awake her; strike! 'Tis time; descend; be stone no more. . . . Bequeath to death your numbness.'"

"And the statue comes alive."

I nodded.

"And then what?"

"Hermione says something like, 'I had faith this day would come, when my beloved daughter would be found and my husband would beg forgiveness.'"

"And then what?"

"Everyone is happy. The end."

She took the book and looked it over. "Is there a movie version?"

"I don't know. It's not the most popular Shakespeare play."

Then we settled down to work, and we actually got some math problems done that day.

■ ■ ■

The receptionist stopped me on my way out of the Learning Center that afternoon. "Larry wants to see you, Sassy."

The receptionist nodded toward an open conference room where Larry Gant sat sorting piles of workbooks. He looked up when I walked in.

"You're Sassy Sullivan, right?" I nodded. "Okay, listen. I've got some bad news. Cassandra Higgins's mother stopped in today after she dropped off Cassandra, and she was unhappy."

"Unhappy?" My stomach dropped, the way it does when a roller coaster heads down the steep part.

"Yes. She says Cassandra isn't learning anything here. She says the two of you have hardly covered any math at all. She says all the two of you do for your hour is talk and tell crazy stories to each other. Is that true?"

"Um, yeah, it's true, but Cassandra's math grades are going up."

"That's what Ms. Higgins said. But she said that's because she's helping Cassandra with her homework at home. After Cassandra comes back from what's supposed to be tutoring."

"Oh." What else could I say? I had no defense. My failure at math had bitten me in the butt yet again.

"That little girl hasn't got time to sit here and listen to your problems. You want a shrink, you've got to pay one. And I'd suggest you find one who's better qualified than an eleven-year-old."

"Are you saying I'm emotionally disturbed?"

"I don't know anything about you," Larry said. "You seem nice. All I'm saying is we can't have you coming here and wasting people's time. We've got to think about our reputation as a place of learning, you know what I'm saying?"

A bit of phlegm rose to my throat. I tried to clear it but my voice sounded froggy anyway. "Yes."

"So I hope you won't be hurt by this but we've got to let you go. I know you're a volunteer but volunteers have still got to do the work."

"I know. I'm sorry. I tried to tell you I wasn't any good at math."

"Yeah, I should've listened to you. I thought you were just being humble."

"No, I was telling the truth."

"I get that now. You still could have made an effort."

"You're so right. I'll leave now."

He nodded and went back to sorting books. I walked out of there as fast as I could so he wouldn't see me cry.

I sat at the bus stop, unzipped my backpack, and stuck my head into the main pocket so I could cry in peace. I felt so ashamed. Not that I wasn't a good math tutor — that wasn't news to me. But that I had let Cassandra down. Because I wasn't a good person. Now I wouldn't see her anymore. And I didn't even get to say good-bye.

That was my punishment.

TWELVE

✉   ✉   ✉

CHRISTMAS WAS COMING SOON. NORRIE WAS GETTING READY for the Cotillon and the house was in an uproar. I went up to her room one night just to lie at the foot of her bed and read while she did her homework. I like to do that sometimes. Of course, we usually end up talking and not getting the rest of our homework done.

I was lying across the bottom of the bed, and she was propped against the headboard, reading and pressing her feet into my ribs, but not in a bad way. I put down my book and watched her face while she read. She was frowning, and her eyes weren't on the pages. They were staring at the squares of color on her quilt, unfocused.

"Are you excited about the Cotillon?" I asked her. Her face drooped into an even less happy expression, but she said, "Uh-huh."

I rolled onto my stomach and squeezed one of her feet through her white gym sock. "What's wrong? Is it Brooks? He's a nice guy. I can picture him being somebody's uncle someday, or grandpa. The kind that writes silly poems just for you on your birthday."

"I know." She picked at the quilt without looking at me. "That's the trouble, isn't it? I'm not ready to be grandma to somebody's grandpa yet."

"I didn't mean it like that," I said. "I just meant that he's nice. Like you can trust him."

"He seems like you can trust him. But that doesn't mean you can. How can you ever know that about someone?"

"I don't know." I have been thinking about this a lot lately. I know how people see me. They think I'm the saintly one. People are always saying I look like a Christmas angel.

But we know better, don't we? I'm not a good person. I volunteered to tutor because I wanted to help someone, and I didn't help her at all. Because I didn't really want to help her. I wanted to help myself. And I was so bad at tutoring I got fired. Fired from a volunteer job. That's pretty sad.

And when Bubbles died, Takey was sad but I wasn't. I pretended to be sad, but I really didn't care that much.

And then there's Wallace. I killed a man. But whenever I try to tell someone, they don't take me seriously. Because I look like a Christmas angel, not a killer. The only person who understands how bad I really am inside is you. And maybe Cassandra.

So Norrie might be right. Brooks seems like a wonderful guy, but maybe on the inside he isn't. Maybe he's mean. Maybe he's secretly plotting the destruction of the human race. How can anyone know? It's just like on the news — whenever someone cracks and kills somebody, the killer's mother and even his neighbors always say they can't believe it, he wouldn't hurt a fly. The guy who shot all those people in the 7-Eleven — that's what his mother said about him. But people are dead. You can't deny it.

"Robbie's mad at me," Norrie said. "About the Cotillon. He doesn't understand: I have to do it. Or everybody will get so upset."

"Maybe he's not right for you if he doesn't understand."

"That's what everybody says. That's what Claire says. But he is right for me. That's the problem. He doesn't understand because he feels how right we are for each other and he thinks I'm denying it by going to the ball with Brooks."

She really looked sad for a girl who was about to have the best night of her life.

"Why do you think Jane's tattoo won't wash off?" I asked. Jane's friend Bridget had drawn a skull and crossbones on the back of Jane's neck and it wouldn't come off. It had been on there for weeks now.

"I don't know," Norrie said. "Maybe she's marked for life."

■　■　■

On the morning of the Cotillon, the house began to fill with flowers. The phone rang and rang; Miss Maura was always answering something, the phone or the door or Takey's requests for chocolate milk and demands to stick 'em up, while Ginger strutted around using her bossy voice on everyone, especially Norrie. Jane sidled through the rooms, peeking at the cards that came with the flowers and sneering. I got something in the mail that day too — a note from Cassandra. She'd left it for me at the Learning Center and they'd forwarded it to my address. It said:

Dear Sassy, I'm sorry my mother got you fired from tutoring. I hope you are okay and have not been hit by any more cars or hockey balls. I hope you don't feel too guilty about you-know-what. Has your sister been telling any more of your secrets in the newspaper?

I have a new tutor who taught me how to multiply fractions. But her stories are boring. I miss you.

Your friend, Cassandra

Norrie came downstairs in her white dress when it was time to leave for the ball. She looked so beautiful and grown up. It felt like she was getting married, only we weren't invited to the wedding. Miss Maura said we would stay home and have our own special Cotillon — the Fondue Cotillon — just her and Jane and Takey and me. We were going to sit by the fire and eat cheese fondue followed by chocolate fondue.

Jane and I were invited to a "Screw the Cotillon" party — sorry, Almighty, but that's what it's called — for people who weren't debuting, at Matt Bowie's house. Matt was escorting Phoebe Fernandez-Ruiz to the ball but his brothers Philip and Sean weren't going. The plan was to crash the Cotillon afterparty at the country club later. Takey threatened to blow our brains out if we went because he didn't want to be left home alone with Miss Maura. He's always home alone with Miss Maura.

But after eating all that fondue, Jane and I both wanted to get out of the house. Jane had been suspended from school for a while by then and hadn't seen any of her friends in a long time.

After Takey went to bed, Jane and I headed out to the Bowie farm in the blue Mercedes. Next year Norrie will go away to college and the Mercedes will pass down to Jane. Then me. We'll see if it lasts long enough for Takey.

Once we got off the expressway and onto the dark country roads, Jane leaned back in her seat and drove with one finger. We saw the bonfire in the distance, from half a mile away over post fences and horse fields. Sometimes when we go to the Bowies' farm I try to picture you as a girl my age, going to a party for the Bowies' grandmother.

The field near the big house was littered with cars. We parked in a faraway row and walked toward the bonfire. I had texted Aisha and Lula and they'd promised to come, but they weren't there yet.

The big house was decorated for Christmas, outlined in white lights with electric candles in the windows and a fluffy evergreen wreath on every door. The pond was frozen over and lit with floodlights. A girl pirouetted on the ice while six boys battled over a hockey puck, slapping at each other with wooden sticks. At the bonfire, Philip Bowie's girlfriend, Katie, handed out marshmallows for toasting and oversaw a huge thermos of hot chocolate.

Jane's friend Bridget to Nowhere came over and said, "Finally you're here. Nobody will talk to me. Come on, let's go inside and see if Sean's in there."

Jane looked at me. "You want to come? See if Lula's inside?"

"Send her out if you see her," I said. I wanted to sit and stare at the bonfire. I threaded two marshmallows on a long twig and held it over the flames until they caught fire. Then I blew them out and ate the charred remains. I wandered over to the pond to watch the skaters. It was funny how the hockey players skated around the pirouetting girl, who acted as if she were all alone on the ice, spinning to some imaginary music. Then I went inside the house. I figured Lula and Aisha must be in there by now.

They were, drinking cider by a big stone fireplace. "Remember when you fell into that hole at my house?" Lula said. Her house was finished a couple of months ago, and that room with no floor has a floor now. It's a music studio, with special acoustics and even some recording equipment. Lula's little sister is very serious about the flute.

"That was so weird," Aisha said.

"I remember," I said.

"It seems like a long time ago now," Lula said. "Did Norrie go to the Cotillon tonight?"

"Yes," I said.

"I hope I'll get to go to the Cotillon when I'm a senior," Lula said.

"You will," Aisha said. "I probably won't." Her family is from Pakistan. They've lived in Baltimore for about twenty years. I know that's not usually long enough to be debutante material — unless her father was the deposed king of Pakistan or something like that, instead of just an orthopedic surgeon. But maybe, when our year comes up, you could use your influence to get Aisha into the Cotillon. I know I'm in no position to be asking favors. But it would be a good deed. You and I could make a deal: I'll go if she goes.

After a while, Jane found us and said we were all going to the afterparty. Lula and Aisha were very excited to ride along with us.

We piled into the car. Bridget and Bibi sat in the front with Jane, and I squeezed in the back with Aisha and Lula and Tasha. Jane played the radio while we drove down the dark farm roads toward the expressway. Even the indie rock station was playing Christmas music. I heard a song I liked, a woman's voice wailing about someone being gone two thousand miles. We sang along to all the songs while we zoomed down the highway toward the city. The roads were pretty busy, it being the last Saturday before Christmas. Everybody was going to parties, just like us.

The club's parking lot was full, so we parked on the street and walked a few blocks. A bitter wind blew. The doorman opened the door for us and music poured out. We looked around. The debutantes had arrived and were draped over the furniture in their gowns and pearls. Claire ran over as soon as she saw us.

"Oh my God, you guys!" she cried. She had news. I couldn't tell if it was good or bad, but she definitely had news. That's how we found out about Norrie running away. Even Jane was impressed.

At first I was scared and worried that Norrie was never coming home. Jane said, "Of course she's coming home," but a flicker of doubt clouded her face. Ever since Norrie met Robbie she's been a different person. We don't quite know her. She's always been the most sensible and responsible girl in the family, and here she was running away with a man who is seven whole years older than she is, leaving our beloved Daddy-o in the middle of her debutante ball, and infuriating everyone else, most of all, you.

Love made Norrie go crazy. I hope it will never happen to me.

THIRTEEN

✉ ✉ ✉

WHEN NORRIE CAME HOME ON CHRISTMAS EVE, SHE WAS LOADED down with glamorous New York presents for everyone. Now she really is a changed person. So grown up, like a bride just back from her honeymoon. I'm happy to see her again but I miss the old Norrie.

Soon I forgot about that because St. John and Sully came home too and the house was full for Christmas, just like it used to be. There was lots of activity and excitement but there was a pall over the house too. Wallace had only been dead for a month and no one seemed to miss him except for me and you, Almighty. You haven't said you miss him but I know you do. I could tell when you and Buffalo Bill stopped by our house the day after the Cotillon. You kept Bill on your lap, shielding him from Takey's squirt gun. I wished you a Merry Christmas and kissed you on the cheek, but you croaked, "What's so merry about it?"

That wasn't like you.

I waited to see if you'd look at me or say something else or dismiss me. But you just stared grimly at the fire. That's when I knew you missed Wallace — and when I knew for sure you hadn't forgiven me.

I was desperate to find a way to make everything better. I thought about the story of *The Winter's Tale*. If only I could make a statue of Wallace and touch it with magic to bring him back to life. I knew I couldn't do it for real. But maybe I could show you how badly I *wished* I could.

And that's when I hatched my Christmas Eve plan.

■   ■   ■

I chopped lines from the play to make it as short and simple as I could, and worked with Takey on his part. Mostly he just had to stand still like a statue. I gave him one other stage direction — it was the most important thing he had to remember. I didn't care if he forgot his lines, as long as he remembered to make that one gesture.

After all the jolly holiday tunes and jokes, we took the stage to play the last scene from *The Winter's Tale* — the scene when the statue of Hermione comes to life. Did you like the wig I wore as the guilty King Leontes? I spray-painted that white skunk stripe on it myself.

Takey made a beautiful statue of Queen Hermione — it's not easy for him to stand so still. When Jane cast her spell over him it really felt like magic. Takey slowly moved his head, then his arms. It was a miracle — the statue came to life. Then Takey touched his first two fingers to his forehead in a familiar salute. Just like Wallace used to do.

That was my special stage direction.

I felt a lump in my throat. I touched Takey's baby skin and could barely speak my lines: "O, she's warm! If this be magic, let it be an art lawful as eating."

I begged pardon for my crimes, and Takey forgave me.

The jolly Christmas audience was spellbound and silent. I don't know what effect the scene had on you. I was too scared to look.

But the next day I got my answer. You told us that one of us has sinned against you. I know I am that person.

My little play didn't move you to forgive me. I hope this confession will.

Sassy

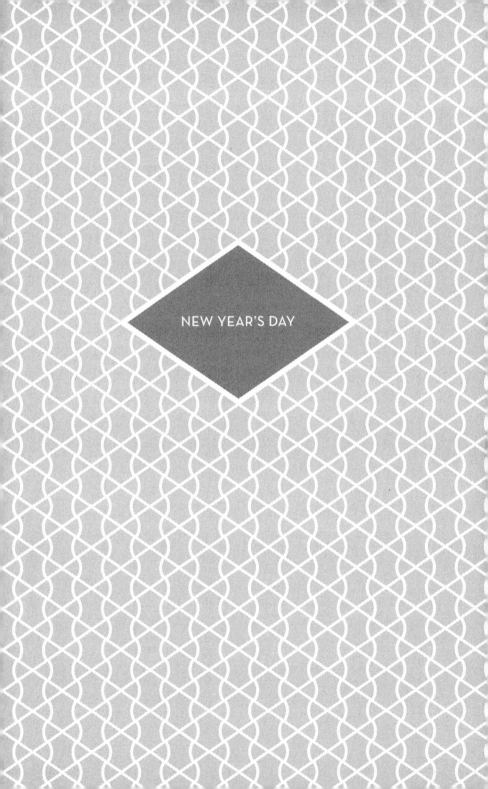

NEW YEAR'S DAY

ON DECEMBER 31, NORRIE, JANE, AND SASSY BROUGHT THEIR confessions to their grandmother. They had to wait until morning to find out what effect they would have on her, if any.

Instead of going out to New Year's Eve parties, they celebrated the New Year at home. Ginger and Daddy-o went out, but all the children, even St. John and Sully, stayed at home and played games — charades and Scrabble and Candy Land and Operation — until midnight. When the clock struck twelve, they blew horns and sprayed each other with Takey's arsenal of squirt guns and laughed and kissed each other, each child grateful and happy to be one of six Sullivans. It had started to snow, so they went outside and jumped and yelled and played in the yard like puppies. In the distance, fireworks burst in the sky as the city marked the passing of time with blasts and booms and cheers.

The next morning, they woke up to Daddy-o's traditional New Year's Day pancake breakfast, with bacon and lots of coffee and cocoa and orange juice. Ginger even made her specialty, sliced grapefruit, which she usually reserved for Christmas.

At noon they all bundled up for the walk to Almighty's house. Six inches of snow had fallen, and the day was bitter cold. The snow squeaked under their boots like Styrofoam. But they all agreed it was a good day for a walk.

They paraded up the long drive to Gilded Elms and entered the house through the kitchen. Almighty was waiting for them in the library, with Buffalo Bill in her arms.

The first thing everyone noticed about Almighty was the change. Her hair had turned white overnight. It had been iron gray for as long as the children could remember, iron gray with one white stripe over her left eye. But now that white stripe had spread over her whole head, which was as snowy as the lawn outside. She looked like a different person. Older, and more beautiful.

She looked, Sassy thought, a bit like Hermione, the statue queen from *The Winter's Tale*.

"Happy New Year to you all," Almighty said. "This is truly the beginning of a new era in the Sullivan family. I have read the confessions submitted to me with great interest."

She paused while Bernice brought in a tea tray and set it on the table. Everyone settled into chairs around the library. Almighty remained standing. She put Buffalo Bill down and he curled up at her feet.

"I would like to read to you the confession that has sealed your fate." Almighty held a folder in front of her and put on her glasses. She stared at the paper in the folder for a tense moment while all the Sullivans held their breath.

She began to read.

Dear Almighty,
I squirted Buffalo Bill with water.

I pulled his tail.

I fed him broccoli which made him sick.

I ate his dog biscuits. They taste like nothing.

It's because of me that you think dogs need rain ponchos.

I'm sorry.

— Takey

The silence in the room was not a comfortable one.

"That's it?" Jane asked. "That's the confession you were looking for?"

"Takey was the sinner." Ginger began to laugh. "You're serious. All this fuss was over Takey teasing your dog?"

"Poor Bill has suffered terribly at his hands." Almighty took the dog in her arms and drew herself up tall. "I will not be mocked. Bill is one of God's creatures and deserves respect like anyone else."

"Certainly he does," Daddy-o said. "But Takey is a six-year-old boy. To hold the future of an entire family hostage over his behavior —"

Almighty flashed him a stony glare that stopped him cold.

"I have received the confession I was looking for, and I will reinstate you in my will. Your trust funds will go on as before, and at my death you will each receive an enormous sum of money. Does that satisfy all of you?"

Dead silence.

"I thought it would. I'm sorry if you're disappointed. Thank you, girls, for your testimonies — they were very enlightening."

The three sisters, sitting side by side, took each other by the hand. They had poured their hearts into those confessions, and now Almighty dismissed them as so much "enlightening testimony"?

"Happy New Year to one and all. I'll see you girls at tea on Tuesday. Good-bye."

The Sullivans grumbled as they put on their coats for the long walk home. "Thank God that's over," Daddy-o said.

"How ridiculous," Ginger added.

Takey took Ginger's hand. "Did I win?"

"Yes, darling. Congratulations."

The incident was bizarre and extremely annoying, but the final result was what they wanted: They had their money.

On her way out, Norrie reached into her coat pocket for her gloves and found a sealed envelope, on which was written *To Norris, Jane, and Saskia* in Almighty's familiar, spidery handwriting. In spite of burning curiosity, Norrie put it back in her pocket to save for the privacy of the Tower Room.

■　■　■

When they got home, the three girls gathered in the Tower to read the letter.

Gilded Elms
January 1

My Dearest Norrie, Jane, and Sassy,
I have been selfish and blind. I have been manipulative. I have been imperious. I confess it.

I have been made crazy by love. I have feuded with my friends and rebelled against my family. I have struggled with fate and identity, with life and death. I have lied, and I have hurt people. I confess all this to you.

My dear granddaughters, I have been just like you. And yet, when I saw your behavior, it outraged me.

But there is one thing I have yet to do: I have not defied death. That is why, Sassy, you were the Sullivan who outraged me the most.

Jane was right: Part of me hoped Norrie would break Brooks's heart. Part of me hoped Jane would tell the world all about it, whatever the cost to my dignity.

But I never expected one of you to be so bold as to believe you were beyond the laws of nature. That boldness shocked me, especially in a sweet, loving girl such as you, Sassy.

However . . . in reading your confessions, all three of them, I understood how truly and deeply you are my descendants. Every action of my life has led to you and your actions — even Sassy's.

And so, my dear Sassy, I forgive you. I forgive all of you. I see how you've suffered, and how you've repented. And I realize now that in spite of my moniker I do not have the power to judge you. I will leave that to the real Almighty.

Go forth and live your lives as you were meant to, and as you wish.

With great love, your grandmother,

A. Louisa Beckendorf

P.S. Don't worry about this so-called brain tumor. The doctors say I'll live forever. I'm unkillable!

"Hmph," Norrie said. "What a fascinating letter."

"Leave it to Almighty to make our lives all about her," Jane said. "But that's Almighty for you."

"She's still a pain," Norrie said. "But now I feel really related to her."

"Because we have a secret together," Sassy said. "The four of us."

They paused to reread the letter and think about its meaning.

"So that's it," Norrie said. "Everything can go on just as it was."

Except that it couldn't. And the Sullivan sisters knew it.

ACKNOWLEDGMENTS

Three books were particularly helpful to me in writing this novel:
Joan of Arc: A Life by Mary Gordon (2000, Penguin Books),
The Winter's Tale by William Shakespeare,
and especially
The Amiable Baltimoreans by Francis F. Beirne
(1951, The Johns Hopkins University Press).

Love and heartfelt thanks to:
SCHOLASTIC:
Becky Amsel, Phil Falco, Adrienne Maria Vrettos

THE GERNERT COMPANY:
Courtney Gatewood and Allison Cohen

TIGER BEAT:
Libba Bray, Dan Ehrenhaft, and Barnabas Miller

RUFFIAN:
Biz Mitchell, Darcey Steinke, Rene Steinke, and Hawes Bostic

LUNCH BUDDIES:
Elise Broach and Bennett Madison

FAMILY:
Will Standiford, Betty Standiford, Kathleen Standiford,
John Standiford, Jim Standiford, and Karen Yasinsky

WONDERFULNESS BEYOND CATEGORY:
Gregory Wilson

Special thanks to Nancy Williams for providing the spark of an idea
(the "GlamFam") which led to this book. In true Baltimore fashion,
we've been friends since we met in kindergarten at age four.

And extra-special thanks to my editor, David Levithan,
and my agent, Sarah Burnes. I'm grateful for them every day.

IN MEMORY OF LILLIAN JAMESON